BOOK ONE

HAUNTED

INTO THE ABYSS

S L DOOLEY

Contact the author: **www.SLDooley.com**

Cover design by Miblart, www.miblart.com

Hardback ISBN: 978-1-956418-11-8

Paperback ISBN: 978-1-956418-10-1

For my sister, Robin
For a lifetime of late night laughter
shared tears of joy and despair
and unparalleled loyalty.
I love you.

Acknowledgements

Returning to the Periferie was both exciting and supremely challenging. I knew Ford's story, but it was so intertwined with the Portal Slayer trilogy, giving the book a voice of its own while honoring the story's history proved a huge task. One that took an entire year longer to write than I had intended. But sometimes stories must find their way to the page in their own time despite demanding deadlines.

Stories aren't spun without a solid support system. I spend unending hours at a computer, with nothing but my fingers moving, not talking to anyone for days, but no book is written in a vacuum. It takes a whole crew.

The love of family is never to be taken for granted. It's the unconditional support and eternal encouragement of those ushered into my deep inner circle that make so many of these stories possible: my husband, **Wil**, my kids, **Joshua**, **Jessica**, **Mariah**, and **Michael**. My precious nieces and nephews, **Ashley**, **Brandon**, **Kadynn**, and **Josiah**, my brother **Stephen** and sister **Robin** and brother-in-law **David**, and my **Mom** and **Dad**.

A special thanks to my cousin **Sean Kight**, who, even if you never read the book, I know you are cheering me all the way.

I choose my closest friends wisely and thus, have few I consider like family: **Barb Allison**, **Judi Cole**, **Karen Sweet**, **Rhonda Revels**, and

Gloria Sinquefield all come from different facets of my life and I wouldn't be the person I am without them.

No one understands a writer like fellow authors. We commiserate and celebrate, sometimes in the same breath. My critique group has seen me through draft after draft: **Jenn Lees, Philip Wilder** and **Patrick (PS) Patton**. The Realm Makers crew know Christian speculative fiction unlike any other group. **Becky Minor** and **Ralene Burke** are my special partners in crime. And the lovely ladies at the Red Herring Society, **Mary Weber** and **C.J. Redwine** are both beautiful and talented and have made me a better writer.

So many more who have poured into my life at one stage or another, shaping and bolstering my career such as it is.

I am grateful to each and every reader who picks up my books and enters into the worlds I've crafted. I am humbled by the many people who have read through my novels, novellas, and short stories. It warms my heart to know others are enjoying the journey through the Periferie.

Not a single word has been written that wasn't prayed over and sifted through God's hand. It is for His glory I write. My prayer, always, is that each story honors him as he has been so faithful to me. All glory and honor and praise go to **God the Father, Son, and Holy Spirit**.

Prologue

Winter, 2001

A strange gurgle caused Ford's skin to prickle along the back of his neck. The aluminum fishing canoe rocked in the gentle, lapping waves of the Texas lake. The heavy, dark clouds made the mid-afternoon seem closer to dusk. He gripped the sides of the boat and stared at his brother.

"Josh? You hear that?"

Joshua brushed his shaggy dark hair out of his gray eyes. A mirror image of Ford. Except for his obvious indifference. How could Joshua be so skeptical? But his brother had stayed true to his word to explore this lake over Christmas break. Reluctantly, yes. But he was here despite the unseasonably icy Texas wind and frigid water.

They peered over opposite sides of the leaky boat. Water sloshed over Ford's Converse high tops, soaking them through.

"I hear something. But"—Joshua scratched the back of his neck—"it could be anything, dude."

Another gurgle and large bubbles popped on the surface of the lake.

Ford gestured out into the water and widened his eyes. "What then?" he hissed. "What could it be?"

Joshua shrugged. "Largemouth bass?" He raised an eyebrow. "Turtle?"

Ford scowled. Though twins, they were nothing alike. Ford's own sense of adventure contrasted Joshua's uptight logic. His own ability to take risks clashed with Joshua's reserve. Night and day, just like their dad always said.

Joshua could deny it, but something was here. Ford would prove it.

He grabbed the oar and paddled closer to the bubbles. He glanced over his shoulder and gave Joshua a wicked grin. "Trust me."

The two words Joshua hated to hear. Especially from him. But this was no fish. Not even a big fish. He'd been here just yesterday by himself and the shadow that passed under the boat had been huge. Nine feet at least. If it had just been a little warmer, he would've dived right in. Maybe.

By the time Ford reached the spot with the bubbles, they were gone.

"How long do you want to wait?" Joshua asked.

Ford suppressed a shiver. But he wasn't cold. In fact, a film of sweat formed on his forehead.

More bubbles. Starboard side.

"There!" Ford pointed.

"I don't see anything," Joshua grumbled.

Ford was already paddling closer. Right into a heavy mist.

"Where'd that come from?" Joshua asked, his voice blunted against the fog.

Ford pulled his oar from the water and glanced around. The mist was considerably warmer. Something bumped the boat. Ford inhaled sharply and gritted his teeth. This was it. He pulled out his underwater camera. An early Christmas gift from the folks.

But how could he capture evidence in virtually zero visibility? This wasn't the ocean where he could see fifty feet or more. This lake was five feet, tops, on a sunny day.

"Ford, this is dangerous. No other boat can see us."

Ford glared over his shoulder. "Who else is going to be out here in this cold?"

"Die hards will fish this lake in the middle of a tornado."

Ford held up a hand. "Five minutes."

Joshua sighed.

Ford gazed out into the fog. This was pointless. Joshua was right. The weather wouldn't cooperate—

The canoe rocked again. A chilly breeze blew. The fog parted slightly. The only sound was the quiet slapping of the waves against the boat.

Ford swiveled his gaze back and forth across the water. Something was here. Not a fish. Not a turtle.

"You know," Ford said, keeping his voice casual. If he could get Joshua talking, he could buy some time. Maybe the fog would lift. "Some say there're creatures, like humanoid, in a lake in Siberia."

"Feels like we're on a lake in Siberia right now, hoss."

Ford rolled his eyes but smirked. "Don't call me hoss. Come on, Joshua. I go to all your games. Even some practices. This is important to me."

Joshua was silent for a moment.

"Okay," he finally said. "But playing football isn't the same as chasing ghosts."

"It's not just chasing the unknown."

"What is it then?"

It was Ford's turn to be quiet. What was it that fascinated him? Not the chase. Not even the rush. It was the thrill of the unknown and the promise of discovery. Whatever it was, since their visit to the supposed haunted house downtown, he was hooked. He wanted confirmation of what everyone claimed to see and experience. He wanted to master his fear. And he wanted the truth.

"If there's something more, a place beyond us, it makes all of this"—Ford swept his hand in an all-inclusive gesture—"worth it."

"Why does there need to be more?"

"Because . . . I don't know, otherwise, what's the point?"

Joshua shrugged and looked over the side of the boat.

"Ford?" he gasped.

Ford followed Joshua's wide-eyed stare into the water.

A black shape beneath the surface floated toward the boat, then under it. The boat lurched to port.

Ford and Joshua both yelled. Ford's expletive would have received a sound reprimand from their mother. Probably Dad too.

Ford's ears popped. His lungs struggled to take in air. Like diving and swimming up out of deep water, feeling like he was sucking the last of the oxygen from his tank.

The jolt of fear bloomed into a stout anger. Ford clenched his teeth and plunged the camera underwater, up to his elbows. The boat tipped. Joshua grabbed the back of Ford's jacket and pulled.

Ford snapped picture after picture. The flash looked like aquatic lightning. He wasn't aiming at anything, just pressing the button as fast as he could.

Then it was gone. No shadow. No fog. Just a cloudy December afternoon.

Joshua yanked hard on Ford's shoulder. Ford scrambled back into the boat, his jacket saturated. His chest heaved as he faced his brother. Joshua frowned and shook his head.

"Can we go now?"

Ford fought the impulse to flip through the photos. They were due back, and he was already pushing it with Joshua's temper.

"Right," Ford said, tucking the camera into his soaked pocket and fished his oar out of the ankle-deep water at the bottom of the canoe. A light drizzle turned to a freezing rain pelting his face as they propelled the boat onto the shore.

They hauled the boat up close to the big elm and then struck out through the trees.

As they tramped through the woods back to their home, neither spoke. A thick carpet of leaves masked their footsteps. The tangled branches of the wintering trees silhouetted against a quickly dimming sky.

"Too bad it was too dark to get any good shots," Joshua said as they approached the house. Warm lights shone in the windows. Mom would have dinner on the table soon.

Ford stopped at the bottom step leading to the back porch and glanced at him, expecting a smirk. But Joshua gazed back at him earnestly.

"There's bound to be one good picture," Ford argued.

They hurried up the back porch steps and huddled beneath the awning. "Well?" Joshua tried to grab at the camera. "Let's see it."

"Hold your horses, man." Ford held it away from him before he brought it close to his face and turned it on.

The first was just streaks of gray filled with bubbles. And the second. The third . . .

"Do you see anything?" Joshua asked. For the first time, he sounded genuinely interested.

A slow grin spread across Ford's lips. He held out the camera triumphantly. "Yes!"

Joshua looked at it. He cocked his head one way. Then another. He scratched the back of his neck. "I don't see anything."

Ford looked at the camera. "What?" He held it out again and pointed. "Right there. In the middle of the photo. The darker shadow."

"You mean your thumb?"

Ford yanked the camera back and narrowed his eyes. "I don't know why I even invited you to come along. You don't believe any of this."

Joshua shrugged. "I'm just teasing. It's not that I don't think there could be something out there. I just don't obsess over it like you do. Com'on." He hooked his arm over Ford's shoulder and pulled him toward the door. "You gotta change before mom sees you."

"Yeah, sure." Ford moped inside the house and trudged up the stairs.

"Hey, Ford," Joshua yelled from downstairs. "Mom's got hot chocolate!"

Ford tossed the camera on his bed and pulled off his wet jacket and shirt. He shook out his hair, then grabbed a sweater from the floor, sniffed it, shrugged, and pulled it over his head.

He sighed, picked up the camera, and turned it back on. The photo with the shadow filled the tiny screen. He'd take it to the print shop and get it enlarged. It wasn't his thumb. It wasn't a fish or turtle. Not only did the shape have both light and dark shades, when he tilted the camera just a little, he could make out what could be eyes, a nose . . .

Maybe Joshua didn't want to see it. But there was no doubt about what was in the picture.

Evidence.

One

Summer, 2029

Ford Montgomery floated just below the surface of the silty lake, twenty feet above the sprawling shadow of the submerged hospital. The wet suit was a good idea. Even in late summer, the water's temperature would drop fast as he descended. He took a shallow breath from his mouthpiece. He glanced at his dive computer: fifty percent. That gave him roughly twenty minutes of air before he needed to start his ascent.

How had it taken them almost an hour to find the place?

He looked up at the sunlight glinting across the surface of the blue-green water. It was a clear fall day, helping his visibility. The sunlight dimmed, plunging him into murky darkness for a split second, likely a passing cloud. But his heartbeat spiked. The light reappeared, streaming in shimmering beams through the water.

Com'on Ford, you need to hurry.

He kicked, descending to approach the north end of the hospital. He took a few shots of the exterior. The camera crew would get more tomorrow. Today, only his dive buddy and sole cameraman, Paul, stayed tight on him, filming his progress.

Going any further probably wasn't worth the risk, even for coveted interior photos. Their lights could only illuminate so much and most of the images might not even come out. Upgraded lights weren't in the continually dwindling budget.

Every day he had to prove himself to his team, the executives, to, well, everyone. Every episode of the show demanded some new and spectacular evidence. There was too much riding on this investigation. On every investigation.

Focus, Ford.

Ford sipped a breath and blinked. He glanced around for Paul. He had drifted below, shooting upward, probably catching a cool angle.

Ford swam closer to the entrance, drifting into what had to be the crumbling lobby, eaten away by the lake since 1923. He shone his flashlight down the dark hallway. Parts of it had caved in. Strained stipples of bright light flickered among the shadows. Long ago, new, unreliable electricity illuminating the hall with dim Edison bulbs wouldn't have provided much more light than what he was seeing now. That'd make a good voiceover when it came time to produce the next episode. He'd have to mention it to Ava. Parks and Rec had given them two days in the lake to complete the shoot. Something about disrupting the boaters. Whatever footage he wanted to get, it was now or never.

He held out his hydrophone, a splurge from last season, and waited. If any of the spirits wanted to give him an aquatic message, he'd hear it.

He glanced at his computer: forty percent.

Just a little further. He had time.

He propelled himself forward. The carcasses of medical equipment littered the muddy floor: wheels from an ancient wheelchair, the rattan seat long rotted away. Unidentified pieces of rusted metal, pipe, and chunks of limestone brick were all overtaken by a thin layer of algae. A largemouth bass swam through a gaping doorway as it kept a close watch on Ford before darting into a darkened room. This ward surely held the ghosts of those who came to be healed. And where they died. But whatever specter the fishermen were seeing above the surface must be further inside.

He glanced back and caught sight of Paul. His cameraman turned his arm, showing his wristwatch, then jerked a thumb up. Ford held out his hand, five fingers splayed. He gripped the doorway to push himself deeper into the structure as Paul shook his head, bubbles spraying from his mouthpiece. Ford stopped and held his arm out, spreading his fingers wider. Paul shook his head and put a fist to his chest. Low on air. Ford nodded but continued holding out his hand. Just five minutes. They had time for that.

The schematic, a tattered map from the historical society, had shown a massive patient room down the hallway only a fifteen or twenty feet in, just ahead. He could risk it. Had to risk it. He'd promised Ava who had promised the executives he would capture something worthwhile. The suits had promised Ava: no evidence, no show. Same as every season.

With a few powerful kicks, Ford surged forward and passed the nurse's station. Sediment suspended in the beam of his light. Thankfully, the ruin wasn't deep, allowing some daylight to penetrate the murky waters. A chill ran through him. Iron Lake would be much deeper. How much would be preserved at the Iron family mansion? When the water levels receded to a level that allowed him to dive the prized lake, he'd find out.

Ford gripped his flashlight and shook his head. He had to get through this dive first.

Shelves that might have once held patient files, long disintegrated, loomed like sentries in the open rooms on either side of the hall. Ford swept his light back and forth, back and forth. The building was more intact the deeper he went. Just enough light allowed some plant life to grow. Stunted grasses, invasive lake weed.

On his left, movement; a shadow swept past his peripheral. He swung the light around. Stalks of rockweed waved at him, straining at the dim light filtering through a hole in the wall.

Ford eased his breathing and passed through an opening to a secondary hallway and into complete darkness. Only his beam of light illuminated the green-tinted water and the sludge-covered walls. Cave diving took special skill. Essentially, that's what this had turned into. He could get lost. A ceiling, seemingly intact, could fall in on him.

Joshua would say he was being irresponsible. Ford frowned and blew out a spray of bubbles, cutting out his line of sight for a split second. What did he care? Ford had put himself out there. Finally called the stubborn a-hole.

That was fourteen years ago.

If he couldn't get through a simple investigation without wondering what his brother thought . . .

It didn't matter. He did care.

But he'd hung up after Josh had answered, hadn't he? Didn't have the guts to even say "hello, how you been?" After all these years, Ford still wanted to prove himself as responsible. Trustworthy.

A long-running hit show could do that.

Ford held his camera at the ready. The GoPro mounted on his shoulder would catch anything he missed, but the camera, his trusty Olympus, would cut through the gloom. He snapped a shot. The flash did little to penetrate the dark.

Any minute, a wispy mist, an orb of light, would hover in the darkness. Something he could document. Anything to prove to the world Mercy Memorial held the souls of the patients who took their last breath at the hospital.

Ford took another look at his computer.

Thirty percent.

If he didn't surface now, he risked drowning and becoming one of the ghosts of Mercy. He came to a gaping doorway to his right. He gave the room a quick pass with his flashlight. The walls were still mostly intact.

He continued, his beam of light barely reaching a few feet ahead of him.

This is crazy. You have to leave. It's not worth running out of air.

Even if he found nothing, it was good practice. If the drought continued this time, his next investigation could be the Holy Grail. Iron Town. Not just one hospital. An entire town with more reported sightings than any of his investigations combined.

Josh'd say you're being an idiot.

Ford shook his head.

Stop it with the Josh thoughts.

He glanced around the murky room and passed his light over a rusty sign proclaiming "no outside phone calls." Stalks of lake kelp waved from the corners. Something rushed through the doorway ahead. Ford sucked in a breath. A school of fish.

Twenty percent.

It's over Ford, you need to go. Paul will be so ticked. So will Ava.

Another shadow above blocked the meager, filtered sunlight. Too big for a school of fish. Without another thought of Paul, Joshua, or Ava, he kicked forward.

A glimpse of shadow, just darker than the rest, left the O.R.

Ford snapped a picture even as he swam to follow out in the hall. A dark mist disappeared into one of the exam rooms. He kicked hard, surging after it.

Ten percent.

At this point, he might have to hold his breath to ascend. Hopefully, Paul was faring better.

He peered into the doorway. A cave-like room. The O.R. maybe.

Something. In the corner. Eyes, a face. Ford sucked in a deep breath. His head spun. He punched the button on the camera. One, two, three. It was coming toward him. Distorted, transparent.

Or he was oxygen deprived.

It was closer, right on him. It grabbed his shoulder and shoved him out of the doorway. Up toward a pinpoint of light in the cracked ceiling. Out of the hospital. But it was getting darker, not lighter, at the edges of his vision. He'd been under too long. He took one last breath and held it.

Ford broke through the water. He yanked his apparatus out of his mouth and gasped in cool, sweet air. Then he ripped his face mask off.

"Ford, you idiot!" Paul sputtered, treading water.

Ford grinned, holding his camera out of the water. "I got it."

"You're an idiot," Ava said, her feet planted on the scrubby grass a stone's throw from the waterline.

Ford's producer narrowed her deep brown eyes and pressed her mouth into a tight line. Her curly, black hair was wind-blown and her blue Aquatic Interdimensional Research T-shirt wrinkled. Together, they had collected the investigating equipment, laying everything out on a tarp to dry: a specially retrofitted Mel Meter, underwater cameras, cables, a pile of waterproof flashlights.

The sun baked the top of Ford's head and his shoulders. No clouds offered relief from the summer heat and the nearest trees were up near the parking lot where they would get to haul each bin full of gear.

Ford gave her a long look, his equipment inventory forgotten. His hands still shook from the dive. He had cut it close. But he'd never say that to Ava.

"Seems to be a consensus." He pulled a matching shirt over his head.

"It's not that I don't appreciate your dedication. I do."

He poked his head out of the neck hole. "But?"

"Risks like that make the network execs nervous. And . . . well . . ." Ava shrugged her shoulders. "The last few episodes have been thin as far as evidence."

"Which is why taking a risk was so important. This episode should keep them happy. Everyone loves haunted hospitals."

Ava fiddled with a small flashlight and chewed her lip. She finally looked at him with a soft expression. "I know you would do anything for this show. I understand how important it is to you. It's just a tough industry. It takes a while to establish a solid show. They're just not sure about it yet."

Ford frowned. "Were *you* ever sure about it?"

Ava shook her head. "My butt's on the line as much as yours. With the other paranormal show taking off, the decline in our ratings was inevitable."

"But you think this stuff is BS."

"Doesn't matter what I think. Just what the suits think. And the viewers. You've still got a good number of loyal fans."

"You counted among them?"

"Sure." She went back to taking inventory of the flashlights and organizing them into a plastic bin.

"You know what would put this show at the top of the ratings at the get-go?"

Ava gave him a quick glance, but continued packing.

"An epic, once-in-a-lifetime dive."

"Drowned talent isn't what we're after here."

Ford heaved a sigh. "Okay, I'll be more careful." He gave her a crooked grin and pushed back his shaggy, wet hair. "For you."

Ava rolled her eyes.

He looked over his equipment. Paul had already loaded each tank in stony silence. He'd get over it. Much as the man fretted about pushing limits, he dug it. More importantly, he understood it.

They finished packing. Ford had only worked with Ava for a year or so, but he knew her well enough to let her stew on any of his suggestions before pushing it. Iron Town was an especially touchy subject.

Soon, all that was left were the wet suits, fins, goggles, and cameras, all rinsed and ready to be stowed into plastic bins. Ford turned his Olympus over, staring at the dark screen. If he caught anything, it would go a long way to earning some grace from the muckity mucks. And Ava.

It was just last season when of the execs hinted at faking some of the evidence when the ratings took a dive. But Ford shut that down quick. No way. There was something out there. He didn't need to fake it. He just had to do his job. The mansion. Iron Town. That would be the ticket. He looked back at Ava and winked.

"Been a dry summer." He'd push it a little.

Ava crossed her arms. "I know what you're thinking, but we haven't been given the green light. The managers at the warehouse are giving us the runaround."

"What do they care if we dive in the lake next to their weird little factory? Besides, what they don't know won't hurt—"

"See?" She threw her arms up. "This is what I'm talking about. Unnecessary risks!"

"If the drought holds, I can't *risk* losing a chance to document that town. Think about it"—he leaned in and put an arm over her shoulder—"a three part special. Never-before-seen location. Exclusive footage." He let go and stepped back. "A producer's dream, right?"

Ava pressed her palms to her eyes. But when she lowered her hands and looked at him, a smile played on her lips.

"It could be incredible," he pressed.

She twirled a lock of that curly hair. Ford's grin widened.

She shook her head. "Don't get any ideas. Wait until I give you the okay."

Ford saluted her. "Aye, aye."

One step closer.

Two

Ford zipped his black Mustang in and out of traffic, mulling over his conversation with his brother. He slammed his fist on the steering wheel.

"Get out of the passing lane, idiot," he grumbled and sped around a white SUV. He was already going to be late.

The conversation hadn't gone *that* bad.

Hadn't gone that good.

Calling Joshua had been hard enough when he'd checked on him after the Upheaval. After the world had spun out of control over a decade ago. But Ford had been broke and broken. Nothing he'd wanted his brother to see. Ford had mumbled a "hello, glad you're alright." Joshua had said even less. Ford left the country to see the world after that.

Now, Ford had a show with promise. A steady job. A life to be proud of.

And so yesterday Ford had gripped his cell phone to his ear once again, so hard his hand ached. "How are you?" So lame.

Joshua had been silent for a good long while. Ford started to repeat the question. What else could he say?

"It's been nearly fourteen years," Joshua finally croaked.

"I know. I—I wanted to reach out. So many times," Ford stammered. He switched the phone to his other ear and shifted on his feet, wiping at his mouth. He'd stopped smoking too soon.

"Why now?" Joshua's voice dropped an octave. Ford pictured the dark frown building on a teenage Joshua's face. He knew that look well.

"I'd like to see you." Ford rushed the words, forcing them from his mouth before they died on his lips. "You're my brother. I . . . shouldn't have let it go so long."

"Fourteen years," Joshua repeated. "I looked for you after high school. But you'd just disappeared."

"It wasn't my fault you got picked by a family and I didn't." Ford cringed. Nothing like whining to your twin brother about your bad luck with adoption.

Joshua sighed. "True. But your choices after were your own."

"I was still a kid. I—look, we can reminisce about all my poor decisions, bad habits, and failed relationships over coffee. I think you might be surprised."

"Good surprise or bad?"

"I wouldn't have bothered to call you with bad." Ford swallowed past the lump in his throat, forcing himself to keep quiet through Joshua's silence.

"Yeah," Joshua finally said, his voice softer but still hesitant, "sure."

"Great. Yeah. Tomorrow? Place on Second Street?"

"Eight a.m."

"Um . . . ten?"

"Nine."

"Done. So, I'll, um, see you then." Ford smoothed back his hair, an aching reluctance to disconnect the call paralyzing him. What if Josh changed his mind? What if he was just agreeing to get him off the phone?

No, that wasn't his by-the-book brother. He always kept his word. Ford frowned. Betrayal was his own forte.

"See you tomorrow, Ford," Joshua said, and the line went dead.

Yeah, see you.

Could that have just been yesterday? Ford blew out a breath, puffing his cheeks, as he exited the highway. At the bottom of the ramp, he glanced at the clock, then gunned it through the yellow—maybe red—light. Just ten minutes late so far. Not too bad.

He whipped into the last parking space of Peggy's Lone Star Diner. A patter of rain began on his windshield as he shut the car off. He took a deep breath and exhaled slowly. After all the years of making his way on his own, this was the most important reunion of his life. His only remaining family member. His brother. Waves of indiscriminate memories passed through Ford's mind. A family vacation to White Sands. His old bedroom. The day the missions' administrator called to tell them their parents were missing and presumed dead. The funeral . . .

Ford shook his head, clearing the thoughts. This wasn't about reconnecting with the past. It was about seeking a future. One thing was for sure.

Nothing would ever be the same.

"Your coffee's gettin' cold." Joshua gestured to the cup of black tar the waitress had served Ford. Two plates of half-eaten scrambled eggs and bacon were pushed to one side. Ford shifted on the booth's creaky red glitter vinyl and nodded, forcing a strained smile. He took a gulp from the mug and grimaced. Cold.

The diner was quiet, well past the breakfast rush. An elderly gentleman in a faded ball cap sat at the counter eating a cherry pie in large bites.

Josh sat with his back straight, starched collared shirt, a mustache and goatee sprinkled with gray like his hair, the same dark brown as Ford's but cut short. He drummed his fingers with neatly trimmed nails on the melamine table. Ford ran his fingers, nails chewed to nubs, through his own shaggy mop. Maybe it was time for a haircut.

Ford had done a brief catch-up with his brother. Joshua, the family man. Ford, the wanderer.

He took another sip of coffee and cringed.

Oh yeah, cold.

"So, you have kids, huh?" Ford asked as he signaled to the waitress with his cup.

Joshua's face transformed with a slow grin. "Yeah, Lily. She's fourteen going on twenty. And Holly, my quiet one. She'll be ten next month."

"Wow. A lot happened in ten years. Married, two daughters, divorced, re-married."

Joshua shrugged and nodded, then raised his eyebrows. "No wife? Kids?"

Ford shook his head. "No way. Got way too much on my plate. I've got this new gig." No use in telling Joshua the show was still getting its legs under it.

"Oh?"

The waitress stepped up and filled Ford's cup. She looked at Joshua, but he shook his head.

"Here's the check," she said. "Take your time." She gave Ford a coy smile.

Joshua chuckled as she walked away. "Seems you'd have no shortage of opportunities."

Ford watched the waitress go. "Nope, not interested. Avoid entanglements. Get things done." He dug out his wallet.

Joshua shook his head, also reaching for his wallet. "I got this."

Ford cocked an eyebrow. "I called you."

Joshua stopped and shrugged. "Fair enough. Where'd you go after Russia?"

Ford dropped his credit card on the ticket. "After researching the Baikal Lake? I headed back to the US. I'd been all over Europe, India, Africa. It was time to come home."

"Just out seeing the world? What did all those places have?"

Ford bit the inside of his mouth and studied his black coffee. Finally, he met Joshua's gaze.

"It was research."

Joshua raised an eyebrow. "For?"

"Underwater hauntings. After college, I worked for NOAA. The National Oceanic and Atmospheric Administration. Saved every penny so I could travel. After five years or so I left NOAA. I worked odd jobs all over the world, but eventually I ran out of money. That's when this new opportunity fell in my lap. A paranormal investigation show. Aquatic Interdimensional Research."

Joshua gave a lopsided grin. "AIR?"

Ford took a sip of the luke-warm coffee. "Yeah, well, seemed clever at the time. I'd led a team for several years and, just this past fall, I was approached to start the show." Now that he had begun, the words came easier. "It's just on a streaming network, but it's a steady income."

Why did everything need an excuse to be legitimate?

Ford cleared his throat. "Anyway, it's a good gig and lets me do the kind of research I really want to do."

Joshua sat back in his seat and crossed his arms. "Oh yeah? What're you hoping to find?"

"Answers."

"The same ones as the lake back home?"

Warmth flooded Ford's chest. He offered a faltering smile. "You remember that?"

"I remember freezing my butt off." Joshua was grinning.

Ford chuckled. "Yeah, I'm still looking for what's out there. What's beyond our perception?"

"There's a market for that kind of . . . research?" Joshua's bemused expression sent a burst of angry heat into Ford's face.

He put his forearms on the table and leaned on them. "Yeah, there is. The show's execs seemed to think so. In fact, the ratings doubled in the first six months."

And have declined in the last six months.

Joshua leaned forward until they were eye to eye. "What're you lookin' for, Ford? Really."

Ford opened his mouth, a quick rebuttal dying on his lips as he sat back. "Truth," he finally said.

"To what you think you saw when we were kids?"

The anger returned in a rush and Ford clenched his fists. "Not what I *think* I saw. What I *saw*. You were there. Don't tell me you don't wonder."

Joshua squeezed his eyes shut and pinched the bridge of his nose with his thumb and index finger. When he let go, he shook his head. "Not anymore."

"Why? 'Cause you got a family now?" Something sour bubbled in his gut. Joshua didn't seem phased.

"Because I got"—Joshua shrugged—"look, never mind. It's just, chasing ghosts will do nothing to bring our parents back. Nothing to change your past—"

Ford splayed out his hands on the table and leaned forward. "That's what you think this is?" he growled.

Joshua held up his hands in surrender. "Of course not. This stuff has always fascinated you. In some way, you might even be right."

Ford blinked and cocked his head. It couldn't be that easy.

They sat in awkward silence for several long seconds.

Joshua rubbed the back of his neck. "How 'bout you come over for dinner? It doesn't make sense, us living so close now, not to get reacquainted. I make a mean lasagna and I'm sure Rae would love to meet you."

They were words Ford never thought he'd hear. His chest tightened painfully. He chewed on the inside of his mouth. A dozen childhood memories raced through Ford's mind: riding bikes through town, shooting off fireworks in the field behind their house, fishing in the gulf . . . he could add to those memories.

"Yeah, okay, sure," Ford said. With the agreement, some of the heaviness lifted. He grinned. "Bet Lily looks just like you."

"Ha! She's got my nose, that's for sure. And my eyes. But she's blonde like her mom."

"A regular family man. Better'n an old empty apartment filled with ghosts."

"By your own design."

"Of course," Ford said, without conviction. "Thanks for the invite. It'll be nice to get to know you again."

"Me too. But Ford . . ." Joshua shifted and looked down at his coffee, spinning the handle around before looking back at Ford. "Things are stable. My family is everything."

Ford frowned. "You think I'd screw that up?"

Joshua's expression darkened. "No, I didn't say that. But you should know something." He took a deep breath. "Just before the Time of Testing, Lily was abducted. Her mom got caught up with some weird cult and for some reason, they took Lily. I got her back, but it was a fight. I'll never let anything like that happen again."

"Geez, I'm so sorry. Of course, I'm sure you'd do anything to protect them."

Joshua nodded. "Plus . . . your life is different from mine. I just want to trust that you'll respect that."

Ford's face burned. He knew what his brother was getting at. "No ghost stories."

"Yeah. Just enjoy the family life."

"You can trust me." Ford held up three fingers in a boy scout salute.

"You know what mom said about trust."

"It's ill-gotten gain? Wait. Sorely lost?"

Joshua rolled his eyes. "Trust is dearly sought, tentatively won and easily squandered."

Ford grinned. "Right. Treasure trust."

"Exactly."

Ford leaned forward, his smile fading. "I may be a mess sometimes, and maybe you don't agree with my line of work. But I'd never do anything to compromise your family." He stared hard into Joshua's eyes. "Trust me."

Three

*T*wo Years Later . . .

"Pass the bread, please?" Joshua asked Raelyn, but Ford got to the basket first. Lily giggled. A sixteen-year-old spit-fire. She was the image of her dad, except for her strawberry blonde hair, tied up in a haphazard bun. She sat across from Ford next to her little sister, almost three years younger, and a perfect combination of Joshua's dark hair and Raelyn's blue eyes.

The long farm table held a platter of fried chicken, a bowl of coleslaw, and a tureen of corn. They filled every seat but one. Raelyn's brother, Peter, was giving a late art history lecture at the college. The quaint cottage in the historical part of Torst had become Ford's second home. It beat his empty one-bedroom condo. If he belonged anywhere, it was here. He treasured Thursdays. Family dinner night. Even when Raelyn's brother, casting glowers of judgement, sitting across from him. To Ford's adventure, Peter preferred books. Ford's gambles contrasted with Peter's prudence. Ford grinned. He didn't help matters by poking at Peter regularly.

Ford took his time selecting the perfect roll. Then he handed the basket to Joshua.

Joshua chuckled. He snatched the basket out of Ford's hand, took a roll, and pelted him with it.

"Josh!" Raelyn burst out laughing, but grabbed the roll as she stood up. "What are you two teaching the girls?"

Lily exchanged an impish smile with Ford. He gave Lily a quick wink and crossed his eyes at Holly, causing her to snort with laughter. Then he sat back with a smile and a contented sigh. Both girls were beacons in his solitary and sometimes gloomy existence. Bright life in a world of ghost ships and haunted islands. Holly's eyes lit up every Thursday as he strode in bearing a small treat. Lily leaned in with rapt attention to every word of Ford's latest adventure. The dives in Florida's croc-invested lakes. The expeditions to South American ruins. A trip to Scotland's Loch Awe. The adventures, yes. Never the ghosts.

Two years of these dinners had settled into a comfortable rhythm. But Ford's smile faltered. His stomach turned.

This dinner was different.

He had to tell them. It was his show's last season. The initial popularity had steadily waned. He'd strung along the execs with promises of the Holy Grail. Iron Town. But just when the water levels were nearly low enough, a monsoon would ruin their chances. Even now, the forecast called for dry conditions. Promises, promises.

"Ford? You okay?" Rae asked.

"Yeah." Ford forced a smile. "Sure." He took a bite of his roll.

What would he tell Lily? She might be a moody sixteen-year-old, but she thought he was Jacques Cousteau. But he was closer to Jack Sparrow. She even named his small speed boat the Black Pearl. Without a hit program, he was just Ford Montgomery, loser uncle.

His brother'd be relieved, though. No more ghost hunting.

Everyone ate, chatting about the upcoming school year. Lily pushed food around her plate as Holly chattered about her last year in middle school, which was apparently a big deal.

Finally, Raelyn instructed Holly to bring out the dessert.

Ford swallowed the lump of bread, then looked at Joshua. "Hey, so I've got some news."

"Oh?" Joshua asked and looked up as he took a bite of coleslaw.

Raelyn glanced at Ford as she took the platter with the chocolate bundt cake from Holly. As usual, he had Lily's full attention. She had put her fork down and leaned forward, staring at him.

"So, it looks like they'll be making some changes at the studio," Ford said. He tried to shrug, but it felt more like an awkward fidget. "AIR isn't going to be in the next line up."

"What?" Lily gasped. "They're cancelling you?"

Ford tried to give her a comical grin. "It's the nature of the beast. Don't you worry. I'm going out with a bang."

"I can't believe it," she continued. "It's the most popular show on that channel. Did they say why?"

"Oh, you know." Ford waved a dismissive hand in the air. "There's always something new and shiny. Aliens I think."

"What's the big bang you have planned?"

"Well . . . I'm thinking about doing a three-part series, starting with a river down south and ending with an ocean investigation off the Galveston coast."

Lily's eyes sparkled as she glanced at her dad. "Hey, you think I could go? Since it's the last few?"

Raelyn sliced the cake and handed Lily a piece. "The rules don't change, even if it's the last few shows. Besides, you have camp coming up."

Lily rolled her eyes. "Camp's going to be so lame this year."

Ford glanced at Raelyn and shrugged as if to say "teenagers."

Rae smiled as she passed around more cake. "Why's that?"

"The camp director says we're forecasted to have the worst drought in fifty years."

Ford opened his mouth, but then snapped his eyes on Lily. "What're they saying?" The forecast hadn't changed in a month. But that Lily was bringing it up gave the information a fresh validity. The camp's leaders were even talking about it.

"Camp," she responded and crammed a forkful of cake in her mouth. "Lame," she said around the bite.

Ford shook his head. "About the weather."

She swallowed. "No rain. They're saying we won't even be able to put a boat out on the lake with the levels so low." She looked at her mom. "I don't see the use in going."

Raelyn set down her fork. "Lily, I know camp isn't always fun—"

"It's torture. None of my friends ever go."

"All two of 'em?" Holly chimed in with an impish grin.

Lily glared at her sister.

"I just think it doesn't serve any purpose. If the activities are so limited, there'll probably be just a lot of sitting around. I could do so much here. Like taking on more hours at the grocery store, helping you around the house, helping Uncle Ford get ready for his investigations."

Ford hid a smile. Lily was smarter than any teen camper. She wasn't interested in boyfriends or mean girl shenanigans. Likely, she would've studied the weather to make her case air tight. She might even know something he didn't. It was ridiculous to let his niece renew his hopes, but his heart pounded anyway. Galveston could wait. If they really were in for a drought, Iron Town Lake might be back on the table.

Joshua glanced at Raelyn and then leaned over to Lily. "We can talk about camp, but Ford's work isn't up for discussion."

"Why?" Lily asked, sitting back, cake forgotten.

"That's the rules," Joshua responded.

Lily glanced at her dad and rolled her eyes. "We can't even talk about it?"

"Your dad's right," Ford said, forcing a smile for his niece. "I might be exaggerating a little. Just a mysterious bay." He leaned forward and glanced between Lily and Holly. "Probably sewer gas and tree frogs."

"Eww," Holly added, and then grinned.

Lily scowled at her dad.

"Will you have to go underwater?" Holly asked.

"Probably not."

"So no breath holding?"

"Not this time."

"How many minutes are you up to?" Lily asked. Something about being able to hold his breath underwater for an extended time fascinated the girls. Something exciting about the risk it posed.

"My record is fifteen minutes. As long as I'm not exerting myself."

"Wow," Holly whispered.

As they ate their cake, Joshua picked up a conversation with Raelyn about sales for her latest book. No doubt an effort to change the subject, for which Ford was relieved. They continued to talk while Ford slipped his phone from his pocket, breaking another table rule. He kept the phone in his lap. But he had to see the forecast. He might have missed something. At least for the next ten days. A month's forecast was too iffy. But how long would he really need for Iron Lake to lose enough volume and make it shallow enough to dive?

Two months with no rain at least.

Ford's hands shook as he scrolled through the weather app. No precipitation for the next ten days. He tapped the link for the extended forecast. Nothing predicted.

This wasn't news. No need to get excited. It could be just like every summer—

"Ford?" Joshua snapped him out of his reverie. He pocketed the phone and grabbed his fork, smiling sheepishly.

"Sorry."

"Hey," Lily said as she pushed her plate back and eyed her uncle, her voice smooth and her grin wide. Ford cocked an eyebrow at her. She wanted something.

"Since the next investigation is at a river, maybe, just this once, I could go?"

"Me too?" Holly piped in, never one to be left behind, especially by her older sister.

"Lil—" Raelyn began.

The girl turned to her mother. "It's not in open water. I could stay on the bank, I wouldn't even—"

"Absolutely not," Joshua said, his voice deep with a finality that shut down any further conversation.

For someone who didn't buy into this stuff, Joshua sure got feisty any time Lily talked about joining in.

Lily's cheeks flushed as she glared at her dad. "I don't get why it's such a big deal. I've never got to see Uncle Ford work. Not once."

"Tell you what, Lilliput," Ford said, putting a hand out between the two of them. "Maybe we can plan a trip to Austin and dive Inks Lake. That's one you haven't been to, right?"

Lily's shoulders fell. She gave Joshua a final frustrated look before turning to Ford. "Sure, Uncle Ford."

"Me too?" Holly repeated.

"You too, kiddo," Ford laughed. "We can take out *The Black Pearl*. If it's okay with mom and dad." He looked at Raelyn, then at Joshua. "No ghosts."

Joshua sighed. "A quick trip. Shoot, maybe I'll go too. I need to get some dive hours in. I don't know about getting in that old bass boat, bro. Naming it after a pirate ship doesn't help the leaks."

Ford burst out laughing. "Great! And the boat is more seaworthy than you think. Lily sees the ship inside of her, don't ya?"

Lily nodded and grinned. "I'll bet we could find treasure with it."

Ford had taken both girls out in search of lost gold, playing the role of Jack Sparrow. All they'd found were some broken clam shells. It wasn't riches they'd discovered, but the treasure of time.

"What about Peter?" Raelyn asked. Her brother had mentioned diving with them during their last Thursday dinner.

Ford nodded. Even though Peter wasn't his favorite person, he'd agree to anything to maintain the peace. "Looks like a family outing is taking shape. You too, Rae?"

Raelyn stood and began gathering plates. "I think I could manage that. There's no deadline squeeze yet. I'll hang out with Holly on the boat."

Joshua joined in on clearing the table and the two left for the kitchen.

"Someday, Uncle Ford," Lily said in a low, conspiratorial tone. "I'll go with you on an investigation. I'm sure I can talk them into it."

Ford smiled. "Maybe." But his mind was already back on the weather.

Ford tossed his keys on the narrow table of the dark entry hall as he swung the door closed. The deafening quiet of his condo always stood out after a family dinner. But it had been a good couple of years. Getting to know Josh again, as a man and not a pesky teenage brother. Rae, Holly, and . . . Lily, his partner in crime. The girl had put him on such a pedestal. Ford shook his head. Joshua would kill him if he ever let her near an investigation.

He switched on the entry table lamp and stared around the bleak living room. It was the opposite of Joshua and Raelyn's. A cheap, modern sofa and two mismatched chairs. A round dining table shared the space. Seating for four. He'd hung a few random ocean prints, but nothing sat on the coffee table except the remote.

A hospital waiting room had more personality.

Ford slid off his shoes and strolled to the window. The tenth-floor unit afforded a wide view of the Dallas skyline. The only reason he'd bought it, really. Not a reason to invite anyone over. Not even Ava.

Ford blinked as she popped into his mind. He could see her surveying the room with a pitying smile. The one she reserved for panhandlers and mothers with screaming toddlers. The one she'd given him when breaking the news about AIR. She'd tried so hard to spin in as a positive.

At least now she could move on.

Ford sighed and crossed his arms. Just another nail in the cancellation coffin. She was too smart for a low-rated niche show. Maybe she'd find somewhere to use her talent.

When he'd landed the show, it was like he had finally found a solid track to follow. Everything revolved around its success. Aside from his family, it was his life. But the thought of not working with Ava was the last bucket of water on the already dwindling flame.

Retrieving his phone from his back pocket, he crossed to the kitchen and pulled open his refrigerator for a bottle of Coors. He checked the weather again. For years, he'd kept his eye on the summer forecast. He'd finally put it out of his mind. Until tonight. He should call Ava about the possibility of diving Iron Town. She hated the idea, so he'd have to start building his case soon.

Lily would love to go.

If Joshua and Raelyn let her stay home from camp, he could give her a special job helping him with the prep. Joshua would never let her tag along. In fact, until she turned eighteen he, himself wouldn't risk the liability. But maybe she could confirm some of the research. They could dub it a history lesson.

Ford levered off the beer top and took a swig. He meandered to his to his office and picked up a pile of bills on the wide desk at the center. He shuffled through them. Electricity. Car payment. Personal loan.

Ugh. And now, unemployed.

He tossed them back on the desk and took another long draught from the beer. If he really could dive Iron Town Lake, maybe the execs would reconsider.

"It's not just the water levels, is it?" he murmured and meandered back to the window.

B&K Sciences and their warehouse overlooking the 5000-acre body of water. They owned all the land and, to their request to dive the lake, they had given them an unequivocal "no." Not just once.

Ford drained the rest of the beer. If he couldn't get the owners to go along with the plan, he was up a creek with or without a drought.

It wasn't just the show. It was old Iron Town, the lake, the mystery surrounding them both. Something about the drowned mining town outside Silo was going to shed light on more than just paranormal proof. If he could capture evidence from that dive, he would shed light on the entire profession.

Heat crept up his neck as he considered his next steps. If he could prove that whatever was down there was more than air-pockets and light reflections, he could come away with the truth, not just about that lake, but about the paranormal world entirely. About his life and what he was doing here on this planet. It wasn't just his career, or his life. It was his afterlife. His soul.

Ford strode back to the kitchen and tossed his empty bottle in the trash.

With or without B&K's permission or Ava's blessing, the second the water levels were even close, he was going.

Four

The waiting room was stone silent. Inside the B&K Sciences building, gray tile floors met pale gray walls adorned with a few large black and white skylines hung almost as an afterthought.

Ford sat on the edge of a molded melamine chair. Orange. Horrid color. They should've stuck with gray.

He tapped his heel, but the echo made the emptiness worse. Would they let him in? Would they agree to his request this time? What would Ava say if she knew he was here asking to dive the lake again? He tried to suppress a grin. She'd blow her top.

But what choice did he have? Just last week she'd said the show was on the chopping block. The Iron Town dive was the ticket to ratings. And this one place stood in the way.

A man opened the opaque door. Finally.

"Mr. Montgomery?" He was exactly what Ford was expecting. Mid-thirties, skinny with a white, collared shirt tucked tight into light gray slacks, sensible loafers. Messy brown hair framed a thin face and blue eyes peered behind wire glasses. One hundred percent nerd.

Ford tugged his leather jacket tighter over his T-shirt and glanced at his jeans. Should have upped his game.

"That's me." Ford gave his signature smile. Disarm. Win over. He stood and held out a hand.

The man shook it. "Dr. Charles Beaghley."

Ford raised his eyebrows. "Dr. Beaghley? Would that be the 'B' in B&K?" Ford hadn't met this scientist before.

"The very one. But call me Charles. My dad, Dr. Beaghley Sr. was the founder." It was Charles' turn to smile, relaxed and friendly, but his eyes narrowed slightly to a shrewd gaze. "Will you follow me to my office?"

"Thanks."

Ford followed Charles back through the doorway down a cold, stark hall lit with bright, florescent lights. No office paintings lined the walls. No plants to soften the edges. White paint, white tile.

"So," Ford said as they descended a set of metal stairs. "What type of science do y'all get up to?"

"Mathematics," Charles said without turning.

"Pretty advanced math. I mean, quantum theory is a bit more than long division."

Charles glanced over his shoulder but continued his silence.

Ford could mention the Large Hadron Collider, but maybe having it dismantled by the government was a touchy subject. He let it go.

They came to the landing and followed another hallway, this one carpeted and darker.

"Here we are," Charles said. He held open a simple wooden door and ushered Ford into a darkened room with a single desk and a row of metal filing cabinets lining one wall.

"I'm an oceanographer myself," Ford said. Science. That's it. Find common ground.

"Oh?" Charles circled his desk and sat down. "Please," he gestured to a chair. "What does an oceanographer do?" He steepled his hands and looked at him with a slight cock to his head. Quizzical but polite. This was the dance. His guard was up. Ford would never get what he wanted. A little more work to be done.

Ford chuckled. "Oh, it came in handy during the Upheaval. All those oceanic volcanoes. I was on a boat every day analyzing, reporting back. Had to do my fair share of number crunching while we looked for the cause. Nothing like what I'm sure you all do."

"Perhaps not. Do you feel you contributed to the end of the Time of Testing?"

"Who knows? It all just stopped, didn't it?"

Not going well. Redirect the conversation.

Ford leaned back casually. "I understand there was quite a bit of activity right here at your warehouse."

Charles's eyebrow shot up and his lips tightened for a split second. Then the smile eased back into place. He sat back and folded his arms. "You heard about that, did you? It wasn't nearly as exciting as the news made it out to be. Same as you, I suppose. Number crunching."

Ford sighed. "Look, I appreciate you all have proprietary concerns for your . . . mathematics. I'm not looking to get into your business. I'm just interested in the lake."

Charles was already shaking his head. "I'm sorry Mr. Montgomery. Like I said on the phone. We take our privacy very seriously. If we allow you to dive the lake, next it will be someone wanting to explore the forests. We acquired the surrounding land for the express purpose of ensuring our boundaries were not violated. Your show would do exactly the opposite."

"What if we made the location a mystery? I'm sure we could spin that to intrigue the audience."

"Nothing is really kept secret these days, now is it?" His smile was fading.

"We'd make it quick. In and out. You wouldn't even know we were there."

Charles cleared his throat. "I wish I could help. I really do. But some of our work is very sensitive." He glanced at a folder in front of him and pulled at the corner. He was quiet for a moment, as though considering something.

Maybe Ford had done a better job convincing him than he'd thought. But Charles finally shook his head and met Ford's gaze.

"Though I'm sure you have a worthy show, I just can't allow you in our lake." He stood and stuck out his hand. "I'm sorry."

Ford didn't move, but cocked his head. "You're familiar with the show?"

Charles let his arm drop. "I am. It's an interesting premise. Ghosts in the lakes? That's your theory?"

Ford shrugged and gave his most disarming grin. "It's an intriguing question, isn't it? An entire town is down there for us to explore and find out."

Charles took off his glasses. "What does your brother think of all this?"

Ford's smile froze. He tried to swallow, but his throat only constricted. "How did"—he cleared his throat—"what's my brother got to do with this?"

It was Charles's turn to shrug. He thumbed the folder again. "We don't live in a particularly large town. One of our previous employees was a friend of his."

Ford pressed his lips together. It didn't matter. "If my brother could vouch—"

The door behind Ford opened. He craned his neck to see a pretty brunette poke her head in. "Dr. Beaghley?" She startled at Ford. "Oh! I'm sorry, I didn't know you were with someone. Steve would like to speak to you if you have a moment. He says it's urgent."

Ford turned back as Charles gave a curt nod and stood. He paused as though he might ask Ford to leave, but when Ford didn't move, he sighed. "Could you wait here just a moment?"

Ford folded a leg over his opposite knee and leaned back with a smile. "Of course."

Charles slid the folder off his desk into a drawer and strode around his desk.

"What's the emergency . . ." he asked as the door closed behind him and their clacking footsteps faded.

Ford stood and stretched his back. He glanced back at the door and then eased around the desk. He opened the drawer and grabbed the folder. After another quick look at the door, he peeked inside. At the top of the first page in bold was "Montgomery."

"What the . . ." Ford whispered.

Footsteps marched up the hallway, growing louder. Ford crammed the folder in the back of his jeans and jerked his jacket over it. He slammed the drawer closed and rushed around the desk. As Charles opened the door, Ford was there to meet him.

"Hey," Ford said, sticking his hand out. "I can see you're really busy here."

Charles shook it uncertainly.

"I'll get out of your hair," Ford continued as he skirted around Charles. "Would you mind seeing me out?"

"Of course. I'm pleased we came to an understanding about the lake."

Ford waved away the comment with a chuckle. "I can't say I'm not disappointed. I'd hoped to convince you, but you run a tight ship. Policy is policy."

"Yes, well . . ." Charles gestured for Ford to follow. "This way."

They walked down the hall, up the stairs, and out the door to the waiting room without speaking. Ford strode to the exit. "Thanks again!" He called over his shoulder and was out the door and jogging to his Mustang before Charles could respond.

He sped out of the parking lot and down the narrow street, the folder still in the back of his pants. He'd be long gone before the man noticed it was missing. On the highway, he pushed his speed to just fifteen over the limit as he raced down the road back to Torst.

Of his many exploits, theft had not been among them, and his hands shook with the rush of adrenaline. He leaned forward, tugged the folder from his waistband, and plopped it on the passenger seat. For the next fifty miles his gaze strayed from the road, over and over, to the quarter inch thick manila folder with his name in it.

They knew his brother. Somehow, they seemed to know him. Who was B&K Sciences? Why was their blasted lake so important?

And what would they do when they discovered the folder missing?

"What do you think?" Ford set the cup down and nodded toward the curled, yellowed, torn parchment. No bigger than a page ripped out of a spiral notebook, it lay on the table next to the manila folder he'd pilfered from B&K. He watched his brother scan the paper once more. They were back at the diner where they had met two years ago. It hadn't changed a bit.

For four weeks, Ford had poured over the folder's contents. Printouts from his show's website. A page summarizing Joshua's military career. Copies of Rae's book covers. Nothing top secret or anything. But strange to have a folder on their family. There was even a copy of a news article about Lily's rescue after the Upheaval, her mom's picture at the bottom.

"I know you don't like to talk about it," Ford said, "but why would they need a report on Lily's abduction?"

Joshua had told Ford the story about Lily going missing after dinner a year ago. Lily's mother had kidnapped her and hidden her away with some cult. Joshua's adoptive parents were instrumental in getting her back. Joshua had never mentioned it again.

Joshua shook his head, then rubbed his eyes with the heels of his hands. "I really don't know." He tugged the article, carefully cut from the *Dallas Morning News*, from beneath the other random papers and stared at it. "I haven't seen Amy in years," he murmured. "You know she didn't spend a minute in jail for abducting Lily? I tried to keep up with her, just to make sure she stayed away from us, but she dropped off the face of the Earth not long after. The cult, too. Disbanded after all the publicity."

"Almost the same with B&K," Ford said. "I tried every search on the Internet to find out about them. Aside from a one-page website, they're nonexistent."

Joshua raised one eyebrow but kept his gaze on the article. "Oh, they exist."

"Dr. Charles says you know a guy who works there?"

"Worked, yeah." Joshua sighed, tucked the article back in the folder and spun the parchment back around, looking over it. Finally, he pushed it back to Ford. "What do you want me to say? An old piece of paper with some cryptic message." He stared at Ford for a moment, then shrugged. "Tell me again how you got it."

Ford snatched it back and cleared his throat.

"Given all the weird sh— stuff that happened twelve years ago, I would think you'd pay more attention to cryptic messages. I mean, is there anything out of bounds? Earthquakes, world conflict, volcanoes? After the Upheaval everything changed. It's like everyone's holding their breath, waiting for it to happen all over again."

Joshua rubbed the back of his neck. There was something he wasn't saying. Ford could almost hear the gears working in his brain.

"Like I said," Ford continued. "I went to talk to the people at the old warehouse."

"B&K."

"Right. They're a strange bunch of geeks, but I got a meeting—"

"Unbeknownst to your boss."

"Producer, not boss."

"Still waiting for you to bring her to dinner."

Ford gave an annoyed wave, swatting the comment away. "They took me into this basement office, all secretive. Seriously"—he gave a dry chuckle—"I thought they might lock me in a room and do experiments on me.

But he had this folder with a bunch of stuff about us. Like some kind of spy portfolio. So I—"

"Stole it."

"You gonna keep interrupting, hoss?"

Joshua gave him a half grin. "Don't call me hoss."

"You wanted to hear the story again."

Joshua raised his eyebrows and gestured for Ford to continue.

"Right, so I took a folder with our name on it. Our *birth* name." Ford shrugged at the twinge of guilt. "What'd they expect?"

"What happens when they come looking for it?"

"I'll deny it. He can't prove a thing."

"No cameras were in the office?"

Ford shifted in the vinyl seat. "If I'm caught, I'm caught. They'd have to explain why they're keeping tabs on us."

"Read it again," Ford said, pushing the parchment back to his brother.

Joshua shook his head but picked up the page.

A line of Moses
one of twelve descendants
A wayward son
will mend the bond once broken
to banish the Schade and
those overtaking mind and body,
wholeness to the temporals
until the appointed time

Ford sat up. "Who're the Schade? What's a temporal? An appointed time? Could it be talking about another Upheaval?"

Joshua frowned and shook his head. "You're saying you found some kind of prediction in the basement office of a science warehouse?" But he wouldn't look Ford in the eye.

Ford slumped in his seat. "When you say it like that, it sounds ridiculous. But there has to be some reason they had a file on us." He placed the parchment back inside the folder and closed it. He'd probably never know.

Joshua held out his hand. "If it means that much to you, I'll read over it this week. You're right, it is a strange thing for B&K to have a folder on us."

Ford plucked the note back out and handed it over. "What about this friend who worked there?" he pressed.

Joshua nodded. "Gabe McKany. A good friend. Still is. I haven't seen him in years, though. After he quit the company, he and his wife moved to New England." He stared down at the table, far away from the diner.

"Why don't you give him a call?"

"Oh, we talk every once in a while. They just had their first baby." His eyes snapped up to meet Ford's. "You ever think about it? Settling down? Wife? Kids?"

Ford burst out laughing. "Boy, if you want to change the subject, you just go for it."

Joshua grinned and rolled the parchment up like a small map. "Rae worries about you."

"No doubt about that. I still can't get over what she did with my place. Tell her not to fret. I'm perfectly content with my job. Besides, I have Lily and Holly."

"Well, they love their Uncle Ford." Joshua turned serious. "I'll take a look at this, but it might not have the answers you're looking for."

"Then I'll just have to keep looking."

"Fair enough," Joshua said, tossed a ten on the table, and slid out of the booth.

Ford scooped up the folder and followed him out of the diner.

"Let me know what you find out," Ford called as he headed for his car.

Joshua nodded but ducked into his truck without comment.

Ford ran the conversation over and over as he drove to his condo. He stomped up the steps. He wasn't angry. Just frustrated no one understood why the dive was so important. His own twin brother holding back. He knew something. That much was clear.

The key stuck as he unlocked the door. He finally yanked it out and opened the door to his condo, slamming it behind him. He tossed the folder, a stack of bills from the mailbox, and his keys on the entry table. Skirting around the new sofa nestled on a soft, trendy rug, he flipped on a chrome lamp on the updated end table. Raelyn had made the condo feel a little more like a home. The only thing she couldn't decorate out of it was the stale scent of disuse. He was rarely here. Even with the nice new appointments.

He strode to the refrigerator and reached in for a beer before returning to the living room and flipping on the TV. The weather channel.

He knew about earthquakes in Mexico, flooding in Alabama. A tornado in Oklahoma. It's all he watched. And the Texas drought continued. Two months with no rain. It wasn't good for any Texan. Except for Ford.

But just this morning, they had a new forecast. Rain was coming. He was out of time. If he was going to dive the Iron lake, it had to be now.

He swigged his beer, then paced back and forth in front of the TV. He'd need help, at the least from Ava and Paul. But whatever they produced, it would have to be good enough for the execs.

A quick interview at the lake. That's all they could afford without the chance of being caught. Donny, a local investigator, had been around the lake years ago. He might be willing to meet out there on short notice. Ford took a deep breath and crossed to the worn dining room table. One item Raelyn had not replaced. Layers of maps, both land and nautical, covered the surface. He shuffled through them until he came across the Iron Town map, circa 1929. If the town was anything like Mercy Hospital, the lake might have eaten away much of it. But it was the stories that held all the intrigue anyway.

Glowing lights. Strange moaning. Mists and shadows. The dive had it all. Add to it the possibility of B&K somehow connected to the Time of Testing. He would find something.

He pulled the map of the lake over the town map and traced the series of circles where he'd estimated where the town might lay.

No, *had* to lay.

He wouldn't have the luxury of searching, diving over and over. He had to hit it on the first try.

He couldn't wait for next week. Or even this weekend. It had to be now. Or he could kiss AIR goodbye.

Five

"Doesn't matter." Ford shifted the cell phone to his other ear as he packed the hydrophone into its case. "We can be in and out before the storm comes. Once it starts raining, our opportunity is gone. With the drought, the water levels are down twenty percent. Plus, we won't have to deal with as much stirred up silt."

Ava was silent on the other end of the line. Better to give her a few minutes to ponder. The more time she had to process, the better his chances of her buying into the idea. Unfortunately, it was time they didn't have. He'd been prepping his gear since five a.m. He glanced at his watch. Seven.

"Ford," Ava began. "We could set it all up, get you and Paul in the water and some *geek,* as you call them, could show up and shut the whole thing down. You're already on thin ice with them."

"We're on thin ice with the studio, too. If we take this chance, we'll have something to show them."

"What makes you so sure this is the Holy Grail? Why are you so obsessed over diving this particular lake?"

Ford looked at the digital camera he was still holding. The lake was special. But not just for the ghosts he hoped to encounter. If Ava understood, she'd have to say yes. He sat down at his table.

"Look, I've never told anyone. This was the last place I was with my dad before he died. Just him and me. The warehouse was there, but no one had ever heard of B&K, so we had free rein back then.

"It was a perfect morning. Fish were biting. Dad was telling his usual stories. But then we heard this hum. Seemed like it was all around us. Just got louder and louder. Then these shadows just rose right out of the water. Dad started the motor and we got out of there quick. The only time he'd ever talked to me about my ghost hunts. Er, well, urban exploring back then. He said, 'We don't fight what we see as much as what we don't see.' He was a missionary. A man of God. If he acknowledged something was in that lake, I have to know what's there."

"It makes sense why it would be so important to you," Ava said gently. "And your dad was right. We do have a spiritual fight."

Ford stood up and stuffed the camera in his bag. "Sure. Besides, I've already called in a separate team to help. We'll shoot it just like we talked about. A quick interview out of sight of the warehouse." He appealed to the producer in her.

"What team?"

"Just some fellow investigators. They've encountered some strange things around the lake—"

"So they've been there?" Her tone was accusatory.

Ford raked his hair out of his eyes. "Everyone does it. Urban exploration just like when I was younger. They haven't been on the actual lake. Just the land surrounding it. The point is, they've got something to share."

Ava sighed. "This just keeps getting better and better."

"Exactly."

"I was being sarcastic," she grumbled.

"I know. But this really could be our best show. If we just take a chance."

"Better to leave the producing to me."

Ford grinned. "Of course. You're the boss. I trust you to make it great. I'll give you Donny's number so you can coordinate with the other team. See you there, then?"

"Argh! Yeah, why not? It's just my career."

"This could help you move on to bigger and better things."

The thought of not having her around wasn't something he wanted to entertain right now. But she'd made it clear this was a bunch of baloney to her. Just a job to get her foot in the door.

"Yeah, we'll see," she said. "I don't know how good our end product will be. We can't use drones. And I'll have to interview Donny and the gang while you and Paul dive."

"Sounds like a plan."

Ava sighed. "Okay, I'll grab Paul and we'll meet you at the lake in, say, two and a half hours?"

"Great."

Not exactly great. That put them in the water around ten at best. But he wouldn't argue.

"See you in about two hours. Hey, and Ava? Thanks. I don't think you know what this means to me."

"I understand more than you probably realize. But it doesn't mean I agree. See you soon."

"Yeah, see ya."

Ford disconnected the call and dropped it in his pocket. He slapped his laptop closed and tossed it in the bag with the rest of the gear. His heart thumped. He took a deep breath and let it out slowly as he surveyed the living room. He could spend another hour packing more flashlights. More batteries. Another GoPro. But he had enough equipment. It was time to go.

He pulled his phone from his pocket and opened the weather app one last time. The weather app forecasted rain to start about three. It was cutting it close.

The phone buzzed in his hand, and a name appeared: Joshua.

Nope. Not today. While they were at Inks Lake, he'd made the mistake of telling his brother where he'd be. Out of an abundance of caution. In case he needed to be bailed out.

Or rescued.

No, not rescued. He hadn't needed Joshua's help in over a decade. But with the approaching storm, things could always go wrong.

He let the call go to voicemail, zipped up his duffle, swung it over his shoulder, and hurried out the door.

As he drove out of town, he flipped through his playlist. A snippet of Floyd, then some AC/DC, Ozzy. Then he punched off his stereo and drove in silence the hour-long trek north to the south side of Silo. Businesses became small country homes. Rolling hills took over with cows munching green grass. Finally, he passed the warehouse. Razor wire had been added to the top of the chain-link fence surrounding it. Like a prison.

A few miles more, before the bridge, he turned right, down the gravel road toward the lake. His pulse pounded and a headache throbbed at his temples. B&K had closed off the warehouse like some kind of fortress. What if they had closed off their access to the lake?

Sure enough, the large gate was secured with a serious padlock. Ford chewed the inside of his cheek. Hopefully, the trip to Lowes had been worth it.

He leaned over into the floorboard, grabbed the bolt cutters, and hopped out of the car.

The cicada's hum rose and fell, otherwise all was silent. The dry summer heat had turned swampy and thick, and sweat immediately broke out on the back of Ford's neck.

He hurried to the low gate and got down on one knee. He gave one last glance over his shoulder and into the trees crowding the road on either side. Then he positioned the cutter on the padlock. The tool sliced right through. He tossed the chain into a pile of leaves and swung the gate open. Best Ava didn't know he had to break in.

He drove the mile and a half to a dirt road hemmed in by scrub oak and tall pines. His mustang bounced in and out of potholes. Occasionally the trees parted, revealing bits and pieces of the sparkling sapphire Iron Lake, laying at the bottom of a fifty-foot limestone cliff to his left. He slowed as he approached a clump of pines. Not a soul in sight. They'd have to stay hidden among the trees until they were ready to get in the water. Once exposed on the lake, they'd still have to swim out at least a hundred yards to get to the dive spot where the map showed the southernmost start of the town.

He got out and popped open his trunk. As he pulled out his dive bag and dropped it on the rocky ground cicada began their chittering swell right above him, louder and louder before abruptly cutting off.

Already sweating, he squinted up at the morning sky. A few fluffy white clouds spotted the otherwise clear blue. The calm weather, combined with the limestone lakebed, made the dive conditions near-perfect. But that didn't mean something wasn't building. After all the talk of a drought, his weather app called for a twenty percent chance of rain by noon. A full thunderstorm by three. The water levels still weren't optimum, but the rain would blow his chances entirely.

He meandered toward the cliff side overlooking the lake and peered between the trees. The B&K Sciences warehouse perched like a sentry tower across the water, high on the cliff and only five hundred yards across at this narrowest part of the reservoir. They would have to navigate a current this close to the river's inlet. At least with B&K owning acres and acres of the surrounding land, the company had assured nothing else was built up around.

He cupped his hand and gazed west where the dam was out of sight. No boaters, no one fishing. Just water for miles and miles.

He glanced at his watch. Any minute, Ava and Paul would show up. The Torst Texas Paranormal Research Team should arrive by eleven, but Ava would take care of the interview. He and Paul would be in the water by then.

"Hey," a soft voice came from behind Ford.

Ford yelped and spun. With her blonde hair in a bun, wearing a faded green tank, and a wet suit half on, the rest dangling at her waist, stood Lily.

Six

"**W**hat in the actual hell are you doing here?"

Lily chewed her lip. "I—uh, I heard dad talking to you about coming here."

"How did you—he didn't—you aren't . . . Lily, you need to go home. You found this place all by yourself?" Ford shook his head. "Doesn't matter." He stepped forward to take her elbow, but she stepped back.

"Just hear me out," she said, a stubborn set to her jaw Ford knew only too well.

"Nothing to hear, darlin'. You can't be here. Not only would your dad kill me, this may be the most dangerous dive I've ever done."

Lily rolled her eyes. "We've dived way more dangerous."

"Not like this." Ford glanced up at the road. Where was Ava? "Even if your dad gave me his blessing to take you, I wouldn't. It's not him this time. It's me. I'll be going deeper than I've ever gone, staying longer, and exploring further. We'll have to move fast. Not just because of the storm but because we're not supposed to—"

"Dive this lake."

Ford gave her his sternest dad face, which wasn't hard. He now had a small taste of dealing with an obstinate teenager. "I don't know what you heard, but yeah, we don't exactly have permission to be here." He took a deep breath. "Lily, please. This is important to me."

"I know, Uncle." Lily opened her gray eyes wide. "That's why I want to join. I know this is the big one. Think about it"—she smiled and swept her hand across the sky as though presenting something—"a family investigation," she said in a deep presenter's voice. "Joining the AIR team, junior investigator and niece, Lily Spurgin." She stopped and looked at him, her smile fixed in place. When Ford didn't react, she folded her arms and set her feet. "Dad's at a convention and mom's locked away writing. Holly's with friends. We'd be back before anyone knew we were gone. C'mon Jack Sparrow. Let's go to world's end together."

Ford shook his head. "No way. Not this time. Even Jack Sparrow protected what was important to him." He looked over her shoulder. "How'd you get here anyway?"

She shrugged. "I parked down the main road on a dirt lot and hauled my stuff up before dawn." She shook her head, not to be thrown off topic. "Dad's always been *over*protective. My abduction when I was little keeps him from letting me do anything. But I'm not a baby anymore."

Ford grasped for an explanation she could understand. Something that wouldn't insult her desire to be grown up.

Lily pressed her lips together and took a deep breath. "This one's important to you. More than any of the others. Is this where you think you'll find the shadow people?"

Ford startled, then narrowed his eyes. She paid more attention than he realized. It didn't really matter if he insulted her. She had to leave.

"I don't have time to argue with you." He glanced at the sky through the trees. Were the clouds already building? No, they were as docile and innocent as when he arrived. For now. "You need to go home before the crew gets here."

As though on cue, the roar of a car motor sounded from the road. The black AIR van rounded the corner and trundled to a stop next to the mustang. Paul jumped out of the driver's seat and joined them, with Ava right behind.

"Hi," Paul said, holding out a hand to Lily. "You part of the Torst team?"

"No," Ford growled. "She's leaving."

Lily stepped forward and shook Paul's hand. "I'm Lily, Ford's niece."

"Ohh," Paul said, glancing at Ford, eyebrows raised.

"Hi, Ava," Lily said over Ford's shoulder.

"Hey, kiddo." Ava looked from Lily to Ford and back. In her usual manner, she calculated the situation, weighed the pros and cons, and came to a decision in record time. She stepped around Ford and ushered Lily toward the trees overlooking the lake. "Your uncle's right," she said softly as they walked away.

"Com'on." Paul gave Ford a light punch. "Ava'll take care of it. We gotta get everything ready. Rain in the forecast. Not a monsoon, but the sooner we get going, the better."

"Right," Ford said, keeping his eyes on Lily. She had crossed her arms and was shaking her head.

If they weren't in the water in the next hour, they might as well go home.

Ford started hauling gear from the van while Ava spoke to Lily.

"Easy, man," Paul said. "It'd suck to break the equipment right before the epic dive."

Ford handed him the Orcatorch. "Yeah, this flashlight really set me back."

Paul nodded. "Just go easy. We'll get everything down to the beach. You got the GoPro?"

"It's in the bag. Both sea scooters are charged."

"We'll cover twice the distance with those babies. They've got, what, a three-hour charge? Should be enough time."

"If it starts raining, we won't even have that."

At 10:30, a thumping beat grew from down the road. Tires crunched the gravel as a rusted minivan rounded the corner. It came to a stop and a burly blond man, who looked like a stocky Swedish body builder, hopped out.

"Yo!" he called as he walked over. He was followed by a young woman, looking to be not much older than Lily, with thick glasses and bright green hair and a skinny black man with a stuffed backpack.

"Hey, Donny. Keep it down, will ya?" Ford shook the blond man's hand. "We don't need to advertise we're here."

"Sure thing. This here's Shawn and Amber," Donny said.

Ford forced a smile, though he flitted his eyes toward Ava and Lily. "Nice to meet you. This is Paul, my cameraman and that"—he gestured to Ava—"is my producer, Ava."

"She's a bit young," Donny chuckled.

Ford scowled. "Not the blonde, the brunette."

"Gotcha." Donny winked.

Ava turned away from Lily, shaking her head, her mouth in that tight line that meant she was frustrated and considering options.

"You must be Donny," Ava said as she approached and held out her hand. "We spoke on the phone."

"Yep." Donny nodded to Lily. "We got an extra?"

"No. She isn't staying," Ford snapped.

Ava gave him a dark look. "Can I speak to you?"

Ford's stomach sank. He didn't have time for this.

They walked back to the van. "I think I've convinced her it'd be best for all of us if she goes home," Ava said in a low voice.

Ford sighed and closed his eyes. "Thank God. Paul and I need to get the gear down the cliff. Can you make sure she leaves and get the interview done? Maybe she can hitch a ride with Donny back to her car."

"Of course. But you could call her dad and let him know she's here."

Ford ran his hand through his hair. "I can't tell him she's here. I'd get blamed somehow."

"But it's not your fault. She came out here entirely of her own accord, right? No suggestions from you?"

"Of course not." He shook his head. "Fine. I'll call him. But he may just get the whole thing shut down."

Ava shrugged. "Then it wasn't meant to be."

Ford narrowed his eyes at her, but held back his retort. Ava always believed in a higher power guiding events.

He pulled his phone from his back pocket and punched Joshua's number. It went to voicemail.

"Hey there. So, you know that dive I talked about? The one out at the Iron Lake. Well, I'm here and we had a visitor. Lily insists on coming along. I'm sending her back home, but I'm on a major time crunch, so I won't have time to make sure she gets there. Check in with her, okay? Sorry."

He tried Raelyn's number and left a similar message. Then he stalked back to Lily.

"Get your stuff loaded." He gestured to her dive vest on the ground.

Lily crossed her arms and looked as though she might argue. But then her shoulders slumped. "Fine," she murmured and moved to pick up the vest.

"Where's your tank?"

Lily grinned sheepishly. "I already took it down to the lake."

Ford closed his eyes and gritted his teeth, taking a breath to calm down. She could have blown the whole thing if she'd been caught.

"I was here too early for anyone to see," she said, as though reading his mind.

A wave of tenderness overtook his frustration. She was just like him. Even a better version. "I promise, kiddo. We'll do a really cool dive soon."

"Sure, okay." Lily grabbed her key off the driver's seat and plopped down.

Ford ruffled her hair through the open door. "Ava can help you get your tank. Be good." He turned and strode back to the van.

"I want you partially suited up," Ava said as she passed by Ford. "Goggles on your head. You know the drill."

While Paul lined up their tanks, scooters, and dry bags behind a tree nearest the cliff, Ford did as he was told and soon he was in character, giving a quick intro.

"The local paranormal team," he said into the small camera Ava was holding, "has seen lights and received an EVP that said 'stay away.' EVP stands for electronic voice phenomenon. Spirit voices. At forty feet, even with the lower water levels, this will be our deepest dive to date. But we're determined to search for the lost souls of Iron Town."

Ford gave an intense look at the camera.

"Okay, good," Ava said and lowered the camera. "We'll do voice over for the information about the flooding in '23."

Ford looked at his watch. Eleven o'clock. Already running behind. He checked his phone. No calls.

"Get in the water," Ava said. "I've got this." She nodded to Lily, who was still fidgeting in her car.

Ford turned to Donny and held out his hand.

"Thanks for coming out, Don," Ford said.

"Sure thing! Glad to help. Good luck down there."

It took nearly an hour, hiding behind maple trees and evergreens as best they could, to get their tanks, fins, bags, and gear down the cliff. The lower water levels, so critical to the dive, left them exposed to the warehouse longer as they traipsed across the gravelly beach.

Dark clouds had gathered on the horizon. Ford kept an eye out for any movement from the warehouse five or six hundred yards across the lake, but it might as well have been abandoned. If everyone stayed busy in their basement offices, no one should be alerted to the small crew setting up on their property.

Ford rolled out the laminated nautical map and held it out for Paul to see. "Remember, we're headed for the dead center of the lake. We can use the DPVs to get out maybe three hundred yards to conserve air. Then we dive straight down."

"Sounds like a plan."

Paul jerked his head up, and Ford spun around.

"Lily!"

She had her goggles on her head and her tank on her back.

Ford clenched his fists. "I cannot believe you would do this. Where's Ava?"

"Still interviewing the Torst Team."

"You're not going."

She drilled him with her gray eyes. "I'm going."

"You see those?" Ford pointed to the DPVs. "That's the only way we're getting down there and back. You try to swim it you'll spend all your oxygen before you even reach the dive spot."

"Maybe for you, old man." She gave him a broad grin, but it faltered when Ford continued to glare at her. Her shoulders fell. "You always said what you do is important. I just want to be a part of it."

Ford pushed a stray clump of hair out of her eyes. "I get it, really. But your dad would kill me. He might even disown me for you being here in the first place."

"I left him a note telling him it's my idea. He can't be mad at you."

"Look," Ford said gently. "I promise, one of these days you can join me. Just not today, okay?"

Tears welled in Lily's eyes. But her jaw was set in defiance.

The girl didn't cry easily. This meant a lot to her. Maybe . . .

Ford shook his head. *No way.*

"I'll just follow you out there."

"You wouldn't."

"I can do this, Uncle Ford. Honest."

Ford shook his head. "You'll go, even if it means you'll drown in the process?"

Lily rolled her eyes. "I won't drown."

"Ford." Paul touched his elbow.

Ford followed his gaze. The billowing gray clouds were closer. He was out of time. It was now or never. Ford let out a few choice expletives under his breath.

He looked back at Lily. "Okay. You don't let go of me." He glanced at Paul. "Give her a flashlight. One of the good ones. We'll have to cut our time. You okay?"

"Right as rai—"

Ford gave him a sharp look.

"I'm ready," Paul mumbled as he handed Lily the Orcatorch from his pack.

They waded into waist-high water, slipped on their fins, fitted on their goggles. Ford drilled Lily with what he hoped was a fierce glare. "Right with me."

She nodded vigorously, eyes wide and sparkling.

Ford lay out in the water and flipped on the DPV. Lily clung to his vest as they jetted out into the lake. When Ford had counted off roughly three hundred yards, he nodded at Paul. He inserted his mouthpiece, then angled the sea scooter downward. With Lily in tow, Ford descended into the darkness.

Seven

Even with a clear sky and high sun, the darkness enveloped Ford immediately. The granite bottom, lack of rain, and absent boaters did little to provide for clear visibility. Silt and dead leaves hung in the blue-green waters. The beam of his flashlight, strapped to his forearm, penetrated maybe twenty feet down before diffusing into nothingness.

The heat of the summer sun, absorbed by the wetsuit, was drawn away immediately. But the cool water held a familiar comfort. Even with a job to do, the silence eased Ford's nerves. The steady descent lifted his heavy spirit. Surrounded by the calm, silky waters, his head cleared. He tried to relax, steady his breathing as the DPV powered him down. But he looked to his right at Lily, clinging to his dive vest, and his peace evaporated. He might as well be in the middle of a hurricane. Her grey eyes, wide and excited in the diminishing daylight, sent a stab of guilt into his gut. What was he doing?

Get in. Get the evidence. Get out. It wasn't just the storm. Or B&K. Now he had a bigger reason to hurry. The sooner he could get Lily topside, the better. But Ford fought the impulse to power to the bottom. Instead, he swam steadily with frequent glances at his charge. This dive was too important. Critical. If he didn't give enough material for Ava to work with, it would look just like any other investigation. This was Iron Town. He was the first to explore the bottom of this lake. Certainly the first to hunt for ghosts.

There could be nothing more than a rubble pile where Iron Town once stood. A bustling community, flooded in the name of progress, may have washed away with the passing years.

No, something was here. There had to be. Or he was finished.

Ford glanced back. Paul was closely filming with the GoPro attached to his DPV. Great perspective, but likely footage they could never use. He couldn't have Lily in the shot. Her presence not only changed how they approached the investigation, but how it would be edited. Ford slowed his breathing. The last thing he needed was to cut it all short because he ran out of air.

He popped his ears and blinked, shining his light back and forth through the blue water, waiting for something to come into view. He felt a tap on his shoulder and flashed his light onto Lily. She pointed ahead.

Ford strained his eyes, looking into the shadows. Then darker shades came into view. Sixteen-year-old eyesight came in handy. Despite her stubborn insistence, the danger in having her even here, a bubble of excitement rose in Ford's gut. Who better to share in his greatest investigation, potentially his greatest evidence, than the one person who believed in his work completely? Paul was only curious. Ava tolerated the show. But Lily was thrilled by the prospect of this hunt. As long as she was down here, he might as well make the most of it.

He switched off the DPV and hooked it to his belt. Then he took her hand and gave a kick, propelling them deeper. He glanced at her. Her eyes lit up in his flashlight beam. Ford nodded and continued on.

The shadow turned out to be what might have been a hill before the lake had been created. Some crumbling debris could have once been a structure. A house maybe. But this close to the surface, storms and even a light current had seen to its demise. If they had time on the way up, they could try some aquatic EVP.

The sunny surface quickly disappeared and darkness pressed on all sides. Twenty feet. Twenty-five.

On they went, passing through a school of crappie. Floating leaves, shriveled and dead, drifted past.

Thirty feet. Thirty-five.

They had to be getting close. It was deeper toward the lake's center than he expected, even with the lack of rain. Cold seeped into Ford's wetsuit.

Forty feet . . .

The drought had done its job. Though murky, the light penetrated somewhat, even this far down. They would just have to be careful not to kick up more silt at the bottom.

A stone wall rose in front of them. Ford fanned his arms and kicked backward to a stop before he and Lily could swim headlong into it. He swept his beam over a broad, smooth space. Something of a roadway. Then another, shorter wall. This was it. Iron Town. This road would have to have been Main Street. The Iron House would be at the far end. They could explore a few of the structures, but they got such a late start, they'd need to make a direct route toward the home of the town's founder.

Lily tugged on him and pointed to a cross half buried in the lakebed. The remnants of the church. He gestured to her to shine her light at the cross. Paul came around to their right, panning from them, down to the cross. Ford snapped off a few shots from the camera dangling on his wrist, then swam to it. He guided Lily to Paul and placed her hand on his vest. Then swam back and put a hand on the cross. People worshiped here. There would have been rows of pews right where this cross sat. Were they here praying when the water came rushing in?

Ava would probably want a voice over with some history about the church. Maybe even a quick cutaway to the interview with the local team and their experiences with the land above. But he'd suggest none of it. Ava usually bristled at any guidance. "Too many cooks in the kitchen."

Didn't matter. She'd kept the show going for two years, and she was good at her job. She would produce a perfect episode. Maybe even a Halloween special.

Ford returned to Lily, grasped her hand and continued following the crumbling road. A depression in the ground caught his eye. It was deep enough to stand out, but no sign of what it was. He couldn't dig around and find out. If the weather, and his luck held, he might make a second dive with the extra tank. If not, this was his only chance to investigate the Iron House. He gave the depression one last look before he waved Paul ahead, took Lily's hand and swam on.

A rusted out model T slumped in the silt. He placed Lily's hand on his shoulder, then photographed it.

They swam down Main Street, passing sagging houses, one still sporting a caved-in roof. Short tufts of defiant lake weed spotted what had once been front lawns. A row of single story structures flanked the road. A large sign half buried in the lakebed silt identified it as the G—n—ral —ore. Ford pointed to it and Paul swam over, snapping some still shots with the Canon. Another building with a steep-pitched roof could have been the schoolhouse.

Lily pointed, first to one side and then the other. Ford nodded at each find, placing her hand on his shoulder as he took pictures. Paul swam ahead, then turned and filmed them coming toward him.

It'd be a cool shot, but Josh would kill him if he used it. They made a good team, actually. Lily making sure they didn't miss any detail, Paul catching the best angles. Maybe when she was older, she could join the show.

Right, and Joshua would never speak to him again.

Ford checked his air: 90 minutes. Then he checked Lily's. Just a little less.

They needed to speed things up. Get to the house, then explore anything else on the way back if they had time. He motioned to move forward.

Up ahead, a strange blue light, faint with no discernable source, pulsed. Ford tried to focus his eyes. It could be an optical illusion. Nothing more than simple sunlight filtering ahead. But they were too deep for the sun to reach and even if it could, the water was a greenish brown, not the blue he just saw. Or thought he saw.

Some kind of environmental discharge? Toxic waste dumped in the water by B&K? He wouldn't jump to conclusions. It might be paranormal. He would rule out any physical cause first. That was part of his job. But his heart pounded with excitement.

Lily squeezed his hand. She saw it too.

They swam closer and closer. Then the house was there. Looming larger than he could have ever imagined: a three-story limestone, mostly intact, steep, gabled roof. Even the metal fencing still stood around it. All perfectly visible in the blue light that poured from the holes that had once been windows.

Ford focused on his breathing. But his heart beat painfully. He'd made it. Finally. The Holy Grail.

He swam to the side of the house, up to the second story, where the gaping window was wide enough to pass through. He stuck his head inside, then stopped. This structure had stood underwater, undisturbed, for a hundred years. Entering may cause the whole thing to come down. Burying him. And Lily.

He turned to her and gave a stopping motion, then pointed at the window. You stay here.

Lily squinted her eyes. He made the motion again. Her shoulders slumped, but she nodded. He placed her hand on the windowsill, then gestured for Paul to go in first. Ava liked when he filmed Ford entering a location.

It would have to be a quick trip. There was no time for any other searches. But the blue light beckoned.

He looked once more at his dive time. Seventy minutes. If he took fifteen minutes to explore, even with the DPV, they would have to surface here to have time for decompression. Without swimming beneath the surface until they were closer to shore, they'd risk being seen by someone at the warehouse. And the scooters' batteries would have to hold out.

But he wouldn't leave empty-handed.

Ford pointed at his watch and flashed his hand open three times. Fifteen minutes. Then he pointed at the sill once more for good measure.

Lily nodded again. Any other girl would have been terrified being left alone forty meters underwater outside a haunted house. But not Lily. She was fearless.

Ford squeezed her hand and ducked into the window. The blue light wasn't as bright as he would have thought from the outside.

A sagging metal bed with rusted springs sat against one wall facing an armoire. Glittering glass littered the floor, the remains of a mirror. Amazing preservation. One hundred years underwater and the floors were mostly intact.

He took out the hydrophone and clipped it to the bed frame. He hooked his scooter on one of the bedposts. Then he swam to the doorway and took pictures of everything inside the room. Paul floated in one corner, filming his work. Then Ford swam backward into the hall. Paul started to follow, but Ford held out a hand, stopping him. He shined a flashlight at Lily, silhouetted in the window. Paul looked back and forth from Lily to Ford, then seemed to understand as he swam back to the window. Ford nodded, then pushed himself from the doorway into the hall. Family photos might have once hung here. Maybe a nice runner on the floor, striped wallpaper, fancy sconces. But those things had disintegrated and floated away in the current, become part of the muddy lake bottom.

He turned left to a wide staircase. Using the curved banister, he pulled himself down to the first floor. The blue light was brighter here. Almost as if working electricity filled the house.

He continued to take photos, not bothering with the flashlight. Without Paul's perspective, the final product would need to be finessed in post-production. But that couldn't be helped. He wouldn't leave Lily alone.

Click, click. A dining room table with floating chairs. A recliner with the stuffing oozing out, waving at him in the current.

The light dimmed. Ford sucked in a breath. But then it resumed its steady glow. So strange. He'd have to do some research on what might be causing it. For now, it was an anomaly. He wouldn't rule out a paranormal source.

They had ten minutes before they had to surface. He couldn't push his luck like he had at Mercy Hospital. Not with Lily here.

A dark shadow wriggled to the left. Ford drifted closer, his camera held out in front of him. He jumped and juggled his camera as a massive carp darted through a door frame and around a corner. He blew out a long breath of air and shook his head.

Dive time: 45 minutes.

That was it. He'd have to get Lily and ascend. All with tales of an unidentified blue light and a blurry photo of a trash fish.

Regardless, he had to go.

He swam back up the stairs. Paul met him in the hall, gesturing wildly to the bedroom. Ford surged forward. Paul had seen something. The shadow of a lost family member?

Halfway expecting Lily to have ventured into the house, Ford swam into the room. But she wasn't there. She wasn't at the window either.

He looked back at Paul, who shook his head vigorously. He yanked on Ford's arm, pulling him toward the window.

A bubble of ice-cold fear rose from Ford's gut. Something was wrong.

He swam to the window and looked out. No Lily. He growled. So much for her word. He gave Paul a questioning tilt to his head, but Paul shook his head again, his eyes wide.

Ford pulled himself through the window, his heart pounding. Paul followed.

Curiosity must have gotten the better of her. He couldn't blame her. They were the same in that way, the risk always worth the consequences. This time, she'd taken it too far.

She might have gone looking for another way in. They didn't have time for games. He swam hard for the back of the house. He forced his breath to remain steady. The blue light was brighter, pouring out of the basement windows. But Lily was nowhere to be seen.

Ford and Paul circled the house twice. Ford's pulse surged in his ears. Would she have gotten scared and headed for the surface? That had to be it. They didn't have enough air to search the house. In fact, if they didn't make for the surface now, they wouldn't make it at all.

Would he be leaving Lily here? Did she drift off in the current into deeper waters and far from shore? Ford calmed his breathing. He'd go back for the spare tank. Come back down. They could buddy breathe on the way up. He waved to Paul to follow him up. He ducked back into the bedroom, unhooked his DPV, flicked it on, and began his assent.

Every ten feet they stopped for ten seconds. But it might as well have been an eternity. Any minute, he would feel her tug on his hand. He would see her fins right above him. Or she would swim up, gray eyes sparkling, excited about something she'd discovered.

But they broke the surface in the middle of the lake without Lily.

Eight

"Paul! Paul!" Ford choked, splashing and spinning circles in the waning light. The horizon was a band of black clouds, looming and swirling, blocking the sun. The water, like ink. A sharp wind had picked up and blew textured waves across the lake.

"Here!" Paul hissed and yanked his arm. "Quiet! We're too close to the warehouse."

B&K Sciences loomed maybe three hundred yards away. But no lights flashed out. No sirens. No voices called for them to stop and explain why they were swimming so near the isolated business in a blind panic.

"She had to have surfaced," Ford gasped.

"She probably got scared. She'll be on shore with Ava," Paul said between gulps of air. "Swim this way."

Paul switched on his DPV and motored toward shore. Ford followed suit, his stomach turning as he put distance between himself and the spot where Lily might have surfaced.

The shore drew closer. Ford's scooter slowed until it was puttering. Paul continued several more feet, then stopped and turned. By the time he made it back to Ford, the DPV was done. Ford strained to see over the waves.

"I had twice the drag with Lily." Saying her name made his head spin.

"Grab hold," Paul said, offering the opposite handle of his scooter. They closed the distance to shore.

Ava was standing in knee deep water. Ford's fins dragged against the rocky bottom.

"Lily!" she shouted.

Ford didn't care who could hear. Still on his knees, he shook his head. "She's not with you?"

"No! Her car's still here but—"

"She came with us," Paul said.

"What?" Ava cried.

Ford ignored her and spoke to Paul. "Bring me the other tank."

Paul nodded, wriggled out of his vest, and yanked off his fins. He waded out of the water, dashed across the beach, and clambered up the cliff, his goggles hanging around his neck.

"What happened?" Ava said, hitching a sob. "I never saw her get near the water."

"While you were filming the interview," Ford said, flicking his dripping hair out of his eyes. "She snuck down to shore. She already had a tank down here she'd hid before we got here."

Ava's hands went to her mouth. She opened just wide enough to talk. "But you went out? With her?"

Ford watched Paul half slid down the cliff with the tank nearly pulling him along. Lightning flashed. Ford counted slowly. At six, a low growl of thunder filled the air.

"She was gonna dive no matter what I said."

Ava pushed her curly hair back with both hands as though trying to keep her head from exploding. "You . . . you should have come back. Why? How?"

"I had her with me almost the whole time, but for maybe ten or fifteen minutes. She was supposed to stay put. I thought she might've come back to you."

Paul ran across the beach and splashed into the water with the tank. Ford turned and let Paul swap the tanks.

Ava paced in the shallow water. "I should have been watching," she mumbled. "I should have made sure she left."

"I'll find her—"

"There, got it," Paul said and gave Ford a shove. "She'll be almost out of—"

"I know!" Ford snapped. "I'll bring her up with my air." He jammed in the mouthpiece, snatched Paul's scooter, and dove back into the water.

With the darkening clouds swallowing up the daylight, he was diving alone, evening not far off, virtually blind.

The blue light. Just watch for the blue light.

But what if Lily was lost? What if she had drifted away from the town entirely?

She knew Morse code. Maybe she would think to flash her light. She had the good one. He'd just have to get down there. She wouldn't have gone far from the house. Anything. Something. There had to be a way to find her.

Ford powered his way to the bottom of the lake, directly toward Iron House, ignoring his heart rate and his breathing. The blue glow was fainter. A whisper of color against the blue-green water. He circled the house once, then again, trying to ease the panic. He had to reserve his air for both of them to return to the surface.

He swam through the window into the bedroom. Leaving the DPV floating in the room, he crossed to the hallway. Down the stairs to the entry. The blue light pulsed from the back of the house. But no Lily. If he was going to search any other part of the town, he had to go now.

Ford swam back out of the house and used the scooter to travel down the darkened Main Street. He peered into a few of the crumbling homes and shops along the way. Back at the steeple, he checked his computer. He was out of time. He glanced once more, praying to see her flashlight. Nothing.

Every breath became more difficult as Ford's throat closed. With only ten minutes left in his tank, Ford ascended without using the scooter. It was as though weights pulled on his ankles. The water seemed like thick syrup. A heaviness in his heart told him he should stay down here until he found her or died trying.

She might still yet have surfaced. He might have missed her on the way down. She might already be back with her car. She might have found a different beach. It was easy to lose perspective. Maybe she made for the opposite shore, swimming with the current.

Without a DPV?

He grasped at each desperate thought. But the hope slipped away the closer he got to the surface.

Ford's thoughts continued to torment him. How could he have let her go? He should have canceled the dive. He should have waited for Joshua to call back. So many ways he could have handled this. Now his niece was in grave danger. And it was his fault.

He broke the surface. The scooter motored him halfway before it died. He put his head down and swam the rest of the way. Ava and Paul didn't say a word as they took his tank and gear, heaving everything to the base of the cliff. The cicada had ceased their chittering. Only the rumbling thunder punched through the silence.

"We've searched the immediate area," Ava said, her voice tight but quiet. "No sign of her."

Ava voiced his last desperate hope, gently but with a hammer of finality. The one person who, despite having every reason, had never judged him. Never asked anything from him more than an excellent show. His chest tightened and his eyes stung.

Droplets of rain the size of quarters fell and thunder rumbled as Ford scrambled up the cliff side. He ran to Lily's car and yanked open the door as though something might be left to give him a clue. He searched the small forest, first whispering her name, then louder, until he was shouting. Let the jerks from B&K find them. As long as he found Lily.

"We need to call this in," Paul said. "She might have ended up on a different beach."

Still more hope. But it was quickly dissipating. Ford ran his hand through his wet hair and nodded. They needed help to search for her.

"Call 911. I'll call my brother." Ford choked on the last word. He hadn't even looked to see if he or Raelyn had called.

"I'll call him," Ava said briskly, leading him to the van and yanking open the door. "Stow the gear. I'm in charge—"

"Ava . . ."

"No, this doesn't need to come from you. He needs to hear it from someone more removed. I'll be able to explain."

"Explain what?" Ford shouted and threw his hands up. "That Lily . . . that his daughter is—" He shook his head and slumped into the open door onto the floorboard. Vomit rose in his throat. He tried to swallow past it, but it was no use. He puked between his knees onto the ground.

"I'll call him." Ava repeated. Her words seemed to come from a great distance.

Ford wiped his mouth with a trembling hand. He needed to keep looking. But his thoughts crowded up behind his thrumming panic. He couldn't focus on where to start. As though in a trance, he followed Paul back down the cliff and helped haul the equipment up. He rubbed at the sweat forming on his brow. Lightning flashed and a few seconds later, thunder. The rain droplets became more insistent, heavy and cold.

Sirens rose in the distance as Ford slumped into the passenger seat. The van doors opened and slammed shut as Ava and Paul loaded their gear. A patter of rain fell on the windshield.

Conversations, hurried movement, frenzied light, cars, flashlights. A voice. So far away. Saying his name.

"Ford?" Someone shook his shoulder. "Ford!"

Ava helped him to stand, handing him an open umbrella. "Joshua's here."

Ford's knees threatened to buckle. It was like a circus, with at least a dozen patrol cars. Men in uniform hurried back and forth, some mumbling into radios attached to their shoulder, others in deep conversation at the edge of the forest. No one had asked him anything. Paul must have run interference.

Joshua stepped up, his wet hair plastered to his head. He held Ford's gaze, his gray eyes like storm clouds.

"Josh, I—"

Joshua punched him square in the jaw. Pinpoints of light flashed across Ford's vision and he stumbled backward, dropping the umbrella. He was instantly drenched.

"Why?" Joshua bellowed, water spraying from his mouth. "Why did you take her down there?"

Raelyn came up behind Joshua and put a hand on his shoulder. Joshua covered his face and sobbed. Raelyn met Ford's eyes. "Tell me everything."

Ford nodded, wiped his face, and took a deep breath. As the rain came harder, they scrambled into the van. Ford and Joshua in the front seats, Ava and Raelyn in the back.

Ford began with Lily's surprise appearance on the beach and finished with his second dive to find her. He left out no detail.

Joshua stared out the window, glassy eyed.

"The blue light was so dim the second time, I could barely see it."

Joshua finally looked at him. "Where was the blue light coming from, exactly?" he strangled out.

"I couldn't tell where it was coming from. Somewhere inside the house. The basement maybe. I never found the source."

Joshua looked at Raelyn. She pressed her lips into a tight line.

"You know something?" Ford said, the surge of hope making him dizzy again. He glanced back at Ava. Though her expression remained neutral, she leaned forward and put a steadying hand on his shoulder.

Joshua glared at him. "All I know is you put my daughter in danger."

"But the blue light." Ford ignored Joshua's dangerous tone and set jaw. There was something his brother wasn't saying.

A tap came on the fogged driver's side door window. Ford wiped at the window to reveal a deputy in a dripping, brimmed hat, gesturing for Ford to roll down the window.

"Mr. Spurgin? Mr. Montgomery?" he shouted over the downpour. "Got someone who'd like to talk to you! We got a tent set up over there!" He pointed to the trees where a white pop-up tent had been positioned. A harried looking man in wire-rimmed glasses paced beneath. Paul stood with his arms crossed, looking wary as he watched the man.

"We haven't found Lily," the deputy continued. "But we got the rescue divers coming."

They clambered out of the van and jogged toward the tent. "I'd like to go—" Ford began, but the sheriff waved him off. "We've got enough help."

When they had all gathered beneath the tent, the sheriff gestured to the man. "This is Mr. Kanabel, owner of B&K ."

"Dr. Kanabel," he corrected. "I'm sorry for this tragedy." The doctor's voice was deeper than his thin physique suggested. He fixed his pale blue eyes on Ford. "If there's anything we can do to help."

"No, no, I'm, uh, sorry—"

Joshua scoffed.

"For everything," Ford finished softly.

Dr. Kanabel shook his head and clucked his tongue. "If you've lost her at the ruin, there are many places her bod"—his eyes flitted to Joshua—"she might be found. But it's a small enough lake, and not terribly deep. That should help in your search. Though the cliffs make the shoreline challenging to follow."

Did this scientist go fishing out on his lake? A bass boat and Fish Hawk depth reader didn't seem to fit his type. Something about how much he knew about the lake felt off, like the wrong note strummed during a guitar ballad. Paul raised his eyebrows at Ford. He noticed it, too.

"I appreciate anything you can do to help," Joshua said.

"Let's just see about finding the girl. Lily?" He looked over Ford to Joshua. His voice was gentle, but his eyes remained cold, scrutinizing.

"Our property is over a thousand acres," Dr. Kanabel continued. "We will make sure every inch is searched."

Ford ran his fingers through his hair. "Thanks, doc."

"Your help is appreciated," Joshua said without taking his eyes off Dr. Kanabel.

The man gave a tight smile. "We would never want any harm to come to your daughter."

Joshua scowled, turned, and strode away with Raelyn behind.

Ava grabbed Ford's arm and addressed Dr. Kanabel. "I hope you understand, we—"

His eyes became chips of ice as he stared at Ford. "Are trespassing."

"Um, yes."

"You have already availed yourself of our property once, Mr. Montgomery. The authorities seem to have this in hand. I ask that you remove yourself from our land."

Ava nodded and looked at Ford. "Come on." She pulled on his arm. "We can ask Joshua if he needs anything."

Ford turned, and he and Paul followed Ava out into the rain and back to the van.

"And do not return," Dr. Kanabel called after them.

"Like hell," Ford mumbled to Ava.

Joshua's truck was gone. Ford shook his head. Maybe he followed the road around the back of the lake. It was something. They were all grasping at anything to do. A task, no matter how farfetched, meant hope.

Ford already knew his next move.

He climbed into the passenger seat and slammed the door. Ava slid into the driver's seat. Paul squeezed in the back next to their equipment and shut the door.

"Ford, we have to obey the law," Ava said, turning the ignition and switching on the wipers. "He'd be within his right to press charges. Or at least file a trespass against you. Under the circumstances, I think it's understandable that he probably wouldn't. But if we push it, he could well change his mind."

She eased the van around a few police cars until she had maneuvered back onto the road.

"I don't care," Ford said as they trundled past a sheriff's vehicle headed the other way. "I'm going back down. I'm gonna swap out the tanks and I'll be back before dawn. Ava, I have to find her. No matter what."

Nine

"You've already done enough," Joshua said to Ford, his words coming out in short huffs as he crammed a flashlight into a dry pack open on his sofa in his living room. He had a towel around his neck but hadn't bothered changing clothes.

He strode to the supplies he'd piled up in the middle of the floor. Raelyn stood nearby with Holly, her face red and puffy, leaning into her mother in the kitchen doorway. Though the young girl had quieted to sniffling, the tears seeming to have run out.

Lightning flashed outside the windows as the deluge continued.

Ava had insisted Ford talk to his brother before going out to find Lily. His level-headed producer seemed to think Joshua would be the voice of reason. Ford had dropped Ava off and gone straight to Joshua's house to do just that. But filling Joshua in on his plan had only made things worse. Now Joshua wanted to go instead.

"Look, she's a smart girl," Ford pleaded. He stood in the entry doorway. "She would have made her way to the surface once she couldn't find us."

"She wouldn't have been down there at all if it weren't for you!"

"I told you, she was already there—"

"But you dove anyway." Joshua stood with a towel dangling in one hand and a bag in the other. He stared at Ford with a challenging glare.

"She was going to follow regardless of whether I wanted her to." Ford braced for another punch.

"Then you should have gone back to shore. You shouldn't have set foot in the lake. You should have waited for me to come get her."

"I know, I know, I *know*. All of it. You don't know how much I regret my decision. I want to make it right."

Joshua shook his head. "Why should I trust you?"

Ford opened his mouth. How could he ask Joshua to trust him? What could he say? He'd done more than shattered his trust. He had destroyed their relationship. The argument was over.

Raelyn guided Holly to the sofa and eased her down before approaching Joshua.

"Sometimes," she said softly, taking the bag from Joshua, "trust needs to be earned back. And"—she took the towel—"the opportunity needs to be offered." She stared hard into her husband's eyes.

In all the discussion, no one spoke of the single fact that should have driven their course of action: Lily would have run out of—

Ford shook his head. "You don't even know where to go!" He punctuated the last word with a fist to the doorframe.

Joshua looked away from Raelyn and blinked at Ford. It was as though a haze lifted from his eyes. He dropped his gaze and stared at the floor, teeth clenched.

"Joshua," Raelyn said quietly. "Ford should go. So should Peter."

"Pete?" Ford asked. What could Rae's brother do? An oil painting of the dive site?

Raelyn sat on the arm of the sofa and turned to Ford. "Describe the blue light. Anything you can remember."

"I—" Ford shook his head. He'd barely mentioned it to the police. What could he say? It was weird. Like nothing he'd ever encountered.

"Like I said, I never saw the source. It uh . . ." Now that it came to it, it seemed silly. If Paul hadn't been there, he might have thought he'd imagined it. "Like I told Josh, it seemed to be coming from the basement of the Iron House. Why?"

"Did it come and go?" Raelyn pressed.

He regarded Raelyn. Unlike Joshua, she was calm, composed, resolved even.

"It pulsed. Just a little. When I went back the second time, it had faded."

Raelyn nodded and looked at Joshua, who sighed and slumped his shoulders. "Call Peter. Tell him to bring his dive gear. And his staff."

"Wait," Ford asked, holding out a hand. "Staff? What do you know that I don't?"

Joshua put truth and trust in such high regard. Why was he withholding information now?

Raelyn handed the bag and towel back to Joshua and gestured for Ford to sit in the recliner. "I think you'd better sit down."

Joshua tossed the items into the pile.

Ford eased onto the edge of the seat, looking from Raelyn to Joshua.

"Com'on sweetie," Raelyn said to Holly. "Let's get some hot cocoa while daddy talks to Uncle Ford."

"Will they find Lily?" Holly sniffed as they left the room.

"If anyone can, Daddy and your uncle will."

"Now, will you tell me what's going on?" Ford asked when Raelyn and Holly were rattling around in the kitchen.

Joshua paced, frowning at the floor. He tucked his hands into the small of his back. Whatever it was, Joshua seemed to have taken on some of Raelyn's composure. Was it hope or resignation? A plan for rescue or recovery? Ford's heart hammered against his chest. He clenched his hands together to hold back the battering ram of panic and focused on Joshua.

"You remember what I told you about Lily's kidnapping?"

"She was just two. It took a year to find her."

Joshua nodded. "We'd just found her not long before you and I talked for the first time right after the Upheaval."

"You've never told me much. There was a cult your ex was involved with. Amy kidnapped Lily. But your folks helped locate her. What does this have to do with the light?"

Joshua nodded again. "Yeah, we'll get to that in a minute. First, the cult. They weren't just your run-of-the-mill extremists. They were *connected* to the Time of Testing."

"You're kidding," Ford breathed. "How? It was nearly a world war. A cult of crazies out of Texas had something to do with it?"

"It's a long story. I never understood why Amy was involved with them," Joshua continued. "Or what they wanted with Lily."

"Who were they?"

Joshua shrugged. "No idea. I have heard nothing about them since. Now"—he stood and began buckling his bag—"about the light. It might not be what I think." He held up a hand to stop Ford's next comment. "But my gut says otherwise. You know about the large hadron collider? The discovery of the fifth dimension?"

Ford frowned. "Sure, it was all over the news. Just before everything went to hell in a handbasket." Ford sat back. "You're not saying . . . you can't be serious."

"Dead serious. B&K not only discovered the dimension, they found a way to get there. Or at least someone from the Fifth found a way here."

Ford's next breath was hard to take. "What?" he strangled out.

Joshua sighed and rubbed the back of his neck. "I know because I was there."

The tea kettle went off, whistling like a distant train. Ford let the noise fill his thoughts. Hot cocoa, Holly, Lily. Family dinners. Normal life.

When the whistle subsided, Joshua continued relentlessly. "It's a place called Alnok."

"The fifth dimension. It's a place." Ford tried to swallow, but his throat refused to work.

A humorless smile twisted Joshua's lips. "Now who's the unbeliever?"

Ford ran his fingers through his hair. "What am I supposed to believe? I mean, it's one thing for a dimension to hold spirits or other beings. You're telling me you hopped an interdimensional train and took a vacation to the fifth dimension?"

Raelyn appeared in the doorway from the kitchen. "It was no vacation."

Ford met her gaze. "You too?"

"I met Raelyn just before we went in," Joshua explained. "There's an entire civilization of beings called Guardians. One of them, Kade, showed us the way in. But one Guardian went bad. Cosyn. He and his horde used three portals to come through to Earth, they call it Earth Apparent, and wreak havoc. They targeted our families."

"Lily?" Ford's stomach turned.

"Yes," Raelyn said. "And Peter. It's why he was sick. There were others. Five of us. They referred to us as Temporals."

Joshua picked up his dive vest and hefted his pack onto his shoulder. He looked at Raelyn. "I'm going to load up and go. Can you have Peter meet us at the lake?"

Raelyn nodded. "Of course. We'll be waiting right here when you get back with Lily." She turned to Ford. "I'll be praying for you."

Ford nodded and swallowed hard.

Joshua looked down at his youngest daughter. "Dad's gotta go."

Holly nodded, handed her mug off to Raelyn, and threw her arms around his waist. He hugged her and kissed the top of her head. "Take care of mom."

Joshua slipped out of Holly's grasp and gave Raelyn a long kiss. "Be back soon."

Raelyn nodded and gathered Holly back to her.

Ford helped Joshua load his dive vest and two dry packs. One with all his equipment. What the other contained, Ford had no idea. They'd agreed to use the tanks from AIR, stored at Ava's place.

Joshua was silent the first few miles he drove. "You met Gabe and Jinny," he finally said.

"They were part of your group?"

"Yeah. Gabe worked at B&K at the time," Joshua said.

Ford nodded slowly. "Right, I remember you saying that."

"Avery was the last to join. You've heard me talk about him and his wife, Penny."

Ford hadn't stopped nodding, his face slack. It was all too much.

"They called our group the Cord. Cosyn used the portals he opened to come through and cause bad things to happen to each of our families. I don't know how the cult was working with him, but whatever the connection, they took Lily on his orders."

"Portals . . ."

"We closed them all," Joshua said. "The three Cosyn opened, at least."

Ford looked at Joshua. "You think there's one in the lake?"

"I do."

"You think Lily went through it."

Joshua's face worked, and tears welled in his eyes. "If she didn't . . ."

The knot tightened in Ford's gut. "Right. Why the lake? What makes you so sure about the portal?"

Joshua stared at the road ahead. He gave a quick glance at Ford. "We destroyed the portals, but Cosyn is still there. Maybe he regained his power. Maybe he's after our families again. The blue light, B&K, Lily missing. It's all too much to be coincidence. Plus"—he looked over his shoulder to change lanes—"you remember that old parchment you found at the warehouse?"

"Yeah."

"There's another one like it. One that our leader in Alnok discovered. It was a prophecy predicting the five of us being there. Told us we were called to protect our families, Earth, and to close the portals."

"You were called. Why you? Why our families?"

"Lineage. Our ancestors were brought to Alnok during the Black Plague as a kind of protected remnant. They lived there until Cosyn drove them out. Our great-great-great grandmother and grandfather were Nahor and Moses."

"So they called you back to where your, our, ancestors once lived."

"That's right."

"What about now? I don't think anyone called me to dive Iron Lake."

Joshua snorted. "Don't be so sure." He glanced at Ford. "You're forgetting the old page from the B&K file."

"What does it have to do with any of this? What's it referencing?"

Joshua flicked the interior light on, then pulled the rolled up parchment from his breast pocket and handed it to Ford. "You."

"Wha . . ." Ford's throat went dry. He coughed and took the paper. "When I showed it to you, you said it was nonsense. Now you're telling me it's a prophecy. And it's about me."

"It fits." Joshua shrugged. "I know it's a lot to digest, and I wish I could give you all the answers. But the first prophecy dealt with each of us specifically. But even more than that"—he took a second page from his pocket—"it literally fits. Open them up. See what I mean."

Ford unrolled the first page, the one from B&K. He smoothed it out on the dash. It was as soft and supple as leather. Then he unrolled the second page. He pressed it against the dash next to the first. The rips nestled together like two puzzle pieces.

"There's a more complete prophecy here," Joshua said. "Read it."

From Earth Apparent, a line of Moses
a child of Micah, one of twelve descendants.
A broken warrior, an unformed leader,
a wayward son
made complete by sword, light, shield,

and sight
will mend the bond once broken.
A cord, brought through fire and ash
to banish the Schade and
shall defeat the shadows, those once
taking mind and body
And bring peace to Alnok, wholeness
to the temporals,
protection to Earth Apparent until the
appointed time.

Ford shook his head. "I don't get any of this."
Joshua smiled grimly. "I believe you're the wayward son."

Ten

At two a.m. Ford and Joshua pulled up to Ava's bungalow in downtown Dallas. The detached garage was already open, the black AIR van parked next to Ava's Ford Explorer. Ford had told her they were coming by to pick up the van and three tanks. He'd hung up before she could ask questions. Now, she stood beneath the porch light, arms crossed. In the dark rain, he couldn't see her expression, but he could imagine it. Pursed lips, narrowed eyes. Suspicious and ready for an argument.

"Let me do the talking," Ford said as they piled out of the truck.

Joshua gave a curt nod. "Got it. I'll grab the bags."

Ford nodded, ducking his head against the downpour, hurried up the driveway and marched up the porch steps. Ava was fully dressed, including a raincoat, and pacing.

"Ava, I need you to understand—"

She stopped and narrowed her eyes at him. "It might surprise you to know, I do."

Ford blinked "You do?"

"I lost Lily first. If I had been paying attention, she never would have ended up at the shoreline. You would never have had to make the choice to call the dive off or bring her with you." She blinked away tears building up in her eyes. "I'm as much to blame as you."

She likely meant the words to have been comforting, but they only bloated his guilt. Yet another person was affected by his decision to let Lily dive. She shouldn't be burdened by what happened.

"I appreciate that. But I made the call. I have to find her."

"Agreed."

"Then you'll give me the keys?"

She dangled them in front of her.

"And the three tanks?" he asked, reaching.

"Four." She tucked the keys into her palm.

Ford held out his arms in petition. "You know I could never let you do this dive with us. We were already pushing the depth. It's supposed to rain all night. There's a reason we haven't dived this lake until now."

Ava shook her head, her curls bouncing. "I'll be in no more danger than you. I'm a more seasoned diver."

"It's not exactly what you think."

"I know this is hard. But I know what I'm getting into."

Ford shook his head slowly. "I don't think you do."

Ava started past him. "We're wasting time. You can argue with me on the way."

He reached out and took hold of her elbow, pulling her close. "This is bigger than a flooded town. Bigger than ghosts. I won't risk—"

Ava cocked an eyebrow. Her brown eyes were warm and her lips soft, parted as though about to argue, but holding back the words.

He drew her even closer. "You don't know the whole story."

She pulled away but grasped his hand. "Maybe not. But I'll see it through to the end."

Ford's shoulders sagged. "Fine. But I'm not letting you out of my sight. No matter what happens, stay right with me. I can't . . ."

. . . lose you.

". . . lose someone else."

"Of course," she said, but she didn't hand off the keys. She pulled the hood of her raincoat over her head as Ford followed her through the rain to the garage.

"What's this?" Joshua gestured to Ava as they walked up. He stood between the vehicles with the gear piled at his feet.

"Joshua," Ava began as she pushed off the hood of her jacket. "I'm so sorry for what you're going through."

"Thank you, Ava, but this isn't exactly what you think it is." Joshua cast a frown at Ford.

Ford shrugged and shook his head. If Joshua could talk her out of it, all the better.

"Funny," Ava said. "Your brother said the same thing. We've got an hour from here to Silo and another thirty to the lake. Plenty of time to fill me in."

She strode to the back of the van, shoulders hunched against the downpour, and squinted at Ford.

Ford rolled his eyes and hit the remote to unlock the doors, joining her as he opened the back doors.

Joshua said nothing as he threw his two packs into the van.

"The scooters!" Ford choked and looked at Ava.

"Front of the garage, plugged in."

Ford let out a relieved sigh. "That's why you're the boss."

"You're just figuring that out?" Ava said. "We'll need to finish charging them on the road. But they should be close."

The two men loaded four fresh tanks from Ava's garage and strapped them in.

"Get in. I'm driving," Ava said.

Joshua climbed into the seat Paul usually took.

"For all the blasted . . ." Ford grumbled as he slid into the passenger seat.

Ava started the van, backed out and was on the dark, wet highway in ten minutes. She turned the wipers on high as the rain pounded the windshield.

Joshua leaned up, sticking his head between Ford and Ava. "All I care about is getting my daughter back, Ava. If you think you can help, great. But if you hinder my search in any way . . . I'll leave you behind without a second thought."

Ford's heart thumped as he looked at Ava. Such harsh words. But her expression remained neutral as she gripped the steering wheel and stared ahead.

"I want to be hopeful," she finally said. "You guys seem to have a good idea about what we're in for." She signaled and changed lanes around a trundling semi. "So what am I not getting?"

Ford swallowed past a lump in his throat. He might as well get the party started. "There were some things I didn't elaborate on with the police."

Ava didn't respond and kept her eyes on the road.

"A light coming from the Iron House," he continued. "From inside it. I think in the basement."

"Why didn't you tell the police?" she asked.

"I wasn't even sure it was real. Or important. Or . . . whatever, I just didn't tell them. The second time I went down I barely remember it. I was just focused on finding Lily. Turns out, the light's not just important. It's everything."

"It's a portal," Joshua said, his voice flat.

Ava didn't react except to press her lips together. She was processing.

Joshua continued, relaying the same story he and Raelyn had told Ford only hours ago.

"That's why Peter is coming. He was as much a part of it as any of us."

"Why not Raelyn?" Ava asked.

Joshua cleared his throat. "She's got Holly to look after. Not just Holly . . ."

Ava looked into the rearview mirror. "Raelyn's pregnant?"

Joshua gave a grim smile. "We found out two weeks ago. We weren't going to tell anyone until we were sure everything was okay. Her pregnancy with Holly was pretty rough. I don't know why they'd go after Lily a second time. Or why they might take her to Alnok, but I can't risk any more of my family."

Ford nodded. "So even if we could find a safe place for Holly, Rae couldn't dive. That's why she didn't dive Inks Lake."

"Of course," Ava said. "This . . . Alnok, you call it. I understand about different realms. I believe there's something. My tía raised me in church. I believe in a spiritual realm beyond our own. I never thought of it as a dimension. These Guardians, they sound like they would help. If Lily is there, wouldn't they protect her?"

"It's impossible to know for sure," Joshua said. "Not if Cosyn, the enemy of Alnok, is back. Or someone took his place. Not all the Guardians are good. Some sided with Cosyn. Then there's Lima."

"Lima?" Ford asked. Apparently, Josh and Raelyn hadn't told him everything.

"There are multiple dimensions. Layered one over the other. I think of it as an onion. We peel back the skin, getting deeper and deeper. But the layers are so close we're practically on top of each other. I'm not a quantum theorist. That's Gabe's department. All I know is there were a few locations in Alnok where we passed into a deeper dimension. We met one inhabitant of that dimension called Velare. She tricked Rae into splitting off and nearly killed her. But in the end, we managed to force her back into her realm."

"How many dimensions are there?" Ford asked.

"Theoretically? Eleven."

Ava signaled and left the highway, heading south on highway 287, the wipers thumping. "Sounds like it's more than just theory. I mean, if you were there."

"You don't believe me?" Joshua asked. His voice held no animosity. In fact, he sounded sad.

"I didn't say that. I mean, who can deny all the stuff that happened? Volcanoes erupting beneath glaciers? Wars ramping up out of nowhere. The Time of Testing was a crazy event. I'm not one to say there isn't an otherworldly explanation. I believe in God, and that's pretty far out there for a lot of people."

Ford suppressed an impulse to grab her hand off the steering wheel and kiss it. She didn't question or argue, simply accepted Joshua's story and offered her support. She seemed to sense his surge of affection and gave him a side eye and a soft smile.

"Now ghosts," she continued. "That's another story. Bunch of tontería, nonsense, if you ask me."

"Well, yes, not ghosts," Joshua agreed. "At least not like what we think of. I saw things that looked like Big Foot, leprechauns, and, yeah, ghosts. Dragons, even."

"Oh, geez," Ford croaked and rubbed his eyes.

"I guess we'll find out what's there soon enough," Ava said as she slowed down, approaching the dirt road to the lake. She pulled off to one side. Yellow crime scene tape sagged where it was pulled across the closed gate.

Ford's stomach tightened. "I forgot the bolt cutters."

"I think we should ditch the van, anyway," Ava said. "We should carry the gear to the beach. Even if they called off the search until morning, there could still be cops here"—she rolled her eyes—"Lord, listen to me, worried about the police."

"It'd still be nice to get a little closer," Ford said as he shouldered open his door.

He jogged to the gate illuminated in the van's headlights. The rain had eased to a heavy mist. He pushed on the gate and it swung open easily. They hadn't bothered to replace the lock just yet. Ford gave a thumbs up as he returned to the van.

Ava ambled the van a few yards past the gate and down a ditch surrounded by trees. "We won't need any of the investigative equipment." She put the van in park.

"True," Ford agreed. "Just our dive equipment."

"Okay," Joshua said as he pulled out his cell phone. "Lemme give Peter a call. He was going to meet us here. I'll tell him where to look for the van."

While he spoke to Peter, Ford and Ava hauled the tanks from the side door. Ford grabbed the smaller of the dry packs from the back.

"Okay, see you soon," Joshua said and dropped his phone in his back pocket. He took the larger dry pack and they hoisted a tank each on their shoulders. Ford carried the extra one for Peter.

Without speaking, they shone flashlights directly in front of their feet and followed the road to the lake.

What had taken half an hour to drive took the trio over an hour, traversing the muddy, pothole-ridden road in the warm, misty rain. They encountered no law enforcement, but by the time they reached the cliff side, Ford's shirt, dried from the rain, was now soaked with sweat and his arm was shaking from carrying the extra tank.

Tire marks crisscrossed the forested area at the top of the cliff, and yellow tape wrapped around the trees. Otherwise, no one would have known anything had happened just a few hours ago.

Ford dropped the tanks and packs and wiped the moisture from his face, then glanced at his watch. 4:37. "How soon 'til Peter gets here?" He tried to keep the negativity from his voice, but Joshua glanced up. He must've heard something in Ford's tone.

"I know you think Peter's just a temperamental artist. But even if he hadn't saved our butts more than once in Alnok, he also led a resistance troop against the government's rogue soldiers during the world conflict. He's got bigger"—Joshua sighed—"let's just say he's tougher than he looks."

Joshua rooted around inside one of the dry packs and pulled a sheathed sword from it, the blade seeming to never end.

Ford took a step back. "What the—"

Joshua pulled it partially from its scabbard and gazed at it with a tender look of admiration. "We were given weapons in Alnok."

"Swords?"

"Well, no, not everyone got a sword. Rae got a . . . well a book."

"Okay," Ford said wearily as he pulled his wetsuit over his shoulders. "Why not? I guess Peter got a magic whistle?"

"No," Peter said, walking up through the trees.

Ford spun around. Peter, with Raelyn's dark hair and pale complexion, but tall and lanky, strode up.

"A staff." He presented a long walking stick about shoulder height and gave Ford a hard stare.

Ford raised his eyebrows and nodded. "Nice." He didn't hide his lack of awe. Joshua may be confident in Peter's ability, but the skinny book worm seemed more teacher and less warrior.

Peter scowled and then looked at Joshua. "Thanks for the tip on where to hide my car." He shifted his gaze to Ava. "I'm Peter."

"Avarilla Ambrello," Ava said as she held out a hand. Peter stowed his walking stick in a holster on his back and shook it.

"Call me Ava," she said.

Peter looked at Joshua. "Gabe should be here."

Joshua nodded and fit his mask on his head. "Yeah, and Rae and Jinny and Avery. But they're not."

Peter sighed. "You sure about this?"

Joshua looked out over the cliff into the blackness. His jaw clenched. "An open portal is the best-case scenario."

"Okay, let's get going, then." Peter quickly donned Paul's wetsuit and gear, fitting his tank over the staff.

With their tanks secured, fins and masks dangling from their vests, and Joshua and Ford each gripping a scooter, the four slid and scrambled down the muddy cliff side, using the tree roots as leverage. By the time they reached the shore, the mist had turned into another deluge.

Ford waded out until the water buoyed his tank. He pulled on his fins and then looked at Joshua.

"Follow me out about 150 yards or so. You and I can maneuver the scooters and Ava, Peter"—he looked at each of them—"use the Orcatorches to give us more light. We'll need it. Hurry before search and rescue show up."

When everyone was ready, with the gray of a late dawn rising in the cloudy sky, Ford rolled over and, with Ava gripping his vest, just like Lily, he switched on the scooter. They stayed on the surface, reserving their air, and made their way to deeper waters.

Joshua's story about dimensions, cults, kidnappings, and Guardians had sounded strangely plausible with Joshua's earnestness. As Ford powered to the middle of the lake to search for his niece, it all slipped back into outlandish territory. Ghosts, yes. Demonic forces, maybe. Alternate dimensions, okay. A realm where Guardians watch over the world and call people to close portals? Not so much.

He had genuine problems. Here and now. His heart pounded, not with excursion, but with a fear that, as they motored through the dark waters, he would see Lily's lifeless body floating ahead.

But if he could believe in the spirits of the long-departed haunting an underwater town, was it such a stretch to buy into a place called Alnok?

Ford watched for the blue light. After all his striving, trying to get into the lake, if he had known to look for a blue light, it might have been bright enough for him to see from the surface. Now, when all hope was on finding the light, he saw nothing. Murky lake water shimmering puce in the rising daylight. No blue lights. No search and rescue. No Lily.

Ford glanced over his shoulder periodically, monitoring the shore, adjusting their trajectory to keep it just slightly to his right. No cruiser lights at their backs. No movement from the shadowed warehouse ahead of them.

Heavy, dark clouds hung directly overhead but left a sliver of horizon for the rising sun. When they had traveled what seemed far enough, Ford pulled his mask on and signaled for them to dive.

He flicked on the mounted flashlight and propelled himself and Ava downward. With Ava on his left and Joshua and Peter just behind on his right, Ford led them to the ruin. The anemic daylight was quickly lost and their lights only reflected silt. A few fish passed in front of the beams. Finally, Ford's light flashed across the first structure. A crumbling, one-story house with the old Model-T in front.

Ford kicked, giving his scooter a boost. The Iron House was just ahead.

Main Street, dark and deserted but for the fish who had made themselves at home, only came into view with the bouncing lights from four flashlights. But the closer they got to what should have been the main attraction, it remained darkened and invisible. No blue light.

Dear God, don't let me have imagined it . . .

The gate came into view first. Ford powered around to the right of the house and to the upstairs window where Lily was supposed to have waited. He switched off the scooter. His throat threatened to close. Waving hair swayed at the base of the house—no, it was just overgrown lake weed.

A delicate hand held onto the window frame—just a piece of molding. Lily wasn't here. But was she inside?

Where was the blue light? Where was the evidence that they would find Lily on the other side of some portal?

Ford waved them through the window and into the bedroom. All was dark.

He hooked his scooter onto the bedframe and gestured for Joshua to do the same. Then he continued into the hall. Still just a black corridor. Far above them, strained light dappled the surface of the water as the day began in earnest. They swam deeper into darkness.

To the top of the stairs.

No blue light.

A current buffeted him, and he spiraled to the bottom of the stairs.

He held on to the banister as Joshua and Peter swept past him to the landing, then on to the elaborate front door. Ava nearly slipped by him, but he grabbed her hand. His heart jack hammered against his chest. Bubbles clouded his vision. He couldn't control his panic.

No way is there a current this strong.

But it increased its pull until he could barely hang on. The beams of Joshua and Peter's lights waved erratically as they disappeared beneath the stairs.

Where is the blasted blue light?

Ford's grip gave out and, still holding onto Ava, he let the current take both of them. They drifted into a kitchen to an open door that could only lead to the basement. Joshua had braced himself against the doorframe, straining against the pull. Peter was nowhere to be seen.

Ford tried to reach out for anything to hold him in place. He'd been in a riptide before, in the gulf. He would have drowned if not for the rescue team who came for him on a jet ski. This current was stronger by a long shot.

Ford's flashlight sputtered out. Then Ava's. They were plunged into darkness.

No light. No Lily. Nothing. It was all wishful thinking. A hope kindled within his desperate heart. He had lost Joshua's daughter. It was all his—

Something flashed. A glimmer of light. A blue light silhouetting Joshua, his sword drawn, held out in front of him and Peter, with his staff raised high above his head. The light grew and pulsed. The current demanded that he succumb to its force. Ford pulled back for a minute. Ava's grip tightened. He squeezed back. He let the vortex draw him toward the light.

Joshua disappeared. Then Peter. Ford squinted his eyes. The light filled his vision. Took over his mind. Nothing existed but the light.

Then all went black.

Eleven

Ford slammed to his knees. He ripped out his mouthpiece, gasping. The world was spinning. He squeezed his eyes shut and gripped the sides of his head to keep it from splitting open. He gagged.

Ava? Joshua?

He tried to speak. Instead, he heaved up a mouthful of lake water.

"It's okay," Joshua mumbled nearby. "I forgot to tell you. Our bodies, they have trouble adjusting to this dimension. Give it a minute."

"We need the seripyn, Josh," Peter said from somewhere behind Ford.

Ford pulled off his mask. His wet hair hung limp in front of his face. He dug his fingers into the soft sand and stared at his hands until they came into focus. Then he sat back and looked out to a blurry blue lake as he shrugged out of his tank and pulled off his fins. No rain. In fact, the sun shone bright and unforgiving into his pounding headache.

The still, humid air was heavy with the tang of vegetation. He squeezed his eyes shut, then widened them to stare at a tall, narrow stone building a few yards away. It wasn't an Iron Town cottage from the ruin. Not even a mini-mansion in Torst. This was a tower straight out of a King Arthur tale. At least six stories high, layers of stone up to a flat turret. Similar stone made up a low wall surrounding the structure.

He traced the tower's shadow across a wide beach and out into the water, where substantial waves crashed on shore. The lake surrounded him on three sides, with land only continuing to the north. In the distance, a few small islands protruded from the turquoise water.

"Let's try to get inside this outpost," Joshua said, helping Ford to his feet.

The world did a full loop, then settled to a steady ripple. Ava was lying on her side, moaning. Ford knelt next to her and swallowed back another urge to vomit. He eased her limp arms from her vest and tugged off her fins before wrapping his arm around her shoulders, easing her to sitting.

"You okay?" he asked, pulling her mask off and pushed her hair from her face.

Ava didn't open her eyes, but she nodded.

"Can you stand?"

Ava gripped Ford's arm and he gently helped her to her feet.

"You feel like puking?"

She took a deep breath and shook her head, finally fluttering her eyes open. "I'll be okay," she whispered and darted her eyes to the tower before settling on Ford.

Ford forced a grin and opened his arms as though presenting the scene to her. "Welcome to Alnok."

Ava nodded, leaned over, and puked between his feet.

Ford held her hair until she could stand, wiping her mouth.

"Better?" he asked.

"A little."

Ford cupped a hand over his eyes and squinted at the sun, then back out at the shadowy water. Further out to sea, the shadow grew darker. Black as night. As though a hole had been blasted into the center of the Earth, swallowing up anything within its vicinity. Too dark to be anything cast by the tower. It wasn't lengthening with the sun's light. It was becoming shorter, faster than any shadow should move.

No, it was advancing on them. Slowly rolling across the water toward the beach, ghostly hands reached out from the darkness as though pulling the shadow along.

"Joshua?" he asked slowly.

"Yeah, I see it."

"That normal for Alnok?"

Joshua took a step back and held out an arm, standing between Ford, Ava, and Peter and the approaching shadow.

He shook his head and grabbed his fins, mask, tank, and a pack, hefting everything over his back or in his arms. They all followed his example.

"Com'on." Joshua and Peter stumbled toward the tower like a couple of drunks.

Ford and Ava struggled through the soft sand toward the gloomy structure. They stumbled through an opening in the short stone wall and up a worn path that led to a large arched wooden door. Joshua threw it open and staggered inside an immense circular stone room and slammed the door shut behind them, shoving a bolt lock into place.

Their feet crunched broken glass strewn about the sandy floor. An overturned bench at the center, a wooden bucket filled with sand, and a busted canoe in one corner were the room's only inhabitants. The far wall was stacked with wooden shelves from floor to wooden ceiling and filled with bottles and jugs of various sizes. The shelves finished at a stairway, the first couple of steps rounding a corner and disappearing.

Ford turned the bench right-side up and sat Ava down. She smiled and nodded her thanks, then gave the door an uneasy glance. "What was that?"

Joshua shook his head and looked at Peter. "You ever see anything like it?"

"Never. But I was only in Alnok a few times. It kind of reminded me of . . . well, I just don't know."

"Are we safe?" Ava asked.

Joshua pulled his sword, stowed in its black scabbard, from a pack and belted it around his waist. "We'll do our best to make sure of that." He glanced at Peter, who drew his staff.

He gripped Ford's shoulder. "The dizziness will ease, I promise." He turned to Peter. "It wasn't this bad before. When we first arrived in Alnok. It came on slowly. I don't recognize that lake either." He gestured out to the water. "But"—he stared around the room—"this reminds me of the Kulum outpost."

"Maybe Kade gave you something for the dizziness while you were unconscious," Peter offered.

Joshua frowned. "I don't think so. But he had the tonic we needed. I don't know what we'll do until we can find a Guardian."

"Kulum . . . that's near Endyle, right?" Peter asked.

Joshua rubbed the back of his head. "If I'm right, yes, the closest kingdom would be Endyle and they're no friends of ours. We'll have to make it to Malvok."

"How far is that?" Ford asked, pressing the heels of his hands into his eyes.

"Too far," a voice echoed just a few feet away.

Joshua drew his sword from its scabbard, and Peter brandished his walking stick. Ava jumped to her feet. Ford had a sudden urge to laugh. Instead, he steadied Ava and focused on not throwing up.

"I am Joshua, son of Moses and Nahor, a temporal from Earth Apparent." Joshua's voice held such authority, such strength, Ford's mirth evaporated.

"Well met, Joshua of Earth Apparent." From the stairs stepped a slim, middle-aged man just slightly taller than Joshua and wearing a brown tunic over dark pants. His sparse, salt-and-pepper facial hair covered tanned, wrinkled skin. He regarded each of them with soulful, brown eyes. His deeply lined face was haggard, but his smile was kind. "I am Harel."

"Why is it we are so bad off?" Joshua asked, lowering his sword. "It took a while to fade when we were in Alnok last."

"That is because you are not in Alnok."

"What?" Peter gasped, his staff dangling in his hand.

"You are not in Alnok," Harel repeated. "You are in Velare."

Ford swallowed and shifted Ava, who sagged against him. "Where's Velare?"

"I should've known," Joshua said, ignoring Ford's question. "It feels different. Smells different."

"Here"—Harel handed Joshua what looked like a large seed—"chew on this." He gave another to Peter, then one each to Ava and Ford.

Joshua cocked his head and looked at it. No way was Ford putting anything in his mouth from this world unless Joshua did first.

"Seripyn?" Joshua asked.

Harel smiled. "Something like that."

Joshua gnawed on it and grimaced. Peter followed suit. The corners of Harel's mouth tugged in a suppressed smile. "You need something stronger for this realm."

Joshua nodded and looked at Ava and Ford. "Go ahead. Doesn't taste any worse than fruit gone bad. It'll help."

Ford nodded and chewed at the seed. Like a peach that had sat out a few weeks past its prime. But the headache lifted and the world righted. He looked at Ava who nibbled the edge without taking her eyes off Harel.

"What's Velare?" she asked.

Harel glanced around and then out the door. "One of the realms of the Periferie," he said without looking at her. "We cannot stay here."

"What's out there?" Ford asked, picking bits of the seed from his teeth with his tongue.

"An old enemy. It is not safe." Harel picked up the sand-filled bucket. "Has not been for a long time, no matter what anyone says," he muttered, then glanced over his shoulder. "This way." He gestured for them to follow him to the shelves.

Ford held out a hand to Ava, but she shook her head.

"I'm better now."

"Kulum was abandoned in Alnok," Joshua said as they followed Harel. "Is this . . . Kulum? Or a Kulum in Velare?"

Harel nodded. "In a manner. But you will find there are greater differences than similarities between the two dimensions. The climate the least of which." He set the bucket down and surveyed the shelves.

"Why is it not safe here?" Peter asked.

"Maybe we ought to send you back," Ford quipped.

"*You* should go back," Peter grumbled. "This isn't exactly must-see TV."

"Too late for any of that," Harel said. "You will have been spotted. The land is not safe."

"Will you take us to Malvok?" Joshua asked.

Harel shook his head. "There is no Malvok. No Herlov. No Guardians. But I can lead you to safety. For now."

"No Kade," Joshua said, looking at Peter. Their downcast reaction told Ford this "Kade" was someone important.

"How did you find us?" Ava asked, slipping her hand from Ford's and planting her feet.

"You are not the first to arrive."

Joshua took a sharp breath. "Lily? She was here?" His eyes bulged from their sockets and he took a step toward Harel.

"She was. Five days ago." Harel waved a hand and shook his head with a frown.

Joshua didn't budge. "Five days? She's been gone less than twenty-four hours!"

Harel shook his head with a scowl. "You think time works the same here? There will be opportunity for an explanation. But now, we must go."

"Go where?" Peter gestured around the small room.

Joshua took another step. "Tell me where Lily is! Do you have her?"

Harel opened his mouth to answer, when a whoosh, like a massive wave crashing onto the shore, came from outside and the door bulged. The sunlight peaking around the edges of the doorway was doused.

"We're out of time." Harel pushed a shelf back and to one side, revealing a dark recess. "They are here." He grabbed the bucket. "Go," he whispered.

Joshua entered the dark space, followed by Peter, Ava, then Ford. Harel squeezed behind them inside a closet-sized room, with hardly space for everyone and their gear, and slid the shelf shut. A light sputtered to life in one corner of the room.

Harel dropped the bucket in front of the hidden doorway. and kneeled down next to it. He scooped up a handful and it bubbled and frothed. As he smeared it into the crack where the shelf had closed it solidified into something resembling concrete.

"This will hold the door closed and give us some time."

"No locks?" Peter asked.

Harel worked his way around them to the center of the room and knelt down. "The substance I created works as well as any lock." He looked up at Peter with a patient raise of his eyebrows. "And a bucket of sand comes in handy for other things."

He placed his hands on the sandy floor and pressed down. As though made of ice, a dark hole, roughly three feet in diameter, melted away from the dirt, revealing a pool of dark blue water.

"You can leave your tanks and vests here," Harel said. "I'll send someone for them."

Peter dropped his tank along the far wall next to Joshua's. Ava and Ford nestled theirs in the grouping, then Ford grabbed Ava's hand.

Harel stood next to the hole. "You can hold your breath for a spell, yes? We will not go far."

"What?" Ava asked.

But Harel sat down with his feet dangling into the hole and dropped into the water without another word.

A crash came from just outside the small room and then a disturbing slithering, bringing to mind the old movie *The Blob*. Whatever had come in from the beach seemed to have made it into the tower.

"Put your fins back on," Ford instructed them as he peered into the hole. "It's big enough to drop in two at a time." He sat down, pulled on his fins and slid his goggles on. He gave Joshua a quick, questioning glance.

Joshua nodded. "We can trust him."

Ford knew better. His brother wasn't sure at all. But some of the shadow seemed to have found a small opening at the bottom of the door and was slithering in.

Ford looked at Ava. "Don't let go. Big breath. Ready?"

She nodded as she sat down across from him. Her beautiful brown eyes were hard with determination though tears filled them, betraying her fear. She yanked on her fins and pulled down her mask.

The shadow was crawling, fingers appearing and disappearing, searching, reaching, drawing close to Joshua's and Peter's feet. Ford squeezed Ava's hand and took a breath. Together, they dropped into the hole.

Ford kicked hard, gripping Ava's hand. He popped his ears, then blinked. A greenish light shimmered ahead, with Harel's silhouette waving them on into a cave-like chamber. It was further than Ford expected, but he held his breath with ease. He glanced at Ava, kicking hard, her gaze trained on Harel.

When they were all inside the cave, Harel swam over and pulled a rough, stone door closed behind them. He pushed a lever into place. Immediately, the water began to drain out. Soon, they were standing inside a cavern with walls honed to a smooth obsidian. Two windows on either side looked out into the deep. Green light streamed in and filled the holding chamber. A door opposite the one Harel shut was carved with elegant stonework and recessed colored gems demarcating it.

Harel glanced at their flippered feet. "You can leave those and your masks here."

The four removed their gear as Harel turned a lever on the ornate door. They followed him into a high ceilinged, cylindrical room with similar round windows as the holding chamber, streaming aquamarine light from the sea. The same ornate stone worked around bits of exposed coral was cut into the walls and inlaid with shining gems.

Ford gazed around the room. "Hey Joshua, you didn't tell me we were going to Atlantis."

Twelve

Lily lifted her heavy head from the cold stone floor. The cave smelled like Gramma's cellar. But worse. Something was rotten. The sun, her only light source, cast a smattering of light from down the tunnel where she'd arrived.

"Where am I?" she shouted, then cringed as her head pounded.

Two days in and out of consciousness on a horse with a strange man dressed like a soldier from Bible times just to be dumped in this sea cave. Warm, moist air moaned through the tunnel. The crashing waves echoed off the walls, closer at times and then further away.

They were getting closer again. Did whoever had taken her plan to let her drown?

No, they'd left a jug of water and a loaf of soggy bread. Why feed her just to let her die?

Morning light was filtering in after a long, dark night. The third day in this cave.

She could venture back down the tunnel. Find an escape. But then what? Every time she gathered her courage, the headache and nausea drove her back to the pallet set up in the center of the chamber.

She pounded her fist on the rough fabric. Surely she had been missed. But how would Uncle Ford know to find her here? She had just swam to the lower floor and then to a basement window for a peek inside. The blue light had filled her eyes . . . before being woken by rough hands shaking her and then forcing her atop the horse.

Maybe she'd just passed out and now she was having the worst and most vivid nightmare of her life.

Another wave of nausea took over any further thought. Lily swallowed as her mouth watered. She pushed her hair back, waiting to see if she would lose the bits of bread she'd nibbled to keep the hunger away. The sickness passed. She took a breath and sat back.

Something slithered in the corner. Something dark, like the shadow of an animal, prowled nearer.

Lily scooted away from it.

"It'sss okay . . ." something whispered. His words were thick, his breathing labored, as though his lungs were filled with mucous.

"Who are you?" she shouted. *What are you?*

"You can call us Bode. We have brought you a gift," the hissing voice continued.

"I want to go home!"

"Sssoon. Try thissss. It will help."

The shadow retreated to reveal a small ceramic bowl on the ground.

Lily stared at it until her body ached from holding the same position. Finally, when it seemed the shadow would not return, she stood, let the dizziness pass, and shuffled to the bowl. A thick, grayish brown substance sloshed at the bottom. She picked it up and sniffed it.

"Ugh! Am I supposed to eat this?" It smelled like rotten fruit and body odor. "Thanks a lot!" she called out to the ceiling.

She returned to her bed and sat the bowl far enough away so she couldn't smell it. Then she lay down and closed her eyes. When she opened them again, the cave walls glittered with afternoon sunlight.

Her new captor had not returned. Lily shivered. Maybe that was a good thing. Unless he was going to tell her where she was and how to get home, he could stay gone.

She grunted as she pushed up to a sitting position and looked at the bowl of thick broth sitting just a few feet away. Not a natural color. Looked like vomit.

Which was all she had done since being rescued. Puke and think.

The blue light was . . . a portal. Yep, that's what it was. No way to deny it, no matter how crazy it seemed. She'd been sucked through it. Maybe like her dad had gone through to the fifth dimension when she was a baby. Wow, what a mess she'd made.

Uncle Ford had tried so hard to talk her out of diving. But she'd forced his hand. *Obstinate.* That's what her dad would say. She wasn't sure of the exact definition, but it fit well enough. This was her fault. She'd let Uncle Ford down. Her dad. Everyone.

Bile rose in her throat. The cave tilted. She squeezed her eyes shut and rocked back and forth. She couldn't even think about escape. She couldn't think about anything.

The stew. Bode had said it would help.

It might be a trick. It could be poison.

She scooted nearer the bowl and stuck her finger in it. Slimy, but it didn't burn away her skin. She rubbed it between her index finger and thumb, then brought her finger to her mouth, licking off the smallest amount.

Gross. Like putrid grapes. But her stomach settled. As she sucked the rest off her thumb, the blurry far side of the cave came into focus. She brought the bowl to lips with one hand and held her nose with the other. She took a sip through pursed lips.

Okay, disgusting, but she felt better.

"Ssseee? You can trussst me," the voice of her kidnapper whispered. She dropped the bowl and stood on unsteady legs. He was nowhere. And everywhere.

"What do you want?" she shouted, glancing from one corner of the cave to another. A shadow stepped out from one of the craggy walls.

"To be friendssss."

"This isn't how friends act." Her voice quivered.

A gurgly chuckle. "How do *your* friendsss act?"

"They, um, they wouldn't do something I didn't want them to." Better, stronger. But her hands shook, and she had to keep blinking away the lightheadedness.

"Isss your uncle your friend?"

"Of course." A sob built up in Lily's throat. "I want to go back to him."

"Perhapsss. In time. Ssstay with usss a little while. We will be your friend. You will ssseee." The whisper faded away. Then footsteps, firm, normal footsteps.

"Sorry about him." A man strolled in from a shadowy opening on the far side of the cave. He couldn't have been much older than she was, with wire-rimmed glasses, a fitted green shirt on a lean body, and brown leather pants. His blond hair was messy but cut above his ears the way her dad would have approved. He smiled, showing even white teeth.

"Who're you?" Lily croaked. He couldn't be one of the good guys. He was too relaxed. Not at all freaked out by Bode.

"I'm Dr. Charles Beaghley. I really didn't expect to meet you this way"—he waved a hand around the cave—"at least not yet. You're a little early." He shrugged. "But here we are. Welcome to Velare."

Lily glared at him. "Never heard of it."

"Of course not." Dr. Beaghley frowned. "But your dad has . . . he was here."

"Liar," Lily whispered, tears stinging her eyes. Could this place be connected to Alnok? The place her dad had gone during the Upheaval?

"In fact," Dr. Beaghley continued. "So were you. But you were just a baby then."

"When I was kidnapped?" Icy fingers tapped on her gut. Her hands tingled. He was part of the cult.

"Now, I know what you're thinking. But your mom was really demonized in that whole debacle. You think she would put you in danger?"

Lily frowned and tried to keep the quiver from her voice. "I don't know. I don't know my mom."

"Ah, well, then we should remedy that straight away." He held out a hand.

"My mom?" Dizziness made her sway. She dug her fingernails into her palms to keep from staggering. "She's here?" A tear slipped down her cheek. The woman, a part of a cult, kidnapped her own child, and then disappeared. That woman was here, in this place full of shadows.

"That she is." The doctor beamed. "She's waiting for you. You must know, she would have come to visit, but she was afraid you might be angry. So many lies told about her."

"I don't understand." Lily had to clench her teeth to keep an angry sob from erupting.

Dr. Beaghley stepped nearer. "Then come find your answers."

Lily glanced at the bowl.

"Ah, that. Yes, well, a necessary evil for us temporals. But worth every nasty gulp. You'll like it here, Lily. I promise."

Lily folded her arms across her chest but didn't argue.

He finally withdrew the hand he had held out to her and shrugged again. "I don't think you want to stay here—"

"No, I want to go home."

"Well, that's not quite possible. Not yet. Until we find you a way home, maybe you could check out Velare?"

"If I go with you, you promise to get me home?"

"If, after you discover all there is to know about Velare you still want to leave, I will see about getting you home." He gave her a solemn nod.

"Fine." Lily wiped the moisture off her cheek and took a deep breath as she straightened her shoulders. Her hair was stringy and she had a horrible taste in her mouth. Spending days in her wetsuit and going to the bathroom in a corner of the cave she felt . . . gross. But maybe there was a shower where they were going. And some decent food. It was worth a chance.

"Just leave your dive gear here," Charles said. "You won't need it."

Lily scrutinized the area of the cave around her gear. A particularly long stalactite dropped from the ceiling next to it, nearly touching the ground. A lighter rock formed a divot in the wall right behind it. Maybe she'd remember where she left it.

And maybe I'll never see any of it again.

But she couldn't wait here for that shadow thing to come back. At least Dr. Beaghley was normal. Mostly.

"The cave is uneven, but you should be okay. Just stay close to me." He gave her another smooth smile. "C'mon. Let's go see your mom."

Flickering torches cast creepy, intermittent light on the walls. The tunnel that led off the chamber opened to another, smaller chamber. Something whispered in the darkness.

"Dr. Beaghley? Are there more of those . . . things?"

"Funny, that. There are, and yet, they all seem to be one. Oh, and call me Charles."

"All one what?"

"Being, entity"—he shrugged—"whatever. But they rule this dimension."

"Why?"

"Why do they want to rule?"

"No, why do you want to be a part of . . . Bode? That's what he said to call him."

Dr. Charles slowed. "Bode. Hmm, to everyone else they are the Schade. I don't know them to be individuals. They operate as one—"

"Like the Borg? Star Trek?"

Dr Charles guided her around a pile of fallen rocks. "Watch your step there. I think that would be as close a comparison as any. And I wouldn't say I became a part of them as much as . . . reaching an agreement. Ours is more of a collaborative effort."

Lily glanced over her shoulder. They were winding their way deeper into the caverns. Dad always said she had his sense of direction. She tried to mark off each turn. But as they passed through another chamber and continued down a third tunnel, she lost track.

"Don't worry," Dr. Charles said. "Not everything is underground." He held out an arm, presenting a spiral staircase just ahead. "The Schade like their dark, wet spaces, but we found a way to compromise. I'll show you."

Lily took one last glance back. Surely her mom wouldn't want to harm her. Maybe she'd get more answers.

Lily nodded and followed Dr. Charles up the narrow staircase. Round and round, they climbed higher and higher. The stone she trailed her hand along became warmer. Finally, with her leg muscles on fire, a light shone above.

Then they were stepping out onto an expansive clifftop. Jagged ridges cut across the stony expanse. Enormous rock formations rose in heavy clumps, towering over them and spreading out in one direction.

But the other way was wide open. A warm breeze blew Lily's hair back, and she breathed in the fresh air as she turned. The sun was sinking in the horizon, sending its rays across the sparkling ocean.

"Ah, the Kaidilas Sea," Dr. Charles said. "Beautiful, isn't it?"

Lily glanced at him. Handsome, yes. Crazy? Definitely. He grinned like she should be impressed by the waters stretching out below the edge of a cliff in an alternate dimension into which they had kidnapped her. For the second time.

"You said my mom—"

"Right, sorry. This way." He eased his way over the white, rocky ground. Some of the surrounding rocks contained deep, sporadic openings—windows. A few even had tattered fabric hanging across them. The doors, obscured in folds in the formations, came into view as they walked past the first cluster of rocks. What had appeared as smaller, fallen stones around the formations took on patterns outlining the base of each structure.

"Do you live here?" Lily asked, gazing up at one of the structures as they passed by.

He shrugged. "Sometimes. I mean, it was built for any of the temporals who came here."

"Temporals?"

"You, me, anyone from Earth . . . Apparent. That's what they call our dimension." He gave her a wink. "Seems appropriate, don't you think?"

"Yeah, sure," Lily said slowly. Nothing about this was appropriate, but he was clearly oblivious to not just the absurdity of his observation, but the depravity of the situation.

They came to a cobblestone path. At the end, a small stoop led to the front door, which was painted a pale yellow. It was the largest of the rock homes so far, with small arched openings for windows and even a few flowers planted along the base of the dwelling.

Dr. Charles gave the door a few raps, and they both waited. The wind gusted, howling through the stone village.

Then the door opened. A blonde woman, resembling the only picture Lily had ever seen of her mother, stood in the darkened archway. She stepped forward and covered her mouth with both hands, tears filling her blue eyes. She had pulled her gray-streaked, dull blonde hair in a sloppy braid. Wrinkles dug deep troughs across her forehead. She reached out with one hand, as though to touch Lily's shoulder, but stopped.

"Lily," she croaked from behind her hand, maybe due to emotion or a lifetime of smoking, or both.

Lily shifted on her feet. "Um, hi . . . mom." What was she supposed to say?

Anything to get home.

This wasn't really her mom, anyway. But then, neither was Raelyn. Suddenly, standing before this woman, lonliness hollowed out her gut. She was no longer hungry. A spark of anger filled her chest.

Her mother dabbed at her eyes with a tissue and glanced at Dr. Charles. "Thank you. I'd like to spend a little time with my daughter. Explain things to her."

Dr. Charles smiled again. Charming man. He really seemed to care.

Lily shook her head and frowned. How would she know that?

"Absolutely, Amy," he said. "I'll go rustle up some food. Can't survive on the seripyn."

Dr. Charles strode away as though he had an appointment to keep.

"I'm sure you have so many questions," Amy said, standing to one side and holding out an encouraging hand.

Lily was two the last time she had been with her mom, but the woman standing before her had landed in jail for her actions. She had never tried to reach out and see Lily. This person with the drawn face and glittering blue eyes was a stranger. But she was a shell of the smiling woman in Lily's one and only photo. A trickle of pity doused some of the building anger.

She entered and slipped past her mom, catching a whiff of what she could only pinpoint as a nursing home scent.

Inside was a neat room with a simple sofa and a few ottomans in a cream color. A counter along one wall served as the kitchen with a basin and what looked like a pizza oven. A wooden table held only two chairs.

Lily spun on Amy. "I do have a question. Why leave me in that cave for three days? Why didn't you come and get me?"

Amy shook her head. "I didn't know you were here, sweetheart. You weren't supposed to be here for weeks."

Lily blinked. Weeks? She was *supposed* to be here?

Amy waved her further into the home. "I know this is all so strange. But it'll sound better with comfortable clothes and a full stomach. I thought we might be close to the same size." She gestured to a blue set of clothes draped over the back of the sofa. "Through there"—she nodded to an open door on the opposite wall of the kitchen—"is my bedroom and a bathroom where you can clean up and change. I'll make us something to eat."

Lily nodded and collected the clothes. She ducked into the darkened room where an oil lamp flickered weakly on a nightstand. She closed the door behind her and tiptoed to another open door that led to a makeshift bathroom, but this one with a high open window, letting in a little evening light.

Lily peered into a pitcher full of water. She poured it into the honed basin formed right out of the stone wall. Then she pulled off her wet suit and rinsed off as best she could, using a chip of soap she found next to the pitcher. She dried off with a threadbare towel and then slipped on the supple, leather-like pants and slim tunic. Her mother was right, the clothes fit her perfectly. She braided her tangled hair and finished it with a hair tie from her wrist.

Like something from Robin Hood. As though she might be one of the Merry Men. Maybe. There was no mirror to confirm it. The scent of warm bread drove out all thoughts of her appearance as her stomach growled.

She made her way back to the main room and to her mother, who placed two bowls on the table flanking a loaf of sliced bread.

Amy smiled. "You look beautiful."

Lily blushed. "Thanks."

She looked at her birth mother. Raelyn had been her mom for the past fourteen years. Yet Lily's heart pounded and her stomach twittered as she tugged at her fresh shirt. This woman might be a stranger, but she was her mom. Her real mom.

Lily sat across from her. She paused only a moment, but with Amy's encouraging smile, she dug into the stew. She'd wolfed down three bites before she realized Amy wasn't eating but just staring at her with a faraway smile. Lily slowly lowered the spoon.

"Why did you bring me here?" she asked.

Amy's smile faltered. "It's not that I wanted to." Her eyes flitted to the front door. "I mean, I've wanted to see you since you were a baby. I've missed you." Her chin quivered.

"But you've repeated exactly what got you in so much trouble before." Lily gave a wary glance around the room. "Last time you were with some kind of cult. Is that what this is?"

Amy vigorously shook her head. "No, it's not a cult at all. A total mis-understanding last time. No one gave me the opportunity to explain—"

"Seemed pretty straightforward." The anger bubbled back up. "You stole me away from my dad and grandparents and hid me away."

"It wasn't like that at all. In fact—well, we'll get to that. But first, you must understand, it's so important that you're here. I hope you'll give me, and Charles, a chance to show you why. There's so much possibility!"

"Possibility for what?" Lily let her spoon clatter into her bowl and stood, food forgotten. "I need to get home. I have school starting soon. And dad will be so worried." She backed away to the door.

"Will you at least hear me out?"

"About why it's important that I'm here?"

"Yes."

Lily crossed her arms. "Why?"

"Because this land, Velare, is on the brink of war."

"I don't see how I could—"

"That's just it. You can help. You are especially equipped to be here. You're meant to be here. As though from birth, you were called."

Lily shook her head. "I don't understand what that means." Tears pooled in her eyes.

"It's okay, sweetheart." Amy stood and rounded the table, but kept an arm's length between them. "It means this special place has been incomplete until you arrived." She stared into Lily's eyes. "Haven't you always felt you were destined for something more?"

Lily fidgeted and looked away, chewing on her bottom lip. "Maybe. But I thought I might do something cool with Uncle Ford."

"Uncle Ford?" Amy blinked, then frowned. "I haven't heard that name in a long time."

"He contacted dad two years ago. He's totally cool. I was diving with him when I ended up here."

"He let you dive with him?"

"Well, not exactly." Lily cracked her knuckles. "I kind of twisted his arm."

Amy gave Lily a sly look. "So you knew the dive was important."

"Of course. It's Uncle Ford's most important dive."

"But it's the one you insisted on joining in."

"No, I always wanted to dive with him."

"But you didn't take no for an answer this time."

"Yeah," Lily said slowly. What was her mom getting at?

"*I* think you were drawn to this place."

"How's that? I didn't even know it existed."

"Why else twist his arm? Why this dive? Because it was important to Ford? Or to you?"

Lily started to argue, but stopped. She'd thought she'd wanted to go because it seemed to be Uncle Ford's pinnacle dive. But could it have been something else? Something deeper that 'drew' her here?

Amy smiled. "Just give me a chance to show you what I mean. There's a grand celebration in a few days. The elders have a critical declaration." Amy reached out for Lily and this time lay a hand on her shoulder and squeezed. "You'll see. I bet in that short time, you won't even want to leave."

Thirteen

Ford held his tongue as Harel led them, barefoot, soaking wet and cold, past a warm, humid room with overstuffed sofas tucked beneath glowing windows. A stone and shell mix created a tan stucco of sorts to cover the floors and walls. But exposed white coral jutted from the walls in various locations. All was cast in the same blue light from small portholes.

Harel hurried them through a maze of serpentine passageways. They passed men and women dressed similarly to their guide. The foreigners received curious glances as the citizens hastened on their way with focus and determination. Ford flinched at a sudden shout, sharp in the enclosed space, though he couldn't determine the distance or direction. Their trek took several more turns.

"Make way!"

Ford turned in time for a man and woman to brush past.

"Anna"—Harel dipped his head to the woman then the man—"Lucas."

Both returned the courtesy without slowing.

Ford picked up his pace and caught up to Harel.

"So, where are we going?"

"I will answer all your questions once we come to a"—he glanced over his shoulder—"private room."

A young man, slightly shorter than Harel, with shaggy reddish hair and a scruffy beard, approached from the opposite direction, bearing a long cloak.

"Thank you, Fitz," Harel said and draped the cloak over his shoulders. He looked Joshua up and down then glanced at Ford, Peter, and Ava. "Best get you into some suitable clothes."

"I'm not worried about my clothes," Joshua said. "Where's Lily? Is she okay? How could she have been here five days? She's only been gone less than one."

Harel nodded, but the creases in his forehead deepened. "She is alive and safe, as far as we know. Scouts followed her and a pawn of the Schade through Theurham Forest. They crossed the rift. They will have taken her to the catacombs."

"What?" Joshua exchanged a wide-eyed look with Peter.

Ford watched the silent communication, then glanced at Ava. She pressed her lips together and folded her arms. Obviously, she didn't enjoy being on the outside of the Periferie Club either.

"The catacombs within Velare," Harel said.

Joshua's face reddened. He clenched his fists. "I know the catacombs. Why do the Schade have her?"

"We have only guesses and rumor, which I will share. Know that she is alive and safe and will be kept so. But we must plan our rescue carefully. This isn't Alnok."

Joshua's jaw flexed, but he nodded.

"As to the time she has been here," Harel continued, "it passes more quickly here than in Earth Apparent. Our days are mere hours for you."

Harel took in a deep breath. "Fitz will take you to your quarters where you can change. I will have a meal prepared where you will meet the leader of Kulum and learn all we know."

"Fine," Joshua growled. "But if we don't leave soon, I have no problem going out on my own."

Harel nodded. "I understand your despair—"

"I'm not in despair. I'm angry. I'm determined to find her with or without help."

"Of course. But without help, you may do more harm than good. There are forces at work here you have never experienced. I repeat: this is not Alnok."

Harel disappeared back the way they had come, and they fell in line behind Fitz. Ford made sure Ava walked ahead of him, then turned to Joshua.

"What's the Schade Catacombs?" he whispered.

"A cave system. It's where we closed the last portal between Alnok and Earth."

"But that wasn't all that was there," Peter said over his shoulder.

Joshua nodded. "Cosyn from Alnok joined forces with a Velarean named Lim—" Joshua caught his breath. "Fitz!" Joshua abandoned his explanation and jogged up next to their guide. "What happened to Lima? Is she the one who took Lily?"

"Lima," Fitz snorted. "Nay, she is under heavy guard and poses no threat. She was but a wayward Velarean who wished to rule over both realms with Cosyn."

"Please," Fitz stopped in front of an ornate, arched blue door set in the stuccoed coral. He gestured for Joshua to enter. "You will find a place to rinse and a change of clothes." He nodded across the hall to another open door and Peter disappeared inside, shutting it behind him.

Ava ran her hand along the smooth wall next to a third room. She touched an exposed bit of coral as though assuring herself this was all real. "This all seems so normal to them."

"I know," Ford murmured. "Some shadow chased us to an underwater kingdom in another dimension. An evil army called the Schade supposedly has my niece. Nothing normal about any of this."

What did you get Lily into?

Ava searched Ford's face. "We'll find her." She opened her mouth as though to say more but closed it and disappeared into her room.

Fitz opened a fourth door for Ford.

"Look," Ford said before crossing the threshold. "I know you're trying to help, but you don't understand. Lily's just a kid. She's probably scared to death. We don't have time for a history lesson over dinner."

"We will waste no time, but you may not understand what you must do to rescue her."

"Whatever it is, I'm in. That little girl"—Ford's throat closed around an unexpected sob and he cleared it—"she may be Joshua's kid, but she's my mini-me. She's my shadow and I'm the reason she's here."

Fitz nodded and gave Ford a steady stare. "Leading young ones into danger is a serious offense. But do not take on more fault than is due."

"Right," Ford grunted and entered his quarters.

A large round window cast an aqua glow over a round bed made of carved stone next to a simple basin of water. He crossed the room to the window. Heat filtered through the clear opening. Bubbles rose out of the sea floor.

Hydrothermal vents next to a window to heat the room. Smart.

He reached out and touched the window, pressing his fingertips to a pliable, rubbery material. Like a clear gelatin that left his fingers damp. It gave a perfect view of colorful fish darting in and out of stalks of seaweed and towering coral in shades of pink and yellow. The scene dissolving into a distant, dark indigo.

Besides the bed, basin, and window, the room was a simple, rough-stone chamber with no embellishments or decoration signifying who the Velareans were.

He turned back to the bed. A pair of dark brown pants and matching long-sleeved tunic, not unlike the clothes worn by his host, lay across a thin covering of white sheets. Eager to get out of his wet suit he stripped off and pulled on the pants. He washed his face and rinsed his hair in the basin of fresh water before tugging the shirt over his head. He took a hair tie from his wrist and combed his hair with his fingers into a ponytail.

Still barefoot, he glanced around the room until he spied a pair of slender boots in the room's corner near the doorway. He yanked them on and laced them. They were made of something not unlike Neoprene. The sole was wider than any boots he'd ever worn, clunky despite their slim material.

He sighed and yanked open the door. The hallway was cooler than his room and deserted. But he could still hear the buzz of conversation just out of sight.

"Hello?"

It was only a second before footsteps rounded the corner. Fitz greeted him with a quick bow. Ava was next out of her room, her curly hair still damp, her face flushed and a deep frown that might have represented confusion or fortitude. Probably both. Her new clothes, the same as his, were a pale green. Peter exited his room immediately after. He wore blue.

Peter looked up and down the hall. "Where's Josh?"

"He is waiting in the dining hall," Fitz said.

Of course, his brother had wasted no time. Ford pressed his lips together. From now on, Joshua wouldn't have to be the first to take on any tasks to lead them to Lily and get her safely home. Ford would be the trustworthy leader he needed. A grieving father shouldn't have to shoulder the brunt of the burden. Not when it was he himself who caused it.

Fitz waved them back the way he had come, and they circled around the hallway. More windows, covered in the clear, gelatinous substance, poured in blue light from the sea.

They followed Fitz through a wide arched opening into an expansive room, the back of which held a rounded window three times the size of the one from Ford's quarters. Harel was at the window, gazing at the liquid landscape, his back to them.

In the center of the room, Joshua sat with his head bowed over an oval table made of the same stone as Ford's bed. Ford strode over to him, meaning to wrap an arm around his shoulder. Assure him of everyone's determination to get Lily. But at the last minute, he veered away and joined Harel at the window. His words to Joshua would be empty until they had her back.

Stalks of broad-leafed seaweed as tall as redwoods swayed in the current. A fish that looked a little like a catfish, but bright yellow with blue markings, darted in and around the kelp forest's leaves. A school of smaller orange fish, like tiny flames, flit back and forth. If not for the steady rise of panic, Ford could have stood at the window for hours watching the life beyond. Another time, he might have shared all this adventure with Lily. No one would appreciate it more.

Another type of fish prowled about the kelp forest. There was no doubt about what this one was.

"A tiger shark," Ford said.

Harel glanced at him. "What?" He followed Ford's gaze. "It is a sirak, but yes, much like your sharks in Earth Apparent."

"Only a lot bigger," Ava said, drifting up next to Ford. She seemed to have shrunk since coming here. Ford checked the instinct to wrap his arm around her shoulder. She had chosen to come. As much as he wanted to comfort her, she needed to find her own strength.

Harel gestured to the table. "Please, have a seat."

Ford sat next to Harel. Ava and Peter chose seats around Joshua. Fitz gave a nod to Harel, then quietly left the room.

"What're the windows made of?" Peter asked as he sat down.

Ford fought an eye roll. *Who cares?*

Harel cocked his head and looked at the enormous window as though he had never considered it. He shrugged.

"Water."

Fitz bustled back in with a few others, trays of food balanced in their hands. Most of the fare was fish of some variety or another. Vegetables, some of them recognizable, were spread across the table. Ford plucked a blue, carrot-looking root from the platter closest to him and sniffed it.

"Eat while we await our leader," Harel said as he scooped a ladle of the vegetables. "We trade with our counterparts to the north for land food."

"So some of you stayed on land," Peter said.

Harel didn't look up from his plate. "A large contingent of Velareans reside in Silom."

"If it's so dangerous," Ava said, leaning forward, "why didn't they choose the protection of the sea?"

"They chose confrontation over cowardice," Fitz said as he plopped down at the far end of the table.

Harel gave him a hard stare. "Our leaders decided protecting their citizens was a greater calling than waging war."

"I can't say I understand what the Schade are," Ford said. "But it seems war is finding its way in every nook and cranny. What makes you think it won't make it here?"

"I agreed to take time for clothes and food," Joshua interrupted, "but we're wasting time. How do we find Lily?"

"Carefully," Harel responded with a meaningful gaze. "As we speak, preparations are being made for our journey. A host of soldiers, supplies, and transportation. We have not been idle. You suppose we have carved out an existence beneath the seas for pure enjoyment? Nay, there is evil about the land we cannot charge into."

Ava leaned across the table and put a hand on Joshua's arm. "I may not understand everything that's going on, but following their lead may be prudent."

"If there's so much evil," Ford broke in, "and that evil has Lily, maybe charging into it is exactly what we should be doing."

"However," Ava continued with an irritated glance at Ford, "a strategy would be wise. Especially from those more familiar with what we might face."

"But why?" Joshua asked, his voice hoarse, strained. "Why do they want my baby so badly?"

Harel nodded. "I will come to that. In fact, it is imperative you understand if we have any hope of a rescue." He glanced at Ford, and Joshua followed his gaze.

"Am I missing something?" Ford asked with an irritated frown.

Joshua glared at him and Ford immediately wished he could inhale the words back into his mouth.

"You don't get to question anything," Joshua said, his tone low and dangerous. "I did everything I could to protect her. To keep her from all of this." He pointed a finger at Ford. "Lily's here because of you. We're all here because of you."

Ford shifted in his seat. "I just, I'm still trying to figure out what this all means. So we can find Lily."

Harel interrupted a retort from Joshua. "It is not by accident you found yourselves here. All of you."

"You're saying Ford was lured," Joshua said. "Lily would have ended up in the Periferie no matter what I did."

Harel shook his head and looked up at the ceiling as if the explanation might be scrawled across it. Finally, he looked back at Joshua. "I would not say lured, but Ford, Lily, each of you are inextricably linked to this realm. There is a greater connection than you can imagine." He glanced at Ava, then past her to the doorway and stood, nearly knocking over his seat.

At the other end of the table, Fitz stood just as quickly and took a step back as though to stand at attention.

"My friends," Harel said, gesturing toward the chamber exit. "May I introduce the leader of our council."

A man with jet black hair set in a low ponytail and full dark beard strode into the room. He was as tall as Harel, but his chest was broader. Or puffed out to appear so.

"Jonis," Harel continued with a bow. "I present to you Ford Montgomery, Joshua Spurgin, Peter Witt, and Ava Ambrello." They all stood.

"Please, sit," Jonis said, gesturing to the table.

Everyone took their seats. Jonis, however, did not.

"So," he said, staring around the table, "word reached us you are missing someone."

Joshua clenched his fists on the table. "That 'someone' happens to be my daughter."

A dark frown passed over Jonis' face. "I am aware." His eyes flitted to Harel before he looked back at Joshua. "If it is aid you are seeking, you must understand, our resources are limited."

Harel stood. "But we can offer some." Though he made the statement, he raised his eyebrows at Jonis as though it was a question.

Jonis nodded. "Of course. I assume you will seek the help of the Silomites?"

"We have no choice. The Schade have grown bolder. Stronger. Sabel will have had better surveillance and may even help with strategy."

A fleeting look passed over Jonis' face. As if he had just tasted something unpleasant.

Harel addressed Joshua. "Sabel is the leader of Silom. She commands a large army."

"I am sorry I cannot accompany you," Jonis said. "As you can understand, my duties are to the inhabitants of Kulum."

He gave Harel a thin smile. "Nevertheless, keep me apprised of your plans. I would not want you to embark on such a perilous journey ill-prepared."

"We will." Harel gave a quick bow.

"Very well." Jonis turned and left the room without a look back.

"He doesn't seem to like us very much," Ford muttered.

Harel offered Ford a sympathetic smile. "We have had fewer dealings with temporals than the Alnokians. Our role has been more . . . supportive of Kade and the Guardians of that realm. But we battle the evil that threatens your world all the same."

"You're talking about the Schade?" Peter asked.

Harel nodded. "Cosyn is a trickster. He wishes to dominate." Harel's words came faster now. It was as though Jonis' visit had spurred something. "The Schade have no such aspirations. They are a hive of wickedness whose existence seems only to torment and destroy all that is good."

"You still haven't answered my question," Joshua said, "about their interest in Lily."

Harel sighed, stood and began pacing. "The Schade are interested in all temporals, but particularly the descendants of Moses and Nahor."

"The two from the letter," Ford said.

Harel cocked his head at Joshua.

"Kade's prophecy," Joshua said. "It seems there was a second part to it."

Harel stopped mid-step; eyebrows rose even as he gazed off into the distance. "How interesting."

"You don't seem surprised," Joshua said.

The corners of Harel's mouth turned up in a small smile. "Little surprises me. But I would like to see this prophecy."

"Of course."

"What about this Schade have to do with our families?" Ford pressed as Joshua retrieved the rolled up parchment from inside his tunic.

"It's a long story," Peter said.

Ford leaned back and looked at him without smiling. "So enlighten me."

"During your black plague," Harel began, resuming his pacing, "Arkon-ai rescued a group of faithful temporals into Alnok. A remnant, you might say. They flourished and eventually established six temporal kingdoms. Many hundreds of years later, Cosyn waged war against them. One by one they fell until only two temporals remained."

"Moses and Nahor," Ava said.

"Yes. Kade, Guardian of Alnok, sent them back to Earth Apparent. You"—he gazed around the table—"are their descendants. But Lily is different. She is the offspring of two of the children of Moses and Nahor. A more direct line."

"That can't be right," Joshua interrupted. "She's not Raelyn's child."

"I know."

"Are you telling me Amy, my ex, she's . . ."

Harel was already nodding. "It seems those born of Moses and Nahor have a particular attraction to each other. It has only strengthened as the line between the Periferie and your world is blurred."

"What does it mean?" Ford asked. "To have both parents from here?"

Harel shook his head. "It is unclear. There must be something for the Schade to want her so badly. We have no time to study the lineage. But I will read the prophecy before we go."

Joshua handed Harel the page. "If there's anything in there that tells us how to rescue Lily, please tell me." His voice was still ragged.

"Of course. We will travel to Silom as soon as possible."

"During the day? The cover of darkness might be advantageous," Peter suggested.

Harel shook his head. "We do not travel after dark. Ever."

"Is there more than the Schade we should be worried about?" Ford asked.

"Too many threats to count," Fitz said. "Which is why Jonis led us beneath the sea."

"You don't seem to be completely sold on the idea," Ava said.

Harel gave a wry smile. "He does what he believes is best for all. We once controlled all of Velare. All but the cliffs and catacombs. But during the Portal Wars, what you call the Time of Testing, something happened in Velare. As Kade saw victory in Alnok, the Schade took more and more land here, marching across the Rift. Jonis retreated to the sea."

"Retreated," Joshua said.

"A protective measure," Harel explained. "But one we cannot indulge if we have hope of finding Lily."

"You said you don't travel at night, but won't we still be exposed?" Ford asked.

Harel nodded. "We will not traverse the land. We travel beneath the surface of the water."

Fourteen

Harel got to his feet, his mild expression now brooding, and waved Fitz over as he spoke to Joshua, Ford, Peter, and Ava. They all stood. With Joris' exit, a tight tension had entered the room. Harel spoke quickly and Fizt fidgeted and paced. Their leader had broken what seemed to have been a holding pattern.

"There is a partial tunnel system we will take from here," Harel said. "We will make for a group of islands call Endyle."

Joshua choked on a sip of water. "Endyle?"

Harel nodded. "Not the kingdom you encountered in Alnok. In Velare, it is a deserted island."

"Except for the encroaching shadows," Fitz corrected.

Harel turned to Fitz. "Indeed. Are we prepared to travel to Silom?"

Fitz nodded. "Yes, every soldier is ready to leave." He gestured for a few of the attendants to follow him out of the room.

Harel snapped his attention to Joshua.

"We can continue our discussion as we travel."

They followed Harel out of the dining hall. What had been a sense of rushed resolve with the other Kulumians marching up and down the corridors had become a controlled panic. Soldiers with spears jogged in pairs ahead of them and out of sight. A woman skirted around Harel, bumping into Ford she raced past, mumbling an apology but never looking his way.

"What's Endyle?" Ava asked, dodging a Kuluman carrying a crate.

"A terrible kingdom with an evil leader," Peter said with a scowl.

Ford raised his eyebrows and looked at the skinny kid. "You know it?"

"I just know about the portal beneath the castle. I helped my sister close it." He gave Ford a steely glare.

Ford glanced at Peter's staff but didn't argue. Evil kings and portals. This was all too much.

They were traveling at an angle, downward and deeper into the subterranean castle.

"Okay, we take the tunnels. Then what?" Joshua asked.

"We will travel to Endyle," Harel said. "You will find no Lord Lachlor there. The island is deserted except for what evil has overtaken it and lurks in the forests and in the shallow waters. But anchored there is a ship. The *Sealight*."

"I thought we need to stay beneath the water," Ava said.

"Aye. An underwater ship."

"A sub?" Ford barked a surprised laugh.

"A submerged ship, yes."

"Why not take it from here?" Joshua asked.

"The currents outside our shelters are too strong," Harel said. "The tunnels will take two days to traverse."

"Two days?" Joshua and Ford asked in unison and glanced at each other. Joshua's expression softened. Some of the ice seemed to chip away.

"What about Lily?" Joshua asked.

"There's no way they'll do anything to her," Ford said. "Obviously, they need her." He was voicing more of a hope than a fact.

"She will be safe," Harel confirmed. "At least for the time being. But I do not know what they want from her. If it is not her life, they may wish to do her greater harm."

"Something greater than death?" Ava asked.

"They might seek to break her spirit and her will."

Joshua stopped short, and everyone stopped with him. "What does that mean? Break her."

Harel gripped Joshua's shoulder. "Through careful manipulation and coercion. But take heart, she is strong. It will take more than they realize to win her to their uses." He nudged Joshua on.

"She didn't just happen to tumble through the portal, did she?" Ford said as they wound to the right.

Harel shook his head. "They were determined for her to be here. They tried a more direct approach when she was a babe. As subtle as their tactics may be, they have been planning her return since. Though I do not know what plans they have for her, I am certain they will not harm her. But . . ."

"But?" Joshua asked. His face was as pale as when they had arrived before Harel gave them the seripyn.

"Be prepared," Harel said. "She may not wish to leave."

Within the hour, they were fitted with slim backpacks and a few basic supplies. Food was all around them. From the fish to the plant life.

They made their way through the castle to an archway so low even Ava had to duck through it. Remaining crouched, they continued through a damp, dim, cave-like corridor carved out of a greenish coral, smoothed but still pocked and dimpled.

"Two days of this?" Ford grumbled. Already, his thighs burned.

Harel, only a shadow ahead of them, glanced back and chuckled.

The tunnel took on a slight incline. Ford gritted his teeth to cage a surly comment. If this took them to Lily, he would crawl on jagged rocks. A slight inconvenience was nothing if it brought them closer to his niece.

Aqua light shone ahead. The incline became a steep slope. Peter stumbled and Joshua caught him as he slid backward. Ford held Ava's elbow as they clambered through a jagged hole into a massive arched chamber, at least twenty feet high. At one time, it might have been a cave, but circular windows cast that same blue glow on a room of intricately carved stone. Elaborate metal scrollwork served as reinforcements in intermittent arches down a tunnel that curved around out of sight.

"Wow," Peter breathed, looking up and turning in a slow circle.

"This is beautiful," Ava said, looking up at the blue water window surrounded by the same scrollwork.

"This is more to your liking?" Harel asked Ford.

Ford's ears warmed. "I wasn't saying . . . I mean, whatever it takes to find her."

Harel clapped him on the back. "I know. This is an old cave system we carved into our own uses. We continued it, building on, following the shoreline. Here"—he pointed beneath a low window—"Fitz saw to your equipment."

They found their fins, goggles, and even flashlights stacked neatly against the wall.

Fitz came through the smaller tunnel, followed by one Kuluman after another. Soon, at least fifty Velarean soldiers, male and female, surrounded them.

Joshua looked over Fitz's uniform. Similar to the thick pants and tunic worn by everyone else, the clothes were finished with heavy stitching and seams reinforced at the chest and shoulders.

"It looks like underwater armor," Joshua said. "Don't suppose we need anything like this?"

Harel shook his head. "Each has his own. We do not keep spares. However, you have all the protection you will need." He gestured to Joshua's sword.

Joshua touched his hilt and nodded, glancing at Peter.

"Well, that's great for y'all," Ford said, taking a step toward Ava. "But what about us?" He put a protective arm around Ava's shoulders.

She looked up at him, eyebrows raised. "I know some Ju Jitsu."

He let go and ran his fingers through his hair. "I know you're not helpless. But even Joshua has a sword. I promised to keep you safe."

Ava smiled. "I know you did. I know you will."

Harel nodded. "We prepared for your arrival."

Fitz waved over a pair of Velarean guards, a stocky man with shaggy blond hair and a lithe woman with short red hair, but about the same age. Harel had addressed them earlier. Ann and Luke or something.

Others began entering the passage through the ornate arch. The man presented a short speargun, not eighteen inches, to Harel.

Ford couldn't help his grin as he took it. "A speargun?" He scratched the back of his head. "Won't have much power behind it."

Harel smiled. "You might be surprised." He gestured for the man to give the gun to Ford. "Thank you, Lucas."

The woman handed Ava a sheathed dagger.

"Thank you," Ava said as she took it and pulled out a serrated blade that looked to be made of blue quartz, deeply veined and opaque. The hilt was a gleaming silver and the handle wrapped in black cord.

"Whoa," Ford said, looking down at his speargun. The tip of the spear was crafted out of the same quartz.

Harel pointed to Ford's pack. "There is a holster in your bag."

Ava turned her sheath over where two bands would attach to a leg harness.

"I will explain the weapons' significance, but we must go—"

"Harel!" a shout filled the chamber and bounced off every wall.

Harel stiffened, but took a deep breath before he turned. "Jonis!"

Standing in the spot where they had just left the smaller tunnel was their leader.

Jonis offered a stiff smile. "You must have misunderstood our conversation about the temporals."

Harel took a step toward the man and gave a quick bow with his head. "Perhaps. You wished me to send them on with supplies." Harel waved a hand at the soldiers, still awaiting orders. "They are well supplied."

Jonis gazed around the room. "Supplies were not to include an army. And I did not just wish it. I commanded it."

Harel leveled his gaze at his leader. "We have a different understanding as to supplies. With clothing and a map, we would only send them to their deaths."

Ava sucked in a sharp breath.

"I only supposed your *command*," Harel continued, "would include their best chance of success."

"I cannot spare so many of our best fighters."

Harel shook his head and glanced over his shoulder. "I should like to keep Fitz, Lucas, and Anna with us. A few dozen have already entered the tunnel."

Jonis narrowed his eyes, but gave a curt nod. He drew a long breath as he looked around the room. "All of you! Back to the keep. We suspect an attack any day. We will need every soldier on guard!"

Muttering and casting confused glances between Harel and Jonis, as the two men continued to stare each other down, the soldiers went back the way they had come. Soon only Ford, Joshua, Peter, and Ava were left with Harel, Fitz, Lucas, and Anna.

For the first time, Jonis glanced at the newcomers. "I hope you understand. I cannot risk the safety of our people for the sake of one temporal."

"That temporal is my child," Joshua said, his voice low and tense.

Jonis clenched his teeth. "I, too, have children. Here. I am sorry." His shoulders relaxed. "Truly. But your being here is only a prelude to what is to come."

"I only care about getting my daughter."

"I fear you will be forced to care about much more." Jonis flitted his eyes to Harel and then turned and ducked back through the opening to the tunnel.

"What's that supposed to mean?" Peter asked, smoothing his hair back and giving his staff a quick touch.

Ford fought the impulse to put a reassuring hand on his speargun. But Peter's gesture of insecurity was not lost on him.

Harel sighed. "Jonis is both wise and stubborn. I cannot fault him for doing everything he can to protect our keep and those in his charge. The Schade have become increasingly bold."

Fitz glanced into the tunnel and up at a window in the ceiling. Swirling water obscured anything of the sea beyond. "The storm increases."

Harel's face darkened. "The tunnel will protect us."

Anna smiled. "We will be well on the other side if anything should happen."

"Has anything breached the tunnel before?" Peter asked as they set out, following the two dozen soldiers who had already left before Jonis arrived.

"In the early stages of its construction, the Schade did everything within its power to destroy it."

"Sending storms?" Ava asked.

Harel gave her a sidelong glance. "They did."

Ford raised his eyebrows and looked at Ava. *Smart girl.*

"Is this storm from the Schade?" Ford asked.

"There have been many aquatic squalls over the years. None could penetrate the rock once we reinforced it with the same material that make up your weapons." Harel nodded to Ford's speargun.

"But you didn't answer her question," Ford said.

"Is the storm one of the Schade's?" Joshua repeated.

Harel shook his head. "It shows no sign as such." But he exchanged a wary glance with Fitz.

"Even so," Anna said, "we will be to Endyle before the Schade could fashion anything strong enough."

"Something about that doesn't give me a lot of confidence," Joshua grumbled.

They continued at a quick pace in silence down the tube-like corridor, casting nervous glances at the arched window along the walls and above. The floor had been finished like a cobblestone path, incorporating coral and shell. Massive pillars bore into the base and anchored the ceiling every ten yards or so.

Ford, never sensitive to smells, struggled to ignore the heavy mildew. Ava covered her nose. Hungry lichen clung to shallow puddles at the edge of the walkway. Movement caught the edge of Ford's vision and he snapped his head around to search the nearest window.

A school of yellow fish, big as tuna, but slender and quick, darted past. Ford watched them swim past the next window and then out into the empty blue void until the swirling waters ate them up. Just behind them, a massive sirak swam by the window, its teeth bared. Ford shivered. They better not end up in the water with that thing.

"We just lost over half of the soldiers," Joshua said.

"We still have a good number," Harel said. "The best."

"But you must've thought we needed all of them," Peter argued.

"It is prudent to be over-prepared."

"You're still confident we can get past the Schade to Lily?" Ava asked.

Harel nodded. "Even if I doubted it, we have no choice. Not just for Lily. War is coming."

Fifteen

Lily sighed as she changed for bed. She tried to sort through everything her mother had said.

You were chosen.

Help your family.

But in her exhaustion, all the words jumbled together. Dr. Charles and her mother's voices overlapped and competed for importance. A fierce army in another dimension. A family legacy established during the Black Plague of the 1500's.

"A war to end wars," her mother had said.

Lily scoffed as she pulled the soft shirt over her head.

Sounded like a bad suspense movie.

"Lily, you are key to ensuring the right side wins," her mother had said.

"The Schade are neutral, but useful," Dr. Charles had chimed in.

Lily shuddered. The Schade were anything but neutral. Only an idiot would believe that.

She crawled into her mother's spare bed in the tiny second bedroom. The sheets were cold, but the sweet jasmine scent was instantly comforting. She snuggled into the pillow and squeezed her eyes tight, tears leaking out.

Dr. Charles was one of the good guys her mother had assured her, He'd helped create a path between Earth Apparent and Velare. Her dad had fought to sever the tie between Earth and these other dimensions. Why would she help undo all that?

Earth Apparent, the only home she knew. But her mother argued that Velare was as much home. Maybe more.

Lily's head ached. She should have taken some more seripyn before she'd gone to bed. Though nothing sounded better than to close her eyes and forget all of this for a while, a deep thrumming fear held sleep at bay.

They were expecting an answer from her. They needed something it seemed only she could give.

"A special place among us . . . you're needed . . . you're important."

I don't feel important. I'm scared. And homesick.

Lily shook her head and rubbed hard at her eyes as she sat up. Crying wouldn't help anything. And now that she wasn't being bombarded with strange and confusing information, something her mother had said surfaced out of the unfamiliar haze. It shone as though hit with a spotlight.

That B&K Sciences was involved. The company *was* the cult. They were the same people who had stolen her away when she was little. Every time she'd asked, her mother had changed the subject. Why? Why was she here? Why did they want her?

Birds began to chirp. Sleep wasn't going to happen. She threw the blanket back and pulled on the Velarean pants and stomped barefoot into the main room. It was still and quiet.

Maybe it was rude, but she needed answers. Surely her mom wouldn't begrudge getting up a little early to continue their conversation. She tiptoed to her mother's bedroom. The door was opened a crack.

"Mom?" she whispered into the darkened room. She tapped on the door. Nothing.

She pushed the door open a bit. The morning light shone from a small window. The bed was empty.

"Mom?" She hurried to the table where an oil lamp flickered weakly. She turned up the flame and looked around the room.

A scrap of paper lay on the table. Lily looked at it without picking it up.

If you're up early, there's some dried fruit and bread on the shelf next to the oven. I will be back soon.

-Mom

"Great," Lily muttered and strode back to her bedroom and changed into the Velarean shirt. She blew out a breath through puffed cheeks and scratched the back of her head. "Now what?"

She could stay put. Wait for her mom to return. Or she could go out and look for answers. Maybe the answers her mom was not giving her. If she, Lily, was chosen to be here, that should mean she was safe. Right?

She chewed her lip and walked to the door, put her hands on her hips and stared at it. She reached out for the knob, pulled her hand back, reached again and took hold of it.

She cleared her throat and shook her head, gripped the knob and turned it. The door swung open soundlessly. Morning had emerged and Lily blinked at the sudden brightness. When her eyes adjusted, she eased out of the stone house and closed the door behind her.

Okay, step one: leave the house. Step two: back to the cliff.

She had entered the portal through the water. Maybe she would see something in the sea to give her a clue about how to return.

She ambled along the pathway of the quiet town. The interconnected homes with their small, uneven windows seemed abandoned. She didn't pass a soul on her way to the cliff side. A seagull cried as she approached. A salty breeze blew her hair back as the sun climbed into the sky, casting warm rays on her back.

Just miles and miles of choppy, indigo sea. In the distance a scattered collection of islets, only dark spots on the water, and then haze and sky.

She could climb to the base of the cliff. Go back down the stairs to the cave where Dr. Charles had found her. That would bring her closest to the way she had arrived. Her dive gear had been there. Hopefully, still forgotten in the dark corner of the cave. But how helpful would that be? She was nearly out of air when she had blacked out. And then what? She would be just as stuck, and closer to that thing that had brought her the soup. Or she could go back to her mother's house.

A stabbing pain in her forehead forced the choice. Back to the house. She couldn't do anything with this headache and the dizziness that was sure to follow.

Lily heaved a sigh and trudged back. She stopped at a few of the houses and peeked in the windows. Where were the people? The inner rooms were much like her mother's. A simple kitchen and seating area. She meandered to the next house and peered inside. A pair of brown eyes met hers.

She gasped and stumbled back. The eyes belonged to a dark-haired boy, a little older than Holly. Not more than twelve or thirteen. He backed away, disappearing inside the house.

Lily stepped back three paces. What was she, some kind of peeping Tom? People lived here. Lily shook her head and hurried back to the path.

"Hello!"

Lily spun around to find the boy following her along the pathway. He was dressed in short, tan, linen-like pants and a sheer shirt, tied at the neck. His hair was messy, but not long. His chocolate brown eyes filled with mirth searched her face.

"Um, hi." Lily glanced behind him. "Sorry about that."

He grinned. "Don't worry, my housemates are out in the sand fields today."

"Oh." Lily nodded like she knew what he was talking about.

"I'm Jonah."

"Hi, Jonah. I'm Lily."

"I know." He meandered towards her, kicking some rocks.

"How do you know who I am?"

"Everyone knows who you are."

"Everyone?"

He grinned. "You'll meet everyone later. I'm about to go fishing. Would you like to come?"

Lily pressed the heel of her hand to her forehead. "I'd love to, Jonah. I just need to do something about this headache."

Jonah gave her a solemn nod. "The seripyn. I'll come with you to your house. Then we can go."

"Sure, yeah."

Her house? When did it become her house?

Lily's mouth watered as her stomach soured. She had to get the elixir now. She hurried back up the path to her mother's house and burst through the door, not bothering to close it. The cup still sat near the sink basin, half full.

Lily threw back the bitter concoction and swallowed hard. She held onto the counter and waited for the effects. Slowly, the nausea passed. The headache eased. She took a deep breath and blew it out slowly.

"Better?" Jonah asked.

"Much." Lily looked around the room. Still no Mom.

Jonah picked up the cup from which she'd just taken the seripyn and sniffed at it and wrinkled his nose as he sat it down. "You won't need this the longer you're here."

Lily gave him a shrewd glance. "Who says I'll be here that long?"

Jonah shrugged and meandered about the kitchen, seeming to be both curious and bored. "Everyone who comes to the cliffs stays." He frowned. "Or at least most of them." His expression cleared, and he looked at her with a bright, happy smile. "Your mom is probably with the rest of the cliffers, harvesting at the Rift."

"Cliffers." Lily nodded. "Hm, that fits. What are they harvesting?"

Jonah shrugged. "A lot of things. Did you still want to go fishing?"

"Sure. You have a pole?"

"Pole?" He chuckled. "We climb down to the shoreline and cast our nets."

"Of course."

"Follow me."

He walked out the door, and Lily followed, shutting the door behind her. If he took her to the shoreline, there might be another way to escape.

"So, where are your housemates?" she asked as she jogged to catch up.

"Everyone goes to harvest. I stayed behind today because, well, I have been ill and have only just now left my bed."

"I'm sorry to hear that. Do you mean your mom and dad when you say "housemates?""

"Nothing like what you have in Earth Apparent. We are all caretakers of one another."

"You're not from . . . Earth? Where I'm from?" She couldn't call her home Earth Apparent.

"I have only ever known the cliffs and the sea."

"I didn't expect to see kids here."

Jonah approached the same opening in the ground from which Dr. Charles had brought her and gestured for her to follow. "There are few."

Then he disappeared down the stairs.

As they circled down the steps, Lily's heart pounded. This is where that thing was. But surely Jonah knew about the creature. If he wasn't afraid, maybe she didn't have to be.

"Hey, Jonah!" she called at the bottom of the stairs and ran into the back of him. He held a finger to his lips.

"Shh. The Schade leave us alone, but they are no friend of the cliffers."

He waved her to an opening on the far side of the chamber. Lily glanced around. Her tank, goggles, breather, were all stacked in the corner with the stalactite.

Jonah stopped just inside the passageway and followed her gaze. "I don't think you will need that anymore."

"No?" Lily said, trying to hide her irritation. He seemed to know a lot more about her than she knew about anything in this strange world. *Velare.*

It was time for some answers.

She followed him through a dark, winding corridor, then right through an even narrower tunnel, out into a smaller chamber and then through yet another shaft. Finally, light shone ahead. They came out of the center of three massive archways onto a rocky shore.

"Blastek Cove," he said, opening his hand and sweeping his arm out to the deep blue waters.

He retrieved a pile of netting folded up against the cliff wall and marched out to the water's edge.

"It's deep here, so watch your step."

"Actually, I'd love to go for a swim." Lily said, pulling at one of her boots.

Jonah's mild expression instantly darkened. "Not here."

Lily let go of her foot. "Why not?"

"It's not a friendly location. We can swim later. I know a place." He held out one end of the net. "For now, I could use your help."

Lily frowned, but shrugged and took the net. "Sure."

They cast the net over and over. Jonah chattered about daily activities on the cliff. Catching fish, cleaning fish, eating fish, storing fish.

"So you said the others were harvesting," Lily pressed. "Like, corn? Wheat?"

"No, what food we don't find in the sea we forage for at the foot of the mountains." He waved vaguely north.

"If not food, what?"

Jonah stopped pulling at the net and met Lily's eyes. She wasn't gazing into the brown eyes of a thirteen-year-old boy. His was the wise stare of a man who had seen much and survived.

"We harvest for the Schade."

Lily waited.

"We harvest dragon's eggs."

"What?" Lily gasped. "Dragons? Like Smaug?"

"I don't know that type, but if this Smaug is a giant lizard with wings, then yes, a Smaug."

"But why? And why for the Schade?"

Jonah squinted his eyes and shook his head. "You don't know why you're here."

Lily barked a laugh. "No. I'm not supposed to be here. It was an accident."

"There are no accidents. Everything has a higher purpose. Every event has meaning."

"What's the meaning of my being here, then?"

Jonah sighed and made his way to a large boulder and plopped down. "This is likely something you should discuss with your mother."

Lily snorted. "Sounds like something my dad would say."

"It is because of both your mother and father you are here. Even more, those who came before. Long ago, temporals lived in Alnok, a land just out of sight of this one. The Schade wished to command the dragons of that realm."

Lily dropped her side of the net. "Why? Why would you . . . would my mom want to help those things?"

Jonah's shoulders drooped. He stared at the ground for a moment then looked back into the three-arched mouth, yawning from the cliff. Then his grave brown eyes met hers.

"It's not that—"

"Jonah!"

Jonah jumped up from the boulder. Lily turned. Dr. Charles strode from the darkness, a bright smile on his face.

"There you are! And I see you've befriended our fair Lily."

Jonah grinned and nodded. The dark expression evaporated. "We've been fishing!"

"Catch anything?" Dr. Charles said as he joined them and looked out over the water.

"Maybe enough for dinner," Jonah said, tugging on his end of the net.

Lily jumped in to help and together they dragged what seemed to be twenty large bass, but with bright yellow fins and small eyes."

"Well done," Dr. Charles said.

"Can you manage without Lily?" Dr. Charles asked, then looked at her. "I'd like to continue our conversation."

Jonah nodded and then caught her eye. There was a warning there. Something that told her what they had talked about remained between them. She pursed her lips and gave him a quick nod.

"See you at dinner, Lily," the boy said.

"Okay, see you." Lily trailed after Dr. Charles back to the caves, keeping a careful lookout for any sign of the dragon eggs.

Sixteen

Ford crunched the coral gravel with each step. The tunnel windows stretched across the ceiling. Trickles of water seeped down the rough, textured walls. The gelatin-like substance contracted as the waters pressed in. A bubbling and churning sea obscured anything beyond. The heavy wrought iron reinforcing the arched ceiling and the damp walls popped and creaked. Just above, thousands of pounds of seawater bore down on them.

Ford took a deep breath, filling his lungs.

Plenty of air. No need to hold it.

Ava marched to his right; her neck craned as she kept her eyes glued on the water windows. Harel and Fitz led with Anna and Lucas farther ahead but still within sight. Joshua and Peter brought up the rear.

"You're sure we're safe in here, Harel?" Ford asked, glancing at the small pools of water collected in divots on each side of the pathway.

Harel nodded, but he flitted his eyes from one side to the other and he quickened his pace.

"So," Ford glanced back at Joshua. "What's the story with Alnok? How are we connected?" Better to talk through the nerves. Even if Joshua hated him for what he did, any conversation might help him feel less like a lousy traitor.

Joshua strode up next to him and hefted his pack up higher. "Mom and dad, our real mom and dad, their ancestors, all the way back to the Black Plague, hundreds of years ago, lived there with Arkonai—"

"Who?"

"The Creator."

"Of Alnok?"

"Of everything."

"Oh." Ford nodded slowly. No way he was touching that. That was Ava's department.

"Anyway," Joshua said. "Arkonai chose seven families to rescue and allowed them to stay. But his own brother, Cosyn, attacked them and drove them out. Moses and Nahor were the only two to survive. We're their descendants."

Ford rubbed the back of his neck.

"So you're a chosen people," Ava said. "Like the Israelites."

Ford rolled his eyes but grinned at her. "Leave it to you to compare to one of your Bible stories."

"She's not wrong," Peter snapped. Ford's smile vanished and he gave the geeky boy a hard stare. He might be the one with the staff, but he still looked like one stiff breeze could blow him over.

"Any reason you never told me any of this?" Ford asked, his stare lingering on Peter before he looked at Joshua. "I mean, two years, dinner every Thursday, and you had this whole other life."

Joshua's frown cleared, and a soft, thoughtful look took its place. "In some ways, I wanted to move on. They were some of the hardest, but most enlightening experiences of my life. But I have my wife and girls to think about. I couldn't divide myself up between two dimensions."

"If it was so important, wouldn't you want me to know?"

Joshua glanced at Ford. "It might have been easy, you know? Demanding some kind of recognition for what our group, the Cord, did to save the world." He shook his head. "I didn't want that."

"But that doesn't answer my question. Why keep it from me? I wouldn't have tried to make you famous." Ford gave Joshua a nudge.

For the first time since entering Velare, Joshua smiled and nudged him back. "You already had so much interest in what I knew to be hints and glimpses of the Periferie. I was afraid if you had the answers to what you saw, you'd become obsessed. More obsessed. When we get Lily and go home, you'll have to decide: give it all up or chase it for real."

"How would I—"

"Portals. Opening new portals. That's what B&K did."

Ford started to argue but fell silent. This couldn't be it, could it? The answer to his life's work? Was he walking in the place where he'd always simply hoped to capture a photograph?

"What about Amy?" Ford asked Joshua. "You seemed surprised she might be here. To be one of the 'chosen'."

"Yeah, I guess it never occurred to me. When we were here, the Guardians referred to us as the Cord. A family tree listed our names. Her name could have been somewhere on it. But . . ."

"But what?"

"Well, I mean, it's Amy. She's not exactly someone who belongs here."

"Sometimes it's the imperfect who are most often chosen for a higher calling," Ava offered.

Peter snorted. "She's not imperfect. She's bonkers."

Ford cocked his head. "What about—"

The metal groaned as what looked like a tornado of water slammed into the window just ahead, causing some of it to leak around the edges.

Ford reached for Ava, meaning to pull her close. She grabbed his hand and held it.

"I don't like this," Joshua said.

"We can move a little faster," Fitz said, lengthening his stride.

They caught up to Anna and Lucas and continued at a near-jog as a group.

"There are other reasons to reach the *Sealight* quickly," Fitz said.

"Such as?" Ford asked, avoiding the man's heels.

"Jonis gave up the land to the Schade," Fitz said, ignoring Harel's disapproving glance. "But recently they have taken a greater interest in the sea."

"Because of the portal?" Joshua asked.

"That may be part of the reason," Lucas said.

Harel shook his head. "They have sought to wipe us from Velare, whether by sea or land. The portal simply emboldened them."

"Kade used the portal B&K opened to get us to Alnok," Joshua said. "But it was shut down after the Upheaval."

"Not shut down enough," Ava countered.

"But the government came in and dismantled the entire operation," Joshua argued.

Ford shook his head. "I was there. They were hiding something. Whatever they were doing before, I'm betting they didn't stop."

They continued for another half mile in silence. The conversation sifted through Ford's mind. Portals and wars in alternate dimensions. Lily following him to a portal she was meant to go through. A portal he was *meant* to go through. He glanced at Ava, jogging right behind Anna. Was she meant to be here, too?

"So," Ford finally said, huffing as he jogged alongside his brother, dodging the holes on the uneven path. "If we're a chosen people, do you think mom and dad knew?"

Joshua looked ahead thoughtfully before nodding. "I think they did. Raelyn's dad knew. About Alnok at least. I think that's why when you talked about the ghosts you thought you saw—"

"We saw."

"Right," Joshua nodded. "We saw. They tried to redirect your interest. They had a better idea of what it was. The ghosts in the haunted house. The Loch Ness Monster. Aliens."

"All from here."

"If not here, then Alnok," Harel said over his shoulder.

Ford shook his head but was breathing too hard to respond. The headache had returned.

"We are halfway there," Harel huffed. "Keep moving."

"What about . . . the other soldiers?" Ava gasped.

"That is what gives me hope," Harel said. "Our way is clear, or someone would have been sent back to warn us."

"Kulum has the bravest and most capable warriors," Lucas said.

"Wasted ability," Anna mumbled, but Ford caught her words. He was used to listening for whispers beneath the primary noise.

"Why wasted?" he asked.

Anna scowled and shook her head.

"Because some of us," Lucas said, "feel we should be engaging the Schade."

"Instead of hiding under the sea," Fitz added.

"But that's not how Jonis sees it," Peter said.

"Jonis is a valiant ruler and has his reasons for leading the way he does," Harel said and gave Fitz a warning glance.

"Do you agree?" Peter pressed.

"It is not for me to say," Harel said.

"But this may be an opportunity to show him a different way," Joshua said.

Harel didn't answer.

"Tell me about your mom and dad," Ford interrupted. Now that Joshua was talking, Ford wanted to gather as many answers as possible. "Your adoptive parents. I only met them the one time at Christmas."

"They were the best," Joshua huffed. "Best parents anyone could want. Supported me no matter what. Just like our mom and dad." He gave Ford a sidelong glance.

Ford smirked. "No matter how much I screwed up? Is that what you're saying?"

Joshua shrugged. "They never thought you were a screwup."

But you do. And you have every reason to.

Ford stumbled over a protruding rock, and Joshua reached out to steady him.

"How did they find Lily?" Ford asked. Even though they'd been virtually nonexistent over the last twelve months, Joshua's parents were the ones who saved Lily from the cult. If Lily had been here, or in Alnok, maybe Joshua's folks knew something. If they could learn anything to help them get Lily back this time, they should explore it.

Joshua shrugged. "Amy had Lily hidden in a farmhouse with some of her family. We never talked about Alnok. If this cult had something to do with the Periferie, I never knew it. And neither did they."

An ear-splitting metallic squeal echoed, as though the tunnel was crying out in pain. Then an intermittent plink began. Like a bell, the dings coming faster and faster, like a countdown.

Something crashed into the side of the tube, and the metal let out a long screech. Water washed over their feet.

Harel and Fitz continued at a steady jog. Ford kept his eyes on the windows.

They were running in ankle-deep water when another crash came reverberating down the tunnel. Harel stopped short. Everyone splashed to a stop around him. Harel looked at Joshua and Ford, then Peter and Ava up and down.

A steady pounding, deep and consistent, sounded ahead. Harel took hold of Ford's sleeve and yanked it down over his hand, hooking it over his thumb. Ford spread his fingers beneath the snug fabric.

"A hand fin," he said as Harel and Fitz adjusted everyone's shirt.

"Yes," he said. "The boots will act in the same manner. Now move."

They took out at a run as the waters rose.

"If this thing fills up . . ." Peter said.

"We'll be trapped." Ava finished.

Ford caught his foot on a rock and went down on all fours. Water splashed up in his face and his hands scraped the rough coral beneath the pool. Peter ran to help him up as everyone slowed. Ford waved him away. "Go!"

Peter pressed his lips together and dashed ahead as Ford scrambled to his feet. His head was pounding in time with every footstep. The sloshing water spun outside the tunnel. Ford's vision blurred, the blue from the window filling his sight.

"Harel," Joshua gasped. "We're fading. We need the seripyn."

"Just a little further," Harel said. "We're almost there."

The water rose to their knees, then they were wading, hip deep.

A crash rocked the tunnel, vibrating the metal and sending a tremor down the path. Harel glanced at Fitz and they both stopped. Water rushed in.

"We will not make it to the end," Fitz admitted.

"No," Harel agreed. He gave each of the temporals a quick glance, then spoke to Joshua. "Prepare to swim."

Seventeen

"This way," Harel called and waded to the side of the tunnel where a round window bulged.

"What about the others?" Lucas gestured ahead.

"They got a good head start," Fitz reasoned.

Harel narrowed his eyes, looking ahead as though he might see his soldiers. "They would have been moving faster."

Anna placed a hand on Lucas's shoulder. "They can manage the waters. Our temporals cannot."

"Join them if you can," Harel said to Anna. "Either way, get to the boat. Be sure it's prepared to set sail. For the valor of Arkonai." He touched his forehead.

Anna and Lucas nodded. "For the valor of Arkonai," they both said and dashed away.

Harel placed his hand on the window and then looked at Ford, Joshua, Peter, and Ava. "It will be easier if I control the water's entrance. Wait for it to fill the tunnel. Then swim for the surface."

He pressed his palm into the membrane. Water leaked in. Ford reached for Ava and she took hold of his hand, gripping it so hard it hurt.

Harel leaned into the window and his hand passed through, into the sea. Water poured over his head. Somehow, he remained standing, not washing away in the deluge.

The water rushed past them, splashing up the opposite side of the tunnel. It rose quickly, gurgling around Ford's knees, his waist, then past his neck. He swam against the current. He looked at Ava, doing the same.

"Deep breath," he said.

She nodded. "See you topside." She breathed in and dove beneath the surface toward the open window.

Ford glanced at Joshua, then Peter, as they followed suit. Harel and Fitz were already swimming out of the tunnel. Ford took a deep breath and dove, kicking hard against the water and sweeping his arms. He propelled forward with surprising ease.

But once he cleared the window, the water pounded against him, spinning him in a chaotic current. His pack instantly became a counterweight to his own, tossing him back and forth in the flow. Like he was in a washing machine on high spin. Among the frenzy of bubbles, a dim light shone from above. He adjusted his trajectory, forcing himself to remain pointed toward the surface. Something pounded into his lower back. Then scraped against his shoulder. The tunnel, now rubble, was caught up in the storm. He'd be cut to pieces if he didn't get to the surface. Even as the current carried him away, Ford continued to fight his way up.

Finally, the current eased and the storm subsided. The calmer water was clearer, making the surface appear to be just above him. Below, the storm continued to rage, tossing and churning.

He swam hard, but never seemed to gain any distance. They were deeper than he had first thought. He tried to look around for the others. He'd be able to hold his breath for several more minutes, but Ava . . .

Ford slowed his progress and looked down between his feet. The bubbles and foam blocked out anything more than a few yards.

A dark shape passed just under Ford's feet. Too large to be one of their team.

Ford's heart pounded, using up his precious little oxygen. The shark.

Or worse.

Ford resumed his ascent, pushing the water behind him with the fin-like fabric over his hands and powering his legs with the wide boots as flippers. From the corner of his eye, he glimpsed a long tail before it was gone.

The pressure compressed his ears. His lungs burned. They would burst. Dribbles of air leaked from his pursed lips.

Then his head broke through the water. He gasped in the cool air. Harel was swimming nearer the shore.

"The others!" Ford shouted. "Ava!"

Harel turned and gestured for Ford to follow him. "I saw Joshua and Peter! They're just ahead."

Ford shook his head. "I can't—"

. . . lose her.

"You must get to shore!" Harel insisted.

Ford tread in a circle and looked frantically out over the waves. Something bobbed to the surface. A blue tunic and dark, curly hair. Ford hurled his waterlogged backpack toward the shore and swam out after Ava. He grabbed her limp arm, turned her over, and lifted her head out of the water. With her body in the crook of his arm, he swam back for shore as though the Schade and every sea creature from both Velare and Earth were after him.

His feet finally touched sand. He threw Ava over his shoulder, trudging in long strides through the shallow water. Just as he reached the shore, he eased her down on her back, tilted her head back and put his ear near her mouth, listening for breath. Nothing.

Peter dropped next to them and picked up her hand, feeling her wrist.

"She has a pulse."

Ford nodded and pressed his mouth over Ava's, blowing life-giving air into her lungs.

She didn't move.

Not her. Not her.

Ford blew again.

Ava heaved out a mouthful of water. Ford rolled her over as she wretched, coughing and sputtering.

Ford sat back on his heels and wiped away warm tears he didn't know had leaked out onto his cheeks, mingling with the sea water.

As her coughs subsided, Ava looked around, spied Ford, and threw her arms around his neck, sobbing.

"Hey, it's okay. You're okay," Ford murmured.

Ava hiccuped and nodded, pushing back from him with a shy smile.

Ford ran his fingers through his hair. He stumbled to his feet and looked around.

"This is Endyle?" Peter asked.

"It is," Harel said.

"With no castle," Joshua said.

"No need," Fitz said, still breathing hard.

Harel nodded. "Which is to our advantage. Lord Lachlor of Alnok was once a Guardian, before he was corrupted by Cosyn. He labored beneath his own desire for flattery and finery. We do not maintain outposts, villages, or lesser kingdoms. The desire for riches, so long kept in castles with minor kings, is foreign to us, therefore not a stumbling block."

"We have enough trouble," Fitz said.

Harel gestured for them to follow him away from the sea. "Here you will find nothing but a collection of islets."

More and more soldiers were staggering from the sea roughly half-a-mile north of them. Sparse trees stuck out from a sandy island surrounded by nothing more than chunks of land over which a blue, cloudless sky stretched. Across a channel, the mainland seemed small and distant. Water-logged and exhausted, Ford helped Ava to a clearing with shade from a nearby palm tree.

Ava put her hands on her hips. "So now what?" Her voice was rough and raw.

Harel looked at Fitz. "Find Anna and Lucas. Take a few soldiers to the ship and bring her up." He returned his attention to Ford.

"For now, rest. You will soon board the *Sealight* and we will be on our way to Silom." A wistful smile softened his grizzled features.

Peter rubbed his shoulder and shook his head. "Why are the leaders so at odds? Jonis and Sabel. It seems like they could benefit from working together to defeat the Schade on two fronts."

Ford raised an eyebrow and glanced at Peter. The man might be unqualified, but his point was a good one. And his ability to remember names was impressive. Ford only remembered Fitz's because Harel had repeated it so often. Something to work on when they got back.

Harel picked up a few pieces of driftwood and tossed them in a pile. "I don't believe their disagreement is with policy, just implementation. Jonis prefers clandestine strikes and heavy protection. Sabel, she is less cautious, relying on smaller companies to create a barrier between her community and the Schade."

"You prefer Sabel's technique," Joshua stated.

Harel passed his hand over the wood and a tendril of smoke turned to a flame at the center.

Ford scrutinized Harel's hands, looking for a match, flint, anything. But he seemed to have lit it with his palm. Ford looked at Joshua and Peter. They didn't react. Ford shrugged. So the Velareans could light fires by magic. Why not?

Ava sat down next to the fire and held her hands over it. Ford, Joshua, and Peter joined her, circling the warm blaze.

Harel stared at the flickering flames as they grew. He finally looked at Joshua, then at each of them. "I dislike hiding."

"Jonis seems like a tool," Ford said.

Joshua frowned at him.

"Just saying, cutting our legs out from under us, taking back all of our forces."

"He was right to be cautious," Harel countered.

Ford cocked his head. "Why were the storms so strong they caused the tunnel to collapse, anyway?"

They had been so sure of its stability. A solid structure for so long to only give way once they were in the middle of it? Then, after Jonis gave his dire warning, all hell broke loose. He couldn't be the only one to see the possibility of sabotage.

"The storm was worse and the current stronger than I had realized. We built the tunnel to withstand pressure, but not a bombardment of debris. How you all surfaced without being torn apart . . ." He shook his head and held out a bleeding hand.

Ford looked down at his boots. "Seems we were well equipped. Don't know how you designed these, but I've never owned such well made and effective fins."

Peter pulled his sleeve down. "And these are genius."

Joshua hadn't looked up from the fire. He cleared his throat as he stood and stalked to the shore. They all looked at Ford.

"I, um, I'll check on him."

Ford scrambled to his feet, but a wave of dizziness made the trees do a lazy dance around him.

"Ford," Ava said. She rummaged through her pack. "Here." She handed him two seripyn seeds.

"Right," Ford took them. "Thanks." He gnawed on one as he followed Joshua.

"Hey, Joshua?" Ford shivered, the breeze cool on his still-damp skin. The seripyn settled not just his head but his nerves. He handed a seed to Joshua.

Joshua nodded as he took it. "I can't lose her." He said and took a bite.

"Lily? Nah, she's too tough for this place." Ford eased up beside his brother.

"Tough, yeah. But it took me a long time to buy into the Periferie. Into the dimensions."

"Well, it's a mind bender for sure. But kids, they're more apt to accept the outlandish."

Joshua gave him a side glance. "Like you do?"

Ford scratched the back of his neck. "Maybe. I mean, I knew what we saw in the lake wasn't just shadows. Even though all the so-called evidence I got wasn't much more than blurry images and static feedback on the recorder, my gut told me there was something more. This"—he gestured out at the water—"kind of proves I wasn't crazy."

Joshua looked at him. "This is what you've been searching for with all those investigations?"

Ford squinted his eyes, scanning the distant mainland. In a way, it was. He should be overjoyed at discovering the source. Of learning the name of his ghosts. The Schade. But there was no elation. No satisfaction. Somehow, it all felt . . . incomplete.

"I don't know what I've been searching for to tell you the truth."

Joshua nodded. "I just can't imagine what she's going through—" His voice caught.

Ford grasped Joshua's shoulder and turned him so they were eye-to-eye. "We'll find her. We'll get her back. I know I don't—"

"Joshua!" Peter ran up, out of breath. "Something's wrong." He gestured for them to follow.

"Now what?" Ford grumbled.

They walked up to Harel and Fitz deep in discussion, Ava next to them with her arms crossed. Harel looked up, his expression hard.

"The ship," he said without waiting for the question. "It has been damaged."

"What?" Ford laced his fingers behind his head. Heat rose in his chest. He wanted to punch something. What else could go wrong? "How?"

"Can it be repaired?" Joshua asked.

Sure, that's the better question, Ford, you idiot.

"I believe so. But it may take longer than we wish to wait."

Ford let his arms down as Ava stepped closer to him. He glanced at the mainland. "So we hike to this Silom."

"It is not so easy as that," Fitz said. "We may not agree with Jonis on all of his decisions, but there are good reasons we retreated to the depths."

"The land, particularly the forest, is all but blocked by the Schade."

Joshua did a quick circle. "The Theaurham Forest."

"The what?" Ford asked.

Harel nodded. "It is treacherous in Alnok. It is worse in Velare."

"The Schade have taken it over," Fitz added.

"What about the shore?" Peter asked. "Away from the trees."

Fitz looked at Harel, his mouth a fine line.

"Do you have a boat or canoes? We could stay in the shallow waters," Ava said.

Fitz nodded, but Joshua stiffened.

Ford looked at him. "What's wrong with the water?"

Joshua frowned over the darkening seaside. "There's just as much danger out there."

"Nahesekai." Peter said and Joshua nodded.

"What's that?" Ava asked.

"An ancient sea dragon," Harel said. "It does not venture past the storms, so our province is safe, but here, in the open waters . . ." He shrugged. "Our smaller boats would leave us vulnerable."

Ford rolled his eyes and threw his hands up. "Of *course* there's a sea dragon. So we have three choices. We wait. We hike. We paddle."

"We can't wait," Joshua said, shaking his head.

"We cannot hike," Harel repeated.

"We would cover more ground in smaller boats," Fitz reasoned, looking at Harel with raised eyebrows.

Harel nodded. "Perhaps. But we only have three boats and only enough oars for two."

"How many will a boat hold?" Ford asked.

Harel glanced at the four of them. "Three."

Ford let out a long breath. "So some of us are walking."

"I'm taking a boat," Joshua said.

"Me too," Peter added.

"We're not splitting up," Ava said.

"Agreed," Ford said.

Harel nodded. "I will send our troops to the mainland. They will advance along the shore. But we will reach Silom ahead of them. Once there, we must wait for them. I will not advance on the catacombs without them."

"Even with the Silom troops?" Joshua asked.

Harel exchanged a quick glance with Fitz.

"What *now*?" Ford exclaimed.

"Sabel has fewer numbers," Harel said. "And of those, I do not know who will volunteer to go."

"I thought they were all about fighting the Schade," Ava said.

Joshua shook his head. "This is a rescue mission. Not an assault."

"Yes," Harel said. "Our ongoing battle with the Schade have a strategy of its own. It does not include . . . rescue missions. Sabel may resist taking part in our plan to rescue Lily."

"Then why go there?" Peter asked.

"She knows the land better than anyone. She will know the paths to take and the ways around the Schade. We cannot do this without her."

"Fine," Joshua said. "We have a plan. Let's get to it."

Harel nodded at Fitz, who hurried away. He turned his attention back to the four of them.

"It will take until nightfall to ferry the troops across the channel. Then we make for Silom."

"How long will it take us to get there by boat?" Joshua asked.

"If we take no breaks," Harel said, squinting into the setting sun, "this time tomorrow."

"We should rest," Ava said softly, looking at Joshua.

Harel nodded. "Yes, it will be a long night."

Eighteen

"Why were you gone all day?" Lily asked her mother as she watched the fish sizzle in the pan. She played it cool. She would keep Jonah's secret. This wasn't a test—well, yeah it was a test. If her mom told her about the dragon eggs, then she could get more information. If she didn't . . .

Amy turned the fish over with a wooden spatula and shook her head. "It's not unlike back home. The Velareans eat, breathe, sleep, just like us."

Lily pulled two plates from the cupboard. Her mom was going with the non-answer. "So you were farming? Gathering food then?" She kept her voice neutral. It was a little like probing dad for answers. If her mom was to be trusted, she had to come clean.

Amy sighed. "There's still so much to explain."

Lily let the plates drop onto the table with a clatter. "What do the Schade have to do with all this?"

Amy looked at the plates with wide eyes before turning back to the stove. She pushed around the fish for a moment, then gave a decisive nod. She faced Lily. "Let's dish up some dinner and I'll tell you what I can."

"Okay," Lily said and moved to one side as her mom slid a filet on each plate.

They settled at the table with plates full of fried fish and something like diced blue carrots.

Lily picked up her fork but stared hard at her mother.

Amy took a bite and chewed slowly, then swallowed. "At home, there's a secret group called The Quantum Six. Dr. Charles is part of that group. They're scientists who have done work for the government, important companies—"

"They opened the way here?" Lily tried to keep the accusation out of her voice.

Amy nodded and smiled. "In a way. They funded the work after the Time of Testing so B&K could get things moving again. It's just miraculous. I mean, everyone knows about the opening to the fifth dimension, but here, Velare, is totally unknown."

"But why?" Lily would not let her mother off that easily. This history lesson didn't answer the mystery of the dragon eggs. "Did you go visit them today?"

Amy gave her a quizzical look as though the question was ridiculous, then her expression cleared, and she smiled again. "I know it's hard to imagine, being so young—"

Lily leaned forward. "Try me."

"There are some very bad people in Earth Apparent. There's a battle no one knows anything about. The Schade have offered a way to combat them."

"Are you sure it's not the reverse? The Schade don't seem on the up and up to me."

Amy shook her head and took a large bite. "They're creepy," she said around the food. "I'll give you that. But that's just because we've been taught to fear dark, shadowy things." She swallowed. "But they're here to help."

Lily took a bite. It tasted like a wad of putty. Could her mom be right? Maybe the Schade were just misunderstood. The hair on her neck stood on end. No way. If her dad taught her anything, it was to trust her gut. But her mom seemed completely convinced the Schade were a great bunch of . . . things.

"So are the Quantum Six here?" Lily asked. "Do they stay in Velare?" Maybe they had something to do with the eggs.

Amy shrugged. "Not to my knowledge. I don't have a lot to do with them. I work mostly with the elders—"

"Are they who you were with?"

Amy gave her an irritated glance. "I'm getting to that."

Lily nodded and smiled. No use making her mad. Use honey, not vinegar. Another of her dad's sayings. A distant twinge plucked at her heart.

"Okay," Lily said. "Tell me about the Quantum Six."

"There's no one smarter. Fifteen years ago, they started working with B&K Sciences."

"The company that discovered the fifth."

Amy nodded. "Yep. Not in any official manner. Just offering some consulting to the scientists who were running the show. But when the Time of Testing put everything into chaos, the volcanoes and the world conflict, the Q6 took on a larger role."

"Dad says the chaos was *because* of the evil we can't see. He never explained much, but I think it's safe to say he was talking about Velare as much as Alnok."

Amy leaned forward, her brow deeply furrowed. "Your dad didn't explain much because he doesn't understand. He thinks what I did, taking you when you were little, was to harm you. But it's just the opposite." She smiled and sat back. "Now you're really here. Just like we wanted so long ago."

"We?"

"Me, the leaders of the Q6. Lily, you have to understand, you coming to Velare is so important to Earth Apparent. More than you know. But you'll come to understand. Maybe your dad will, too."

"What's so important?" Lily took a breath and stabbed at some of the carrots. "Did it have anything to do with what you were harvesting today?" She shoved the bite into her mouth and kept her eyes on her plate. This had to be it. Her mom had to come clean about the eggs or get caught in a lie.

"It does," Amy said slowly. "The next time I go, I'll take you. In the meantime, I want you to get to know some of the Velareans. Someone in particular."

"Not one of the Schade."

Amy chuckled. "No, no. They only meet with the Q6. And there's not 'one' Schade. They're more of many parts of one. They share one mind and mission. It's a perfect society, really. No arguing, no one fighting for their own needs. Just the good of the group."

"Sounds efficient," Lily mumbled.

"Efficient and effective. You haven't even seen the best parts of Velare."

Lily finally looked up. Her mom's face was glowing with a rapturous smile. Something tugged at Lily. Compassion, love, maybe even a little hope. "The sea is beautiful," she conceded.

"The sea, the forest, the mountains. If it weren't for the councils, this would be paradise. A virtual Eden."

Lily raised her eyebrows. "Not everyone agrees with the Schade?"

"No." Amy scowled. "Selfish cowards. They've always stood in the way of the Schade entering Earth Apparent. But they've lost a lot of their control."

"I don't think I like the idea of those things having anything to do with our home."

"They are already a part of it." Amy reached across the table and squeezed Lily's arm. "It's a lot to take in. I just ask that you keep an open mind."

"Why is it so important that I be here? What do I have to do with any of this?"

"A long time ago, thousands of years, our ancestors were a part of Alnok."

"Dad's told me the stories. The Black Plague. A group was saved out of it."

A pain stabbed Lily's temples and she winced. Amy nodded, obviously understanding, and left the table. She retrieved a bottle from the bottom shelf and brought it back.

"Here," she said and poured a dollop out into a spoon. *Like medicine.*

Lily took the spoon and gulped the foul liquid down. But the slimy consistency and rotten taste was worth the instant relief and boost.

"Better?" Amy asked.

"Much."

Amy looked down at the table and frowned. "Now, where were we? Oh, the ancestors. So decades later, they were called back. We, temporals I mean, have a special part to play. Unfortunately, the Guardians in Alnok have misread some of the prophecy. That's what the elders here say."

Lily choked. "Prophecy?"

"I only know bits and pieces, really. What I'm trying to say is, we were meant to be here. You, me, even your dad."

"Dad said they closed the portals to the fifth dimension. Why would we be called back?"

Amy's eyes misted and she gave Lily a wistful smile. "That's part of the beautiful mystery. But someday all the dimensions will become one, and we will have helped usher in that reality."

Lily's stomach soured and the little fish she had eaten turned to stone. Her mom had swallowed whatever this was, hook, line, and sinker.

Someone rapped on the front door. Amy scooted from the table and hurried to open it.

"Oh, hello Jonah." Her mother was clearly disappointed.

"I wondered if Lily would like to come out. The sun is about to set."

Lily was up from the table and striding for the door before Amy turned around.

"I'd love to."

"Oh?" Amy frowned.

"I might as well get to know some locals." Lily grinned.

Amy's face softened. "Of course. But not too long. I have a lot I want to show you in the morning and I'd like for you to get a good night's rest. Plus, nights are best spent . . . indoors." She chewed on her lower lip and the frown returned.

Lily nodded, hesitated, and then gave her mom a peck on the cheek as she slipped past. "I'll be back soon."

She shut the door behind her before her mother could object. Breathing in the salty, humid air, she followed Jonah up the path back to the cliff side. Though the knot remained in the pit of her stomach, being outside her mom's house loosened it a bit. Plus, answers might be a little more straightforward with this young Velarean. Especially about the Schade.

"You will love this!" Jonah said, darting from one side of the path to the other. He scooped up a rock, then pitched it away in favor of a stick.

Already the sky had deepened to a vibrant orange. Fluffy clouds reflected the light in soft pinks and peaches. At the cliff's edge, Jonah sat and dangled his legs over the side. Lily eased down next to him and folded her legs under her. She gazed out over the water as the sun melted into the horizon.

"You're right," she said.

"I am?"

"I love this."

"Oh!" Jonah laughed. "I am glad."

"Everything about Velare is beautiful. But Jonah"—she turned to face him—"I'm afraid of the Schade." Kids understood fear in a way adults couldn't. He'd give her an honest answer.

He nodded, his brown eyes darkened in the setting sun. "I don't blame you. They're secretive and hide in the corners of our world. They are beyond our understanding. Which makes them scary."

"But you don't think I should be afraid."

He shrugged. "That is not for me to say. You don't need to be. They have powers that have guided and formed Velare for a lot longer than we've been here. But even as powerful as *they* are, everyone was looking forward to *you* being here."

Lily turned to him, the sunset forgotten. "What do you mean the Schade have been here longer than *we've* been here? I thought this was your home?"

Jonah rubbed his lips together and sifted through the dirt with one hand. "It is. I was brought here as a baby by my parents. They died when I was three, so I was adopted as a Velarean."

"Do the Schade just live in the caves?" Lily lowered her voice. Somehow, this seemed more like a forbidden conversation. Like the dragon eggs. Otherwise, her mother surely would have said something.

Jonah glanced behind him. "I, uh, yeah, I guess so." He hurled a rock out over the cliff.

"You don't know?"

Jonah fidgeted and scooted away from her. Lily leaned back, realizing she was almost in Jonah's face.

Jonah hopped up. "It's not really important. But you are. Once you are here, you are Velarean. You become part of the family." He held out a hand and gave her a hesitant smile. "That is a good thing."

Lily took his hand, calloused and warm. "I wouldn't mind having you for a brother," she said, dusting off her behind. "But what about the others? The Velareans opposing the Schade? Are they wrong?"

Jonah screwed up his face and looked at the sun as it bid its last farewell. "I think they want the same thing as the Schade. They want to control Velare. They just see going about it differently. I heard Dr. Charles talking one day. They've split in two. Some went to the waters. The others went to the mountains. That's one thing we have over them. We live in harmony. No one questions the Schade, and the cliffers prosper."

"Why would my mom hide the fact they were harvesting dragon eggs today?" Maybe Jonah was just joking. Maybe he'd come clean.

"She might think you won't believe her. Dragons aren't common in Earth Apparent, are they?"

Lily burst out laughing. "No, not unless you count movies and books. I'd like to see them. The dragon eggs."

Jonah bit his lip. "I could show you. But I could get in a lot of trouble." A slow grin grew. "But I think we could get past the cliffers and the Velareans."

"Like a quest."

"Yes!"

Lily was silent as the first stars winked into the twilight sky. Both her mom and Jonah, even Dr. Charles, seemed to think the Schade were just misunderstood. But the one shadow that had greeted her, Bode, there was no way it was on the good side.

You've seen too many horror movies.

Maybe.

Maybe she should keep an open mind. Like her mom said.

Jonah walked her back to her mom's house, quietly swinging a stick.

"Lily?" Jonah said softly, without looking at her. "It is good that you are here. You'll be the one to bring us all together."

"The Schade and Velarean Counsels?"

"Velare and Earth Apparent. You will be the one to bring the dimensions into one."

Lily's heart pounded. Her mom had alluded to something like this.

"How can you be so sure?" Her face flushed. Over and over, she kept hearing how she was so special.

Jonah stopped and looked up at her, twilight settling around them. "The prophecy."

Sweat formed on her upper lip. "What do you know about that?"

"I've just heard rumors. But I overheard some of the elders talking about it." He stepped closer to her. "They talked about 'wholeness.' That doesn't sound so bad, does it?"

"No, it doesn't. But sometimes interpretations can be wrong." Lily smiled and ruffled his hair. "I'm glad to have a friend, regardless."

Jonah returned the smile. "Me too."

He walked her back to the house and skipped away. But Lily stood for a few minutes looking at the closed door. She didn't have to go in. She could get to the stairs and find her way back to the sea. Maybe she'd meet up with some of the other Velareans.

Maybe she'd end up running into the Schade. A more likely scenario.

Jonah could be right. If there was a prophecy that talked about someone, not her, who would bring the entire world together. That would be pretty awesome. A utopia where no one fought.

She sighed and put her hand on the door handle. Or they could have it all wrong.

Nineteen

Lily was up and dressed before her mother had finished setting breakfast. She looked at the plates. Buttered bread and fruit.

Thank God, no fish.

A week had passed with fish for nearly every meal. Fish and vegetables. Fish and noodles. Fish and fish. But it had been an uneventful week. A week of making friends and making peace. No Schade. No conflict. Her life in Earth Apparent felt a million miles away.

Amy smiled and looked Lily up and down. "You have a big day planned?"

Lily took a giant bite of the bread and shrugged. "Jonah was going to show me a watering hole they use to swim." She looked up at her mother. She still didn't entirely trust her, but they were developing an easy, natural relationship. It had to be some innate maternal bond. Something she'd never have with Raelyn. Not even her dad. Maybe this is what Raelyn and Holly experienced.

"Is that okay?" Lily asked. Best to show her some respect.

Amy bit her lip. "The Cliffers rarely venture too deep into the sea. Not even with boats."

"Jonah promises this is a safe spot."

"I suppose he would know. Just stay in the shallows."

Lily grabbed a peach and stood. "I will. I'll bring back some fish for dinner."

Amy beamed. "That would be wonderful. I'm going to The Rift today, but I'll be back by sundown and we can cook together."

Lily hugged her mom. "It's a deal."

She took a gulp of the seripyn straight from the bottle. It didn't even taste so bad anymore. She smacked her lips. The sliminess was the same. She waved as she opened the door and dashed out.

Dad would never have let me go to the ocean alone.

Had she ever made dinner with Raelyn? She hadn't really shared much of anything with her parents. Affection for Amy bloomed in Lily's chest as she grinned up at the clear sky.

She skipped through the town as other Cliffers left their homes, busy about their day. They numbered just over three dozen. Some gathered vegetables from small gardens. Another climbed a ladder into a tree to bring down huge apples. A man with sandy blond hair, dressed similarly to Jonah, looked up from shelling peas and waved, smiling at her. Others greeted her as she made her way to the opening of the catacombs.

Where else had she ever been so welcomed?

But the steps down into the cave system dampened some of her cheer.

"I'll leave you alone if you leave me alone," she murmured as she reached the bottom of the stairs. Same cold cave. Now she'd have to remember how to get out.

But here, in the dark, a purple glow shone in the corners of the small chamber. It got brighter at one end.

Might as well go where I can see.

As she drew closer, the light faded and appeared further down a corridor. From behind her, something made a soft squelching noise. A shadowy form disappeared behind a stalagmite.

She hurried around a corner and followed the light into another chamber and another tunnel. Then she was in the large chamber where she had first awoken. She glanced around the corner next to the stalactite. Her tank and vest were still there with her goggles and fins.

Might come in handy.

She shook her head. Not today. Now that she could traverse the caverns, she could come down here whenever she wanted. She could take her things and set out to sea to find home. Anytime.

She followed the uneven path to the arched exit. She breathed in the moist air, forcing away the remaining thoughts of gurgling shadow monsters.

"Hi Lily!" Jonah called from the shore. It was low tide, and the beach was wide and sparkling in the morning sun.

"You ready?" Lily asked as she approached the water.

Jonah nodded. "The tide is low. That's good." He looked serious, which made Lily smile. "Just don't go too deep, okay?"

Lily ruffled his hair. "Of course. I'll follow your lead."

Jonah looked at her as if to see if she was patronizing him, but seemed satisfied and ran ahead. "Last one in is a dragon dropping!" he called.

Lily caught up easily, and they ran, side-by-side in the wet sand. The day was calm and sunny, with the whoosh of the waves filling her ears.

She grinned and waved at a few Cliffers casting nets in the sea and they waved back. "Hi Jabez! Hi Sarah!" she shouted as she ran past.

They followed the coastline until they came to a turquoise lagoon in a perfect half-moon shape. A small grotto with a trickling waterfall tinkling into the pool stood on the far side.

"Jonah! It's beautiful!" Lily was already removing her boots.

Jonah beamed. "And it's perfectly safe. Just don't go past those rocks." He pointed at a narrow jetty fifty yards out to sea.

Lily waded out into the cool water, her pants and tunic acting as a wetsuit. Then she closed her eyes and lay out on her back, floating to the center of the pool. Complete peace. Total calm—

A splash sent water up her nose. She sat up sputtering and coughing, wiping water from her eyes.

Jonah giggled and swam away.

"Oh, no you don't!" Lily swam after him.

She caught him and dunked him. Until the sun marked mid-morning, they splashed and played. After climbing up the grotto and jumping into the water over and over and playing Marco Polo, Lily finally flopped onto the beach, exhausted.

Jonah sat next to her.

"It's so quiet here," she said, digging at the sand with her fingers. Unusual given everyone was here, not at the Rift.

"Hey," Lily said slowly. "How close are we to the Rift?"

Jonah looked north and shrugged. "Half a day's journey, I suppose." Then he looked at her, narrowing his eyes in suspicion. "Why?"

"Just wondering. I mean, no one's there. Seems like it might be a perfect time to—"

Jonah shifted his eyes back to the catacombs and then north again. "I don't know . . ."

"You said you'd take me. This is the ideal opportunity." She could see Jonah working it out. He wanted to go as badly as she did.

"Okay," he whispered, as though suddenly surrounded by Cliffers. "Grab your boots. We have to hurry."

Beneath a dry, leafless tree, its mangled roots exposed, Lily scrambled down an opening in the crusty earth. The sun had sunk low in the sky. They'd taken longer to get here than Jonah had estimated. Even if they hoofed it, they wouldn't make it back before dark.

"This way," Jonah waved her over, his voice echoing.

Crouching low, Lily followed the boy down the tunnel, leaving the light behind.

Should've brought my flashlight. Uncle Ford's Orcatorch. The one he gave her when she had followed him into the depths of the lake.

She took a deep breath as the memory caught her off guard. She stopped short as one by one, Ford, Dad, Holly, Raelyn, Peter, made a split-second processional across her mind. With one blink, they were gone.

Thankfully, she didn't need a flashlight. The purple light shimmered in every crevice. Glowing here, radiant there.

"How far, Jonah?" she whispered. The light pulsed ahead.

"Just around this corner," he said over his shoulder, and disappeared to the right.

Lily followed, edging against the tunnel into complete darkness. Where was the light?

"Jonah?" she said, her voice quavering. The echo suggested a larger chamber.

"Here," he said, and a flame flickered to life, casting deep shadows on his face.

He held up a crude torch made of a thin branch wrapped in cloth. He swept the torch at his feet.

Lily gasped. Not much bigger than her air tank, lay a greenish egg with smooth scales the size of her thumb, nestled in a collection of dry branches. Next to it, a yellow one, perfectly smooth with no scales. Another blue. A quick count revealed a dozen at least.

Jonah grinned. "Told you."

Lily crossed her arms. "I believed you. It's just . . ." She kneeled down next to it. "Can I touch it?"

"Sure."

Lily reached out and laid her hand on the top of the egg. She glanced up at Jonah. "It's so warm! I wish they still had their mom." She ran her hand along the sleek surface, the scales perfectly spaced.

"Maybe dragons don't have families like we do."

"Maybe. You don't think they'll end up . . . bad do you?"

Jonah shook his head. "Dragons aren't good or bad. Like all animals, they can be either. It depends on who controls them."

"Like a trainer?"

"Yep. The Alnok dragons were controlled by Cosyn. He made them bad. He used them as weapons against Periferials and temporals."

Lily crouched next to the yellow egg and stroked its smooth, leathery surface. "Why isn't this one scaley?"

"The scales form on them the older they get. It means they're close to hatching."

"So, these baby dragons won't be bad?"

Jonah's face darkened. "Not if I have anything to do with it."

"But you're not sure."

"Dr. Charles says they won't be."

"But . . ." Lily stood and raised her eyebrows, gesturing for him to continue. He had to trust her by now.

Jonah shrugged. "I just don't see why we need them at all. Dragons are powerful and free. What use do we have to control them?"

"Maybe for protection. My mom says the Velarean councils are in conflict. That there may even be a war between them. If we could influence them, maybe we could ask the dragons to keep the councils from trying to take over the Cliffers."

"I've never seen anyone from the councils." Jonah had lowered his voice and looked warily toward the exit. "We should go. It'll be dark by the time we get home."

"Okay, you're right."

Jonah led the way out. The purple light was gone. Maybe she had imagined it all along.

"Jonah," Lily said, jogging next to him as the sun set to their right. "Have you ever seen a dragon?"

"No, this will be the first time they have a clutch intact for them to hatch."

"What do you mean?"

"Eggs laid by a single dragon must all be together. If one is missing, none will hatch."

"How soon do you think the oldest one will hatch?"

Jonah looked at her with a grin. "Soon."

Twenty

"What about the page I found at B&K?" Ford asked Joshua as he gave a hard sweep with his oar. "The prophecy?" It was still weird to use archaic terms.

At first light, they had loaded three wide, raft-like canoes made of smooth wooden planks and low seats. They paddled along the shore, less than fifty yards out. Harel and Fitz passing a paddle back and forth between them in the first boat, Joshua and Peter doing the same in the second, and Ford and Ava bringing up the rear. Ford held the paddle away any time Ava reached for it. Now, nearing noon, they approached a bend in the shoreline. The trees from the forest had steadily drawn closer. Though the sun poured its sparkling rays into the treetops, the woods remained in shadow.

Joshua dug his oar into the water for a few strokes, then let the boat coast for a moment. "I thought the words only spoke of Alnok. What we were called to do there. Closing the portals."

"We didn't know there was more to it," Peter added.

"Were you a part of it?" Ford asked testily. He wanted to have this discussion with his brother. It wasn't fair to lash out at Pete. But rescuing Lily seemed best suited to himself and Joshua. Even Ava's presence was a burden.

Peter sighed and looked down at his hands. "More than you know."

"Maybe," Ford conceded. It seemed Peter had played a role no one had yet detailed. "But this second part. Does it mean we were always going to come here?"

Joshua nodded. "I can only guess it's like before. Kade had full faith in the legitimacy of every word of the first prophecy and its power to foretell events."

"But what about . . . Lily?" Ford finally asked the question. What he had wondered since being in Velare. How did she fit into all of it? If she was *meant* to be here, maybe he wasn't solely responsible for her disappearance.

You don't get off that easy.

Joshua shook his head. "Whatever we're meant to do here, it can't involve her. War is no place for sixteen-year-old girls."

Ford grimaced and hunched his shoulders, giving a few hard strokes. War. That's what this was. He was battling not just against the ghosts of Velare, but what he'd been chasing for some twenty years. Something, he was realizing, that was far more than ghosts.

"I have learned," Ava offered, "accidents are often where miracles are born. Your prophecy names no names. We don't know all the purposes."

"Indeed," Harel called over his shoulder. "Arkonai alone can see all ends. We will rescue Lily from the Schade, but what part she may have in this is yet to be seen."

"Her part," Joshua said, his voice low, tense, "if she has one, can be played from home. Not here."

"Of course," Ford said. "Whatever it takes. I'll get her home. I promise."

Joshua shot a look over his shoulder. "Don't make promises about which you have no control."

Ford flinched. His statement was one frequently said by their mother.

"Do you think Kade knew?" Peter asked. "About the second prophecy Ford found at the warehouse?"

Joshua paddled for a moment without answering. "I don't think so. If he had more direction, deeper answers to his questions, he would have said. Now that I think about it, they're not really even that different. The two prophecies. Complementary even. Battling evil, working together. It fits."

"Fighting evil is a quest shared by all," Harel said. "We do not fight our battles alone. It is a daily choice whether to enter the fray or stand back and watch the conflict unfold."

A breeze sighed through the forest. Ford squinted through the trees, trying to see around the trunks. Shadows seemed to move all around. Darting from one tree to the next. But they were just regular shadows, nothing like—

A shadow stopped hard, seeming to watch them pass.

"Harel?" Ford called.

Harel glanced back, and Ford gestured to the trees. The Velarean gazed into the woods and then nodded.

"As we come around this bend, we should put more water between Theaurham and us."

"We can't go too deep," Joshua warned.

They rounded the corner; the trees dipped their roots into the waters closest to them. Shadows, black and inky, leached out into the waves. Ford watched them draw nearer like an opaque oil spill.

"Harel?" he asked.

"I see it!" Harel called back. "Out to sea!"

"Wait!" Peter shouted as he pulled his staff off his back. He lowered it into the water, causing a series of ripples. The shadow made an arch around the ripples, drawing no closer to the boats, but neither did it retreat.

"Can you hold them off?" Joshua asked.

Peter squeezed his eyes shut. "Maybe for a little while. They're strong."

"Quickly, then," Harel said. "If we can make the river, we can petition for Sabel's help and additional protection."

"And be out of this sea," Joshua added.

While Peter trailed his staff in the water, they raced across, each boat slicing through the waters. The Schade stalked them, floating not thirty yards off their port side. An occasional dark hand raised up, pulling the pool of darkness along.

But as the sun made its arc across the sky, glaring off the waters, the shadow slowly closed the space. Peter grunted, but it seemed whatever power he had maintained was waning.

"Josh," he gasped. "I can't . . . I'm sorry."

"Then we have no choice!" Harel shouted. "We must make for deeper waters."

"Harel! We can't!" Joshua shouted. "Nahesakai!"

"The dragon?" Ava cried, rising to a crouch in the boat to get a better look at what had entered the water. "What's in the water?"

Fitz had joined Harel in steering their boat away from shore. "The Schade!"

Joshua pounded his fist on the side of his boat, but followed Harel and Fitz. They paddled until the turquoise waters turned deep blue and the darting fish had disappeared. The shadow of the Schade dissipated, though it remained in the turquoise waters of the shallows.

"Seems it got exactly what it wanted," Joshua said between gritted teeth. "We're sitting ducks for the dragon."

"All the more reason to double our speed," Fitz said and dug his oar into the waters, their boat surging ahead.

The sun radiated a late afternoon heat as they traversed the sea without resting. The breeze had withdrawn its cool relief. Sweat dripped down Ford's back and his temples throbbed.

"We'll need to stop for water soon," Ava said. "If we have some monster to avoid, we won't get far if we're dehydrated."

"She's right," Peter said. "And I could use another dose of seripyn."

Ford glanced back at the tree-lined shore. The shadows had retreated into the forest, but the hair on Ford's neck prickled. Like the forest he visited in Romania years ago. He never saw anything, but he had no doubt something had watched him the entire time he was there.

"We need to get to the inlet," Harel said between gasps. "We are close. Peter gave us an advantage."

"We won't make it," Joshua said, peering over the side of his boat as Peter rowed.

"What'd you mean?" Ford followed his gaze. The water was a perfect indigo. A darker shade of blue glided beneath them. "Josh?" he said, drawing his name out. It could be the shark, sirak.

Joshua and Peter had pulled ahead. Ford glanced over his shoulder at Harel and Fitz.

The dark shape, larger, faster, made another pass. With no wind, the waves tumbling onto shore a fair distance away, and aside from their steady rowing, all was eerily silent.

A horned head broke out of the water. Forcing a giant wave ahead of it, it came roaring like a freight train. Ford scrambled to Ava and steadied her in the rocking boat. The creature dove just before it reached Harel's canoe, a spiked tail rising from the waters, coming down at the center of their boat and breaking it in half.

Both men disappeared into the churning sea. Shards of wood floated from the foamy attack site.

Two heads popped up. Harel and Fitz.

Ford grabbed his oar and steered around Joshua's boat, aiming for the two men thrashing in the deep waters.

"Climb in!" he said when he reached Fitz. Ava balanced the port side as Fitz heaved himself aboard. Harel did the same in Peter and Joshua's canoe. Both boats sagged in the water.

Silence returned, but for their gasping and the lapping water on the sides of the two remaining boats bobbing in the diminishing waves.

Joshua took the oar from Peter and turned his craft toward shore. "We have no choice. We'll have to face the Schade. There's a better chance we escape above water than under."

A ribbed back broke the surface between the shore and their boats.

"The bastard is playing with us," Peter said. "It'll never let us get that far."

Joshua slammed his oar into the bottom of the boat and let out a raw shout.

"Continue to make for shore," Harel said, directing Ford and Ava. "We will get as close as we can."

"Then what?" Peter asked.

"We only need to get to the shallows," Fitz said, taking Ava's oar. "We cannot stay here." The extra weight slowed them to a crawl.

"So we confront the Schade," Ford said, briefly scanning the shoreline. He gestured for Fitz to hand off the oar.

"Doesn't help our odds of getting to Silom," Ava said, her voice trembling.

Ford and Joshua paddled hard for a few feet, but the water parted again, horns rising out of the surface. Then a massive snout and eyes, one glaring and red, a jagged scar where the other once was. Then a mouthful of razor teeth.

It let out a deafening roar. Ava flinched and gripped the sides of the boat. It rose to expose its chest, then dove again, parting the two vessels.

If Ford hadn't turned their boat to coast down the resulting wave, they would have capsized. He turned around, heading back to Joshua, Peter, and Harel but kept them angled toward shore.

Joshua was doing the same just a few feet away. They nearly collided back together.

Joshua stopped rowing.

"Josh, we don't have time—" Ford started.

Joshua handed his oar to Harel and kneeled in the boat.

"Joshua?"

Joshua rubbed the back of his neck. With a tremendous sigh, he pulled his sword from his sheath.

"This sword knows the creature," Joshua said to Harel. "I hope it remembers how to battle it. I'll at least buy you some time." He turned to look at Ford.

"What're you doing?" Ford whispered. He knew. He didn't want to believe it. But he knew.

"If I don't meet you in Silom, get to Lily—"

"No! I'll go!" Ford drew his speargun, nearly dropping it in the water.

Joshua shook his head and looked into the water. "Find Lily. Get her home." He stood and dove into the blue. The boat rocked, nearly tipping Peter and Fitz out.

"This way!" Fitz said, pointing north.

"NO!" Ford tried to dive into the water. A steely hand gripped his arm. He looked down at Fitz. The man looked from him to Ava and back.

"We must make it to shore."

Ford searched the waters once more, then sat down and dug his oar into the water, pushing the boat forward.

Ford, Ava, and Fitz followed Peter and Harel, traversing the shore and keeping to the deeper waters.

They had no more encounters, but with each stroke, Ford's heart pounded painfully. A deep ache that radiated into his arms and gut. It should have been him. He was the better swimmer.

What would you do? You're useless with your gun. You'd just create one more person to rescue.

"Joshua is an accomplished swordsman," Harel said.

Ford gritted his teeth. Underwater? "He shouldn't have gone. How will he defeat that thing? Weren't you just saying we needed to fight each other's battles? I just sat on the sidelines," he mumbled.

"Joshua beat Nahesekai once, hasn't he?" Fitz argued. "Word of his victory even reached Velare."

Ford blinked and then frowned. There was so much he didn't know. About this realm. About fighting. About his brother.

No one spoke. Fitz, Ava, and Ford rotated the oar among them. As the sun dipped behind the trees, casting everything into shadow, a wide inlet came into view.

"We'll be rowing upstream," Harel said, wiping his brow. "But it is a wide river with a slow current. Too shallow for the dragon. We should make Silom not long after nightfall."

"We will encounter their scouts before that," Fitz said with a glance over his shoulder.

"How will we get to Lily? With no ship?" Ford asked.

"We can't risk getting back in these canoes," Ava said.

Harel nodded. "Agreed. I will consult with Sabel. Her people are better acquainted with the land. If she agrees to help, they will know a way."

"If they don't agree?" Peter asked. "You said they wouldn't be keen on a rescue mission."

Ford grunted as he gave another stroke with his oar. His arms were rubber. His heart, a sinking stone. "We'll still find a way."

Twenty-One

"**S** top!" a deep, gruff voice shouted from the canyon's rocky shore-line through which the river had snaked during the night.

Harel slowed his paddling but continued to maintain their position in the current. Just as he had promised, it wasn't strong, but they were all so exhausted they had made little progress. The stars had waned as dawn approached, though the canyon remained shrouded in darkness.

It wasn't just Ford's arms screaming at him. His mind replayed Joshua's leap into the sea over and over. He focused on each stroke, driving them forward, sweat pouring off his forehead. He forced an image of Lily's grinning face to the forefront of his mind. But Joshua's determined glare before he jumped into the sea kept overtaking her sweet face.

With the sudden stop, and his concentration shattered, his throat threatened to close with panic.

Please, no more roadblocks.

"I come from Kulum!" Harel called back. "We seek refuge and aid!"

After a brief silence, a woman's voice came from ahead. "Harel?" A pinpoint of light from a lantern held aloft illuminated a stout figure on a narrow beach.

"Sabel!" Fitz cried, grabbed the oar from Ford, and made for the shore.

Harel let out a sigh and followed. Both boats landed on the beach, their hulls shushing in the fine gravel.

In the pale moonlight, a dozen soldiers wearing dark tunics and carrying bows scrambled down from the rocky precipice. They formed a semi-circle, blocking anyone from approaching the woman. With tight, grim expressions, they held their positions.

Fitz half launched, half fell out of his boat and approached the nearest soldier. Even as Fitz reached for his arm, a smile spread across the soldier's face. They gripped each other's elbow, then the soldier pulled Fitz into an embrace.

Peter yanked his boat onto shore, stumbling to his knees several times. Harel clambered out to assist Peter as Ford jumped out into ankle-deep water, gesturing for Ava to remain seated as he tugged the boat out of the river. He helped her out of the boat and onto shore. They waited, watching Harel and Fitz greet the soldiers. Ava held fast to Ford's hand and the grip steeled his aching heart. Heartbreak raged against relief.

Josh should be here.

The woman approached, a walking stick in one hand, the now doused lantern swinging in the other. The first glimmers of daylight showed blonde hair, pulled back in a tight ponytail. She wore a light brown belted tunic over dark pants.

Surrounding her were a dozen or more soldiers, some with staffs like hers, others with short swords, all looking wary.

"Refuge? Aid, you say?" she asked. Her smile was tender, but a deep frown furrowed her brow, showing her pleasure but confusion about their appearance.

"Aye," Harel said, still catching his breath. "The Schade are at the edge of the forest—"

"Yes, we have been tracking them. It is for you they have ventured so close to our borders?"

"That is true. But there is much more. Too much to explain here."

"Of course," she said, gesturing to the soldiers. "We will take care of your boats. Follow me."

She turned and marched up the beach.

"Jonis knows you are here?" she asked with a glance back.

"He does," Harel said. "But he would not come. And the rest of our party is repairing the *Sealight*."

"What do you need of your ship?" the soldier who had greeted Fitz asked.

"Myrel, it is a long story," Fitz said. "One which involves Alnok and Earth Apparent."

"We have enough trouble of our own," Sabel answered. "You find it necessary to marry three of the dimensions?"

"We were not looking to do so," Fitz said.

"But we chose not to deny the aid asked of us," Harel finished.

Sabel nodded.

Ford cleared his throat and opened his mouth. Peter put a hand on his arm and shook his head.

Ford scowled, but followed his advice. The man may be weak, but he had been to Alnok. Ford could be patient. For now. His brother was gone, and they were dancing around the subject of Lily.

The day had warmed, and the sun had crept into the sky by the time they reached a massive, mossy stone wall. Several soldiers stood on parapets high above them. Sabel let out a whistle and two of the soldiers turned a crank. A part of the wall recessed in and moved to one side.

"Come," Sabel said. "I imagine you are hungry. And tired."

"We can wait for those things." Ford couldn't stay silent. "My brother went after a sea monster and his daughter, my niece, is being held by the Schade."

Sabel stopped just inside the wall. She slowly turned. She gave him a hard look. "I know about the girl." A full head shorter than Ford, shorter than even Ava, she looked him up and down. "We will discuss what has happened. But you must replenish your strength if you wish to go any further. Your chances of recovering your niece are slim."

Ford's face burned, but he caught a look from Peter out of the corner of his eye that made him hold his tongue.

They continued along the river to a wide lake with a pounding waterfall.

"Welcome to Silom." Sabel held out a hand to a modest castle. "We will find food in the kitchens"—she glanced at Myrel—"no need to prepare the dining hall."

When they had settled around a low, wooden table with bread and soup passed around, Sabel looked directly at Ford.

"The Schade have become restless of late. I do not believe those in Kulum have been privy to this."

"We have," Fitz said around a full mouth. "They have ventured from the forests into the shallows of the sea. We have spotted them near our outer fortresses."

Sabel shook her head. "So the waters did not protect as much as Jonis thought."

"Perhaps not," Harel said. "But we have mastered the waters. It gives us an advantage."

Sabel eyed him, clearly not buying it. "I thought you were smarter than that."

"He is our leader."

"So you follow blindly."

"This is the alternative?" Harel said, irritation clipping his words as he gestured around the room.

"I prefer it to following a tyrant."

Harel sighed. "I had hoped you might have changed your views of Jonis."

"Even if I had. He has not. We choose to fight. He, to hide." She waved her hand. "I do not think you came to recruit me."

"No, but our quest to find the girl is more than aid to a grieving father"—he glanced at Ford—"and uncle. The Schade took her for a reason."

"We noticed a shift in their tactics. Always, they set out to antagonize and eventually overtake. They have become"—she squinted and looked up—"purposeful. Targeted."

"They found a target," Ford said. "Lily."

"The lost girl."

"She . . . followed me to an underwater ruin. We came to the portal and she was taken in. We came in after her."

Sabel looked from face to face, Ford, Peter, Ava, then back to Ford. "Your brother. I presume you will attempt to rescue him as well?"

Ford grit his teeth against a buildup of harsh words. "Will you help us?"

Sabel finally looked at Harel. "What do you ask of us?"

"We must get the *Sealight* repaired. I do not know what progress they have made with it. Nahesekai attacked us as we made for the river. Once we have the ship, we will go after Lily. Perhaps we will also push back the Schade from our lands."

Ford's throat closed over his next question. Thankfully, Peter voiced it for him.

"What about Joshua?"

Sabel and Harel exchanged a look.

"We will trust he found his way out of the sea," Harel finally said.

"We're not going after him?" Ava whispered.

"We could spend resources on searching for him," Sabel said. "But we would be less effective in finding Lily."

Ford felt as though someone had taken an ax and split him right down the middle. Rescue Lily. Find Joshua. They were saying both could not be done. But he had to. He'd told Joshua to trust him. He couldn't live up to that promise if something happened to either of them.

"Ford," Harel said softly. "What did Joshua tell you?"

Ford shook his head. How could this be a choice? His choice? Joshua had told him to find Lily. That's what he had to do.

"I will send a contingent south to check on your ship," Sabel continued.

"I will go with them," Fitz said.

Sabel shook her head. "You should rest."

"I will rest while you gather the troops." He raised his eyebrows as if to challenge Sabel to argue.

Sabel shrugged. "As you wish."

"Thank you, Fitz," Harel said.

"You know how to use that?" Sabel asked, nodding at Ford's speargun.

"I—" He touched the grip. "I know enough. But I don't see how much it can help against sea monsters and shadows."

She gave a sharp nod. "Finish eating. Take a brief rest." She held up her hand and shook her head when Ford opened his mouth to argue. "My troops will not be ready until sundown and we will not travel at night. Take this opportunity to recover and perhaps train." She glanced at Harel then looked back at Ford. "We will show you how to use the gun."

"And my dagger," Ava added.

Ford nodded. He pushed his soup away. The knot in his stomach wouldn't let the food settle.

When the others had finished eating, they followed a few of the Silomites to their quarters. It was as though he walked through chest-high water, his arms and legs weighed down as heavy as his heart.

They reached a simple bunker just outside the main castle.

"We did not have time to prepare suitable sleeping quarters," Sabel said. "But your time here will be brief. I trust you will be comfortable enough."

"Thank you, my friend," Harel said with an earnest smile.

Ford looked around the room at a row of bunk beds as Sabel led Ava to an adjoining room. There was no way he would get any rest here. Not now.

Ford woke before dawn. Frantic whispers came from outside. He eased up, fastened his gun on his hip and tiptoed to the doorway. A quiet flurry of activity filled the square. He trudged toward the castle as he pulled his hair back and clipped it. He kept his eyes glued to the ground, though the stare of every Velarean was like a dart aimed at him, an intruder in their realm.

Just find Harel. Make a plan. Get Lily. Find Josh. Get home.

"Oh!" Ford looked up and grabbed Peter's arm to keep from knocking him over.

"Didn't see you there," Ford mumbled. "Where is everyone?"

"Harel went to see Sabel."

"We're wasting time here. We need to get moving."

"Without the ship?"

Ford scowled.

"Until we have protection and transportation we risk never getting to Lily. Harel mentioned you taking some time to practice with your gun. If we're going to have any chance of getting past the Schade, you need to see what they have to teach you."

Ford put his hand on the grip. "What do I need to practice? Point and shoot. I've used them before."

"On your ghosts?"

Ford shook his head in frustration. "Of course not."

"Then how do you expect to beat the Schade?"

Ford snorted. "You're saying the shadows here are the same as the spirits—"

Peter crossed his arms and cocked an eyebrow. "No . . . they're, I mean they can't be—"

"There you are!"

Peter and Ford spun to find Harel smiling as he strode toward them, Sabel not far behind.

"If you will follow me," Sabel gestured to Peter, and the two set out for a level field, with Peter spinning his staff, pivoting, bending, and turning.

"Harel." Ford spread out his arms in appeal. "What are we doing? I appreciate Sabel wanting to get her troops ready—"

"And we await our own."

"Yes, and that. But we could at least find out where they've got Lily."

"And then?"

"I don't know. I just know we can't keep dragging our feet."

"We will be on our way soon. But let me ask you, when you think of the Schade, what comes to mind?"

"I try not to think about them."

Harel gestured for Ford to follow him as he trundled down the hill toward the placid pool near the castle. "Not a bad strategy if they were to leave you alone. But as soon as you try to take Lily, who they assuredly view as one of their own, they will do everything to get her back. You will have to fight them."

"With this?" Ford unholstered the gun, pointing it at the ground as they stopped at the pool.

"With this." Harel placed his hand on Ford's chest.

A knot formed in Ford's throat. It was as though Harel's hand was made of hot coals.

He swallowed. "If that's the case, we're all doomed."

Harel gave him a half smile. "Perhaps not. Take the gun into the pool. Let the water buoy you. Do not fight it, whatever happens."

"I don't understand."

"I trust you will."

Ford stared at him for a moment more, then shook his head and waded into the cool, crystalline lake until he was waist deep. The rumble of the waterfall drummed against his body. With two more steps, he was up to his neck. Something about the water's consistent pressure on his body calmed him. Water always had a way of calming him. He took a deep breath, expanding his lungs, feeling the resistance. Working his arms back and forth, he created large ripples to compete with the ones made by the waterfall. He turned.

Harel was gone. Everyone was gone.

"What the—"

Something tugged at his leg. Ford pulled away, taking two long steps back to shore as he struggled with the speargun. Before he could get it aimed, it slipped out of his hands and plunked into the water.

Ford cursed and took a deep breath, plunging beneath the surface.

He could see straight through to the bottom. The gun drifted just out of his grasp, as though caught in a current. With a hard kick, he went after it. His fingers were almost around the grip when a whisper, deep and euphonious, rippled through the water.

"Ford . . ."

The gun slipped away as Ford stopped. He did a slow circle, looking for the source of the voice. He opened his mouth.

That's dumb. Talking underwater?

"Ford . . ."

He spun again, thrashing his hand angrily.

I've lost the gun!

"What was lost will be found."

Ford's heart pounded. His lungs ached.

Too much has been lost. As though on a roll of film in his mind, the last twenty years flashed by.

His parent's death. Foster home after foster home. Hunting ghosts around the world in abandoned hospitals, factories . . . Iron Town. The portal. Lily. Joshua.

Who are you? What're you saying? What will I find? The gun?

Ford clenched his teeth. How could he be hearing the words so clearly?

"You will find when you seek."

I am! You're saying we'll find Lily?

"With you, nothing is possible. But with me, all things are possible."

The Author? The Creator? Arkonai?

Ford tried to form another question. An argument. But the words slipped away as though carried off by the gentle current. His body relaxed. It all did seem possible. Lily's rescue. Finding Joshua. Getting back home. All without a plan. Without a thought. This was what it was like to finally find . . . something.

No. This was what it was like to be found.

He tried to resist the impulse, the need, to trust this voice. This Arkonai. He was fighting a raging river. Buffeted and slammed into stones of uncertainty and disbelief. Drowning in fear. It would be so much easier to just . . . surrender.

So you will be with me?

"Forever."

How will I know?

"Do not try to understand. Trust."

Ford squeezed his hand. His fingers pressed into the grip of the spear gun. He looked at his lost weapon, appearing out of nowhere. He kicked and propelled himself up and broke the surface of the water. Harel stood on the shore.

Ford swam until he could stand, hip-deep. He stared at Harel.

"Did you find something?" Harel asked.

"I don't know. Maybe. Or maybe I'm going crazy."

"You seem to have absorbed everything presented to you in Velare without concern for your mental health thus far. Is what you encountered beneath the surface of the water so different?"

Ford glanced back at the lake, then down at the speargun. The voice, it had been familiar. Like a memory. All things were possible. If that was true, he had only one option. He looked at Harel.

"I think I know what I need to do."

Twenty-Two

"**Y**ou will now be Lily of Velare!"

Atop a massive, flat boulder, Lily, dressed in a long, gauzy white dress, a gift from her mother the night before, stood next to Dr. Charles as he made the pronouncement. He lifted his hands and spoke to the entire congregation, looking up at them, backs to the cliff and the sea below. The tide was high and had claimed the beach; the waves crashed against the cavern wall and surged into the catacombs. All the cliffers had smiles of adoration as a sigh passed through the crowd. A few even clapped.

Lily faced Dr. Charles but cast periodic glances at the upturned faces. It had been only two weeks. She had gotten to know so many of them in such a short time. Jonah grinned up at her. Lily's chest swelled. She was among friends. They were all so happy she was here.

Her mother, wispy blonde strands of hair highlighted by the morning sun and lifting in the breeze, gave her an encouraging nod.

Her mom had promised this was just an informal ceremony to make her feel welcomed. This seemed like more.

Dr. Charles raised his voice, saying things Lily had wanted to hear her whole life.

"She came to us from a world broken and confused. Like so many wayward, directionless temporals, we now have a pure connection to Earth

Apparent. With Lily's power, together with our army, we will finally find the harmony lost for centuries. It is precisely what the prophecy foretold. For any who doubted"—Dr. Charles's wandering gaze stopped a few times—"now be reassured. We will be victorious."

At the last word, Dr. Charles's attention snapped back to Lily. She looked up at him. His eyes were shining and his smile was tender, fatherly even.

Victorious in what?

A successful community. Harmony with each other.

A soft heat grew in Lily's chest and tears sprang to her eyes. She was accepted. More than anyone at school. More than even her dad ever could. Or would. They didn't view her as some fragile little girl. She had strength. Authority.

She belonged. She was home.

What about Holly?

Her sister had her own mom, Raelyn. They all had their family.

What about Uncle Ford?

Lily pressed her lips together. He would understand.

This wasn't something she thought she wanted. But with Dr. Charles, her mother, Jonah, all looking on with pride, at that moment she wanted nothing else. She grinned back at them.

She had kept an open mind, just like her mother had asked. Over the last two weeks she'd learned so much: gathering fish with Jonah, making dinner with her mom, even a trip to see the dragon eggs. She and Jonah had dreamed up ways to train them when they hatched. She could just see herself riding on the back of one, trailing her fingers through the clouds. Whatever happened, her world outside of Velare was fading fast. And she was prepared to let it go. An image of her dad swam to the corner of her mind, but only an opaque recollection, a feeling really. A distant affection with no anchor. When she tried to conjure up specifics, the memory scattered into a million pieces.

She shivered and tried again. Wouldn't this ceremony have been something he would have loved to attend? Like a softball game.

She frowned and shook her head. Had she ever played softball? Vague memories of running bases touched the edges of her mind. She shook her head. No, that would mean she was part of a team and that had never been the case. This was her team. Her family.

She scanned the cheerful faces. The Schade had all but disappeared. The freaky creatures seemed more a part of a scary dream than something she had actually encountered. But a shadow passed over her thoughts as though the Schade entered her mind. For just a minute. A shiver of fear ran through her. Her hands turned clammy.

Dr. Charles finished her introduction and stepped down from the platform. Lily took a breath and clasped her hands in front of her, squeezing away the nerves, and stepped forward.

"I don't think I deserve this honor," she said, lifting her voice. "But there is work to be done in Velare. Work that will help my home and my family." It was a phrase repeated by both Dr. Charles and her mom. It was strange speaking those same words with such conviction. Had she really even considered what they meant?

It didn't matter. She would learn. She would do anything to hold on to this feeling. To know she was not just a Cliffer, but maybe even someday a leader in the community.

A robed elder stepped forward, and Dr. Charles helped her up onto the boulder. She faced Lily, taking her hands, bringing them to her wrinkled forehead. It was impossible to tell if she was Velarean or, like Jonah, from Earth Apparent. Lily had never met a Velarean. But her mom insisted they were around. That they looked and acted just like temporals. It didn't really matter. No one dwelled on it, anyway. But this woman looked ancient. Maybe that's what Velareans looked like.

"It is us you honor with your wisdom and insight," the elder said. "We trust you will bring unity to our worlds. We also believe that when the time comes"—a shadow passed over her face—"you will defend our people, your people, against those who would seek to do us harm."

The proclamation seemed a bit dramatic. Who would want to harm them? Lily tried to smile, but it felt as though someone was pulling on the corners of her mouth.

"I will do my best," she said.

Lame. But they all seemed satisfied with her answer. What else could she say? She wasn't equipped to go into any battle. That was her dad's department. He was the soldier. The warrior of Alnok.

A sudden vision of her dad, standing in a boat with his sword drawn, washed away her peace from only moments ago. She squinted against the tug of a headache as she tried to draw up a memory of him. But just as quickly as the image came, it disappeared. Whatever defense needed raising, she would have to manage. She could ask mom about it later. The elder cocked her head with a slight frown. Lily forced her smile to broaden.

The sea crashing against the cliff created a lulling backdrop to the buzz of conversation from those she now counted as friends and family. She looked over their heads at the expanse of textured water behind them. The sun glinted off the waves. A white bird dove in and out of the surf.

The elder produced a scepter made of a shining onyx material. Only a few feet long, maybe an inch in diameter, polished crystals and sparkling gems capped each end. She turned to the crowd and held it up for everyone to see. There was a collective "ooh" from the congregation.

Lily fidgeted and tried to find something to do with her sweaty hands and opted for just cracking her knuckles. Lily glanced at Jonah, but his smile faltered as his gaze bounced from the scepter to her. What was he thinking? Lily looked back at the scepter. Something about it gave Lily the creeps. Maybe it was the reverence with which the elder treated it. Almost like an idol everyone was expected to worship. Her old life might be a fog, but the act of idol worship was a big no. She was sure of that.

The elder turned, and holding the scepter in open palms, presented it to Lily.

Lily looked at it. Accepting this gift, the ceremony, the speech, it was all leading to something. An expectation for her to do . . . what?

Boy, would dad have something to say about this.

The sudden thought brought sharp tears. A gut punch of homesickness that sent the throbbing headache into her temples.

Why all these thoughts of her dad? He hadn't even crossed her mind in ages. Whatever he might say didn't matter now.

Wouldn't he be proud?

No, he wasn't here because he had never accepted her. Not really. He was Holly's dad. Raelyn's husband. Lily had waited on the outside long enough.

A film of sweat broke out on Lily's forehead. She glanced at the sea of faces and for a second they blurred. If she took this staff, everything would change. She frowned. There was no way to know this. Besides, what would change? And how?

But she couldn't rationalize away the instinct. Something about this scepter would shift her role with the Cliffers.

Lily cleared her throat and reached out for the scepter, her hand hovering at its center.

Take it.

But she couldn't. Within the dark, honed rod, something moved. A writhing, twisting substance made of—*shadow*—some kind of liquid. Maybe water.

She looked closer. No, it was just a polished stone reflecting the drifting clouds. But the growing revulsion stayed her hand. Along with a heated frustration. Tears stung her eyes. This first act as an official Cliffer and she was blowing it. This thing was just a stupid staff. Nothing nefarious.

She sniffed and wiped at her wet cheeks. The elder smiled.

She thinks I'm overcome with joy. Not fear. Which is exactly as it should be. Lily lifted her chin and drew in a deep breath.

Take it.

A wave of nausea hit her, and she swayed. Dr. Charles was there in a heartbeat and steadied her.

"Take it," he whispered.

Lily nodded. Leaning against Dr. Charles, his hands tight on her arms, she curled her fingers and settled her hand over the cold surface. She sucked in a breath through her teeth as a jolt of heat shot into her palm and up her arm. Dr. Charles gripped her shoulders.

"I, uh. Thanks. This is . . . really something." She fought the urge to vomit. She needed the seripyn. Now.

"I think we should let the newest member of our family rest," Dr. Charles chuckled.

Lily nodded and allowed him to guide her off the makeshift stage. She gripped the scepter. A few of the closest cliffers reached out as though to shake her hand, but she couldn't lift her arms.

Her stomach turned. She gazed into the crowd as they parted. Their long shadows cast by the rising sun seemed to grow. She blinked, but the shadows took over, covering everything, as though an early twilight had descended.

"And maybe a bite to eat," he murmured, steering her past the people.

"Thank you," Lily said. "Yes. Maybe I should lay down for a bit." The words came from her lips, but it was as though she overheard them from someone else.

Dr. Charles led her from the dispersing crowd. Her mom didn't seem to be among them. Down the path, they shuffled toward her home.

"I think my nerves must be getting to me," Lily said, shaking her head, trying to clear the fog.

No, not fog. Even in the darkness, some things were clearer. A memory, vivid and bright, of a meal with her dad, her sister, Uncle Ford and . . . mom.

Not mom. Your mom is here. You mean Raelyn.

"I feel a bit confused."

"It is overwhelming," Dr. Charles said, his voice deep with concern. "I remember my ceremony. Nothing close to this, of course. But it's a day I'll always remember."

"I'm sure." Ceremonies and scepters. A cliff side community in an alternate dimension. Should she be here at all? She didn't even know what they were asking of her.

They made the turn to the stone house, with Dr. Charles's arm still around her shoulder. He opened the door.

"Hi honey." Her mom took over from Dr. Charles in getting Lily through the door. "You need the seripyn. We shouldn't have let you go so long."

"I need to put this somewhere," Lily said, holding out the scepter.

Anywhere. Just get rid of it.

But when she glanced down at it, she drew it close to her body, pressing it against her chest with both hands.

No, put it down.

Lily placed it on the table next to the bowl of soup her mother had prepared for her. Her hand ached as she peeled her fingers off the rod. She sunk down into her seat and took a slurping sip of the brew. Instantly, the headache cleared. Her stomach settled.

She sat back and let out a relieved sigh. She gave the scepter, *her scepter*, a tender look. The swirling substance was mesmerizing. Calming. Comforting. Yes, she was home.

Twenty-Three

"I heard a voice, Harel!" Ford paced the expansive entry. A breeze passed through the open castle doors. Soldiers rushed in and out, preparing for a battle they were long delayed in waging.

Ford had argued away the morning as a slow, angry heat built in his chest. Wasting time was not a useful skill. Ava watched him, her palms pressed together, her index fingers touching her lips as though praying. Ford couldn't look her in the eye. What he'd seen, what he'd heard. She had to think it was crazy.

Ford had tried to convince Harel to set out on foot, but Harel insisted the ship was critical in getting to Lily. Maybe that was the case for many soldiers who might not fare well over land. But what about one sneaky soldier with a magic speargun?

Harel glowered, his hazel eyes flashing. "You may have *heard* him, but you did not listen."

"Heard, listen, either way, I'm not waiting. He said I'd find what I lost. That's Lily. Maybe even Josh. I'm not gonna stand around for one more minute!"

"How do you know where to go?" Peter asked.

"East," Ford snapped.

No one spoke. Fitz, Peter, Ava, Sabel, and a dozen of Sabel's personal guard stood around, watching Harel warily. Harel crossed his arms.

"Joshua spent weeks learning to wield his sword. Will you at least spare the time to learn to use your weapon?"

Ford stopped his pacing. Not fair. Using his brother as leverage. But he relaxed his shoulders, though he couldn't quite release his clenched fists. "I know how. Point and shoot."

"Shoot at shadows?" Ava cried, throwing her hands in the air. Everyone used the same argument. "Look, everyone is eager to get moving. To get to Lily. But you and I are the last people to be questioning Harel's strategy."

Ford growled and shook his head. He should have just left, telling no one. They'd done nothing *but* prepare. Meanwhile, Lily was subjected to the Schade day after day. He looked down at the gun holstered on his waist. He was familiar enough.

"If you agree to spend a few hours becoming acquainted with the spear-gun," Harel reasoned, "I will not stop you from leaving. Although I believe you will be making a mistake. One that may have consequences we do not yet fathom."

Ava unsheathed her dagger. "Maybe you're confident in your skills with the gun, but I don't have the first clue how to wield a knife. I could use a crash course on how to use this without slicing off one of my fingers."

Ford hazarded a glance at her as she raised an eyebrow. He had to look away. She had a way of discerning more of his thoughts than he wanted.

"*Think*," she continued. "You believe you're so tough you could go it alone? I wager rescuing Lily will take all of us."

Ford heaved a sigh and ran his fingers through his hair. This was the Ava he was used to. Firm, logical. He finally nodded. "Okay, okay. We could both do with a little training. I'll give it the rest of today. "

The gun had special qualities meant for this dimension. If he could wield it, he could get Lily.

He drew the gun and held it out in his palms. "What do I do?"

Harel gave a curt nod, then looked at Ava. "I will train you both as best I can within the time you've allotted."

Ava put a hand on Ford's arm, and his shoulders relaxed. Her touch had the same calming effect as the water.

"The sooner we get started, the better trained we'll be," she said.

Harel looked at Peter. "I trust you could use some time to get reacquainted with your weapon?"

"Sure," Peter said, giving the staff an expert rotation around his shoulder.

Show off.

"Come," Sabel said, waving Peter to follow her. "There are a few more techniques I can show you."

"Very well. Fitz"—Harel glanced at his second in command, then back to Ford and Ava—"follow me."

They left the castle and, though Ford was taller than Harel, he had to lengthen his stride to keep up. Ava jogged next to them, with Fitz right behind.

Harel led them to the back of the castle to the pool with the waterfall roughly twenty yards away. The day had grown warm, the sun at the dead center of a blue sky with only a few drifting clouds. The lake roiled at the base of the waterfall, radiating calmer ripples toward shore until the water lapped near their feet.

Harel waded backwards into the pool until he was knee deep. "Nahe-sekai cannot access the Silom Pool. Neither can any other sea creature that would cause us harm." He waved them in.

Ford scanned the rippling waters. He had heard a voice beneath the surface telling him to trust. Nothing could harm him here. But already the words were fading. The memory, fuzzy and dream-like.

"I thought the Schade typically avoid the water? If that's who I'll be fighting, why train here?" Ford asked.

Harel nodded at the waterfall. "We'll be aiming through there."

Ford cocked his head. "How long's this cord?"

Harel smiled. "It depends on what you are aiming for."

Something dark slithered behind the sheet of water. Ava stayed on shore, but Ford joined Harel as he brought his gun up and leveled it at the shadow. "What's behind the falls?"

"Nothing more than an unnamed fear. Something you yourself project. Unlike the Schade, it will not attack. But it can still cause damage. Your weapon is an extension of you. The state of your heart will determine the strength of the strike. Take aim and fire when you are ready."

Ford nodded and brought his left hand under his right to keep it steady. He aimed at the darker part of the waterfall. The shadow didn't move. He squeezed the trigger. The spear launched, bringing with it the slender, white cord, and passed through the waterfall. A slight twinge vibrated the handle.

Ford frowned and looked at the gun.

"What did you feel?" Ava asked.

Ford shrugged. "Nothing."

Fitz touched Ava's arm. "May I?" He gestured to her dagger.

"Of course." She pulled it from its sheath and handed it over.

Fitz hefted it in his palm, then in one smooth motion grasped the tip, pulled back and let it fly at a nearby tree. It stuck into the trunk with a *thwunk*.

"Ava," Harel said. "Perhaps Fitz could give you some training? At the mouth of the river, you will find a variety of targets."

Ava took the dagger back from Fitz and weighed it in her palm as he had done. She held the tip between her thumb and index finger and slung it at the same tree. It hit its mark but failed to pierce the trunk.

She shrugged and looked at Fitz, who gazed at her appraisingly.

"I believe she will be a fast learner," he said with a lopsided grin.

"Indeed," Harel said.

Ava glanced at Ford with lips pressed together and narrowed eyes. The look she held when assessing the perfect shot for an upcoming episode. She strapped the dagger to her thigh.

"Good luck," Ford said with a forced smile.

"Right," Ava said. She and Fitz strode away along the shoreline, chatting quietly, until they had passed a grove of trees and were out of sight.

Harel pointed to a small button beneath the trigger guard, drawing Ford's attention back to their task. "Click this lever with your index finger."

Ford pushed it, and the cord snaked back into its housing. "Handy."

"Yes. Let us try again." Harel waded out of the pool.

Ford nodded and looked back at the waterfall. No shadows. Just clear water rushing down a high cliff and foaming into a blue pool.

"I am confident we will find Joshua," Harel said, just over the roar of the falls.

Ford scowled. "Why bring up—" He glanced at Harel, but just as his gaze left the waterfall, something darted from left to right. Ford focused on the cascade. A cloud cast its own fast-moving shadow across the falls. But it differed from what he'd just seen.

The shadow behind the fall reappeared. Darker, stagnate. Far left corner. Ford fired. The spear pierced the falls. The sensation reminded him of his high school baseball team. When he would knock the ball clean into left field. The stinging vibration was the same. That was just before Mom and Dad died. He had quit the team after that.

The shadow grew taller and darker.

Ford clicked the winding mechanism and drew the spear back into its cradle.

His target continued to spread behind the water, creating a much larger mark. He couldn't miss this time. He fired again.

Same vibration. And the shadow grew larger still.

By the time Ford had the spear loaded and fired again, the shadow filled half the waterfall. He couldn't possibly miss. He shot into the middle of the shadow.

"Ha!" he shouted, his voice echoing off the cliff.

But the shadow bulged, pushing at the water, as though it might not only pass through, but was coming out of it.

Ford fired again and again. Every shot failed to beat back his opponent.

"What'd I do? How do I kill it?"

"The Schade derive their power, in part, from our fear. Our inability to trust the one who brings peace."

"I'm not afraid. I'm ticked off!"

"From what source does anger originate?"

Harel glared at the shadow. His temples pulsed and his hand shook.

"Anger obscures discernment," Harel continued. "It overwhelms logic and drowns love. It steals joy and destroys relationships. All because it is rooted in fear. And with fear, there can be no love. Or trust."

Ford grunted and fired again. His arm ached as he held his stance. His next shot landed in the froth beneath the waterfall, which was now almost entirely black.

He gritted his teeth as he depressed the recoil switch. "Trust what? Myself? If that's the case, we're all doomed."

"It is true. You are sometimes untrustworthy." Harel smiled and nodded. "As am I. And Ava. And Joshua."

"Then trust who?"

"The one who spoke from the water. The voice you heard was Arkonai."

A bitter laugh burst from Ford's lips. "Arkonai. You really think Joshua's Arkonai spoke to me?" Isn't that who the voice said he was? Ford couldn't remember.

Harel smiled quizzically. "You suppose the Creator would not speak to you?"

Ford's smile faded. In all his searches for what lay just beyond his perception, what had he really expected to find? He'd finally encountered something of what he'd pursued for so long. Was he really going to reject it because he didn't understand?

Do not try to understand. Trust.

Ford let out a slow breath. "Okay, not trying," he muttered. "I'm trusting."

He aimed and squeezed the trigger at the black mass, now leaking into the pool. As though in slow motion, the spear flew straight with the cord unfurling. The tip of the spear glinted a bright blue light just before it entered the falls. Rather than a harsh vibration, the handle gave a gentle jerk. The shadow shrank, but did not disappear.

He called back the spear. "Trusting," he said under his breath as he fired again. The shadow backed down into the corner of the foam, crouching, waiting for him to be off his guard. Each time the spear connected, the shadow shrank but never entirely disappeared.

"Why won't it go away?" Ford asked, finally looking at Harel.

Harel gazed into the falls, then jerked his head to signal Ford to join him on the shore. "Learning to trust completely takes time," he said. "And what you are using as target practice is no Schade, but a projection of your own fear and anger." He clapped Ford on the back. "But this was an excellent start. Come, let us have dinner. If we hear nothing of the *Sealight*, we will try again tomorrow."

"Wait..." Ford glanced around. The sun was fading beneath the horizon on his left. "I've been at this all day?"

The speargun dropped from his grasp, his hand suddenly weak and numb. His shoulder burned and his back ached.

"Fighting back our demons is considerable work. Come," Harel urged him toward the castle, "the others will be waiting."

"Hi Ford," Ava said, jogging up next to him and Harel. Her cheeks were flushed, and she had that breathless, joyful look she reserved for a particularly well-produced show.

Ford raised his eyebrows and smiled. "I'm guessing it went well?"

"I think so. I hit more targets than I missed toward the end. And Fitz taught me a little hand to hand combat."

"Alotta good it'll do against shadow figures."

Ava's shoulders fell. "Thanks," she said flatly.

Ford shook his head in disbelief. So they'd both made progress, but wasted a whole day. But he'd done something, hadn't he? He fought back the shadow. It had to be enough. With or without anyone's help.

Ford tossed in his bunk bed beneath Peter in the lower level of the castle. Harel and Fitz were asleep on the other side of the room. Ava had her own bed in an adjoining chamber. After a quick dinner, Harel had insisted they all get a good night's sleep.

But the longer Ford lay on top of his blanket, the tighter his chest became. If he didn't get some air, he'd suffocate.

He eased out of the bed, grabbed his boots, backpack, and his speargun and eased out of the room into the cool night. He waited just outside the door for any voices of protest, but all was quiet. Taking a deep breath, he crept to the gate and peered through a window cut out of the protective wall. The pool shimmered, reflecting a half-moon. He sat down and slid on his boots, then stood and looked back at the water.

Now what?

Muffled conversation came from the castle. Ford hunched over and darted behind the nearest tree. When the voices faded, Ford straightened and pushed his hair back.

Harel would insist on more training tomorrow. Maybe the day after that. All the while, God knew what was happening to Lily. And Joshua.

"Okay, Arkonai . . . God," he whispered. "Whoever. You said to trust. So, here's me trusting. I'm gonna go back to the sea and then head east. With any luck, Josh will be waiting on the shore, no worse for wear and we'll get Lily, come back for Ava and Peter and go home. Sound good?"

Ford waited. No response.

He could swim under the water and listen for the voice. But what if the answer was no? If he left now, he could put his plan into action and ask for help along the way.

Perfect.

Ford buckled his speargun to his hip and threw on the backpack. He planted solid steps as he headed south to the gate, his head on a swivel and his ears perked for noises.

Just before the gate, he grasped the thick, rough stone of the wall and clambered up, swung himself over, and climbed back down. So far, so good.

Lanterns radiated warm, yellow light around the castle. He skirted around a few soldiers on watch. Then he cut west down the hill to the Silom Pool and the thundering waterfall, and waded into the tepid water. A few scouts came near, their words muffled. Ford took a deep breath and went under. He swam several yards until he could feel the river's current pulling at him.

Once he was sure he had cleared the gate, he poked his head out of the water even as he floated down river. It took every bit of strength to fight the current and make his way to shore. Paddling the river and swimming in it were very different. He banged his knee on a rock and scraped his hands in the gravel.

Finally, soaked and sore, he stumbled onto the bank. He hurried, favoring his bruised knee in the near-dark. He stopped once for a swig of seripyn from his flask. Amazing stuff. Like Red Bull on steroids.

The moon passed over and the first glimmers of dawn put the cliffs into sharp relief. He followed the river, gurgling to his right. He wanted to celebrate, but his gut did a slow flip as he approached the sea and the sun made its appearance. It was too quiet.

He stood at the shore, gazing out over the silvery, choppy water, then to the clouds building in the west. Joshua could be at the bottom of that sea. Hot tears filled Ford's eyes.

No, he was too good a swimmer. He had a magic sword. He knew this land. His brother might already be rescuing Lily from the catacombs.

Ford shivered. Was Joshua's sword any match against that monster in the water?

"Let's just get this done," he muttered and started east.

He strode through a thick grove of trees, their canopy blocking the sun as it rose ahead of him. Thunder growled in the west.

He hadn't counted on a storm . . .

It didn't matter. What was a little rain? He'd come through a lot worse. He was making progress and that's all that mattered.

A blast of chilly wind swirled through the trees, sending a barrage of leaves down on Ford.

Great. A *cold* rain.

He hunched his shoulders and put his thoughts on Lily. She was so like him. Adventurous, impulsive, curious. But smarter. He couldn't stop a smile from lifting the corners of his mouth. She was a spitfire. No way the Schade would get the better of her. She'd fight them off. His eyes burned as his smile fell. Fighter or not, how would she stand up against those elusive shadows? She shouldn't have to. She should be at camp right now. The camp she didn't want to be at. Yet another similar trait. Loners.

The clouds gathered faster than the sun could rise, and daylight never made a solid appearance. Ford broke out of the trees, giving him a clear view of the sea. Something floated along the lapping waves. A dark puddle, ten feet offshore, moved contrary to the surrounding water. An oil slick of sorts. Ford slowed.

The wind whistled as he studied the strange spot from a distance. He took a few trepidatious steps. Part of the puddle rose from the water. Ford stopped. It bubbled and bloated, bigger, darker.

Ford took a step back. The puddle took shape. The shape of a man. Or the shadow of one.

"Oh, God," Ford whispered as his stomach sank to his knees.

The Schade.

Twenty-Four

F ord raised his gun and aimed.

Just trust. Just trust.

He fired. The spear disappeared into the mass of darkness. The cord held taut. He'd done it. Whatever the Schade were made of, he'd pierced it. He'd—

A hard yank nearly ripped the gun from Ford's hand. He held on, his shoulder wrenching painfully. He pulled back, gripping the handle with both hands. His feet dragged through the wet sand.

"No, no, no," he grunted, punctuating each tug.

But the shadow was gobbling up the cord. It was drawing Ford to it. Fifteen feet became five in seconds. The toes of his boots splashed into the edge of a surging wave.

Then the pulling stopped. A tendril of shadow edged out like a searching finger. If he continued to hold on to the gun, the shadow would take hold of his hand. Or worse.

But he didn't let go. The smoky shadow seemed to caress the cord, lazily winding around it. The very tip of the protruding black mass hovered in front of Ford's hand.

The shadow held the cord taut. A whip of wind pushed at Ford's back, as though urging him forward, and sending his hair into his eyes. The protrusion dissipated like smoke blown away. The main mass bristled with frenetic spikes of pitch black shadow. A flash of lightning lit up the darkening sky. Then a deep roll of deafening thunder vibrated the air.

Ford hit the switch, forgotten until now.

The cord reversed with a jolt, and the spear bounced and dragged along the waves until it returned to its chamber. Ford fell back and splashed in the shallow waters. The shadow billowed up, fifteen feet tall. Black as night. It divided into two as it shrank. Then three. Then a dozen, his own height. At the center, one shadow took on more form than the others. Head, shoulders, arms, legs. It pulled away from the rest of the shadow, as though struggling to break free. Rain burst from the storm clouds, seeming to wash away the shadow as a face took shape and became a medium flesh-color. Dark brown hair, cut short, gray eyes.

"Ford!" Joshua shouted and leaned forward, fighting against the shadow holding him. He reached out as his hand took on definition.

"Joshua!" Ford bellowed, scrambling to his feet. He waded toward his brother on lead-weighted legs.

"Help me!" Joshua cried.

Ford took a step into the waters as a wave surged to his thighs, pulling at him as it receded, putting him off balance. He splashed headfirst into the sea as another wave came over his head. He flailed in the water, swallowing a mouthful. Sputtering and splashing, until he regained his feet and backed out of the water. Joshua rushed toward him until he was just five paces away, still waist deep in the water, reaching for Ford.

Ford started to launch forward to pull him from the water. Joshua smiled.

Ford froze and frowned, his heart pounding painfully. Adrenaline pumped from his chest up into his temples and sent tingles into his fingertips.

"Josh?" Ford took a hesitant step forward.

Joshua's smile evaporated. "Hurry! I'm almost free!" He reached further.

Another blast of lightning lit up the surrounding army of shadows in the water. They squirmed in the frothy waves and around Joshua's legs.

Ford took another step forward, wading back out into the waves, warm tears mingling with the sea water and rain. He was so close to saving his brother.

"Hold on! I'm coming!"

Ford held out his hand, nearly touching Joshua's fingertips. But another wave knocked him off balance, though he kept his stance.

"Okay, God! A little help here!" How could he trust a being who literally wanted to cut his legs out from under him?

"Ford!" Joshua stretched out from the shadows, straining.

Ford took another step forward. He would do this. He would save his brother. So close . . . so close . . .

Another shock of lightning, longer and brighter than any other, exploded around them. Ford brushed Joshua's fingertips.

Joshua's hopeful smile turned to shock. He gasped and looked down. Protruding from his chest was the tip of a blade, flashing in the downpour. Joshua grabbed at it, his mouth working.

The blade plunged further. Joshua's face was a mask of shock, pain, and anger. His eyes locked on Ford. Ford froze, arms and legs numb. He heard nothing. Felt nothing. He couldn't take the next breath.

Then the place where the blade pierced Joshua's chest disintegrated back into black smoke. The rest of the shadows dispersed. And with them, Joshua.

"No!" Ford's paralysis broke and he scrambled after his brother, reaching for his hand.

"Joshua!" He couldn't lose him. "God, NO!"

Ford tumbled headlong into a solid form. Firm hands gripped him under his arms and hauled him to his feet. He was face-to-face with Joshua. Fully formed, scruffy beard, drenched Joshua.

"What in the—"

"Hang on." Joshua pulled Ford out of the midst of the dispersed shadows. "We're not through yet." He stood next to him, his sword raised and ready. He nodded to the speargun hanging limply in Ford's hand.

"Get ready with that."

"I don't know . . . how did you—"

"I'll explain later. Right now, we've got this to deal with." He gestured to the Schade, assembling and reforming into one solid mass.

"It's no good. I don't know how to get this to work."

"You can't. You're only the wielder. The power comes from another source."

Ford wiped the rain out of his eyes and looked down at the gun.

The voice. Arkonai. He had to trust.

Okay, I'm just gonna shoot. You hit the mark.

Ford aimed at the approaching dark mass.

"For Lily," he whispered and fired. The spear shot through the center of the shadow, just like before. But the smoke substance dissipated, as though being washed away by the rain. The spear dropped to the ground. Ford hit the switch and brought it back.

The smoke floating on the waves gathered together again. It formed a dark lump on the shore. Ford fired. The smoke melted into the waves, forming the puddles again. As Ford brought his spear back, it regrouped again. Joshua splashed out to it and stabbed it through the middle. The shadow form leaked back out into the sea and vanished.

"Nicely done, bro," Joshua shouted over the wind and rain. He dropped his sword. Ford caught him as he fell to his knees.

"Where did you come from?" Ford said, hoisting him back on his feet. "What's wrong?" He made sure Joshua was steady, then felt over his chest. No blood. No wound. He pulled him into a tight hug.

"Geez, I thought I lost you, bro."

"Not that easy." Joshua grunted.

"Sorry." Ford let go and gave him a pat on the shoulder.

Joshua gave him a tight smile as he picked up his sword with his left hand and sheathed it. "I'll explain on the way. The Schade will regroup. It'll take more than a sword and spear gun to wipe them out." Joshua started out into the water where the Schade had disintegrated, but stopped short and turned around. "Where's everybody else?"

Ford glanced over his shoulder. "I, uh, left them back in Silom."

Joshua gave Ford's face a full once over and then nodded. He needed to offer no other explanation. If anyone understood, Joshua would. He knew what it meant to take care of those he loved. And he surely understood Ford's determination to prove he was just as steadfast. Just as trustworthy.

"Joshua, your hand." Ford looked at the charred skin on the back of his brother's right hand.

"Yeah." Joshua narrowed his eyes and cast a glance at Ford. "Hurts like hell, too." He held it out for Ford to inspect.

"The sea monster?"

Joshua didn't answer. There were no puncture wounds. No missing fingers. This wound wasn't from sharp teeth. Fire? Surely he'd have more than a singed hand. The black spot was solid, like a mark of some kind. Clearly defined and black as pitch. Hopefully, wherever Joshua was leading them, they had doctors.

Joshua began staggering along the shoreline.

"Where are we going?" Ford gasped.

Joshua motioned him to follow. "There's a bay up ahead," he called over his shoulder.

Ford shook his head in frustration. They ran, side-by-side, in the pounding rain.

"How do I know it's really you?" Ford shouted.

Joshua shook his head. "Don't be an idiot!"

Ford glanced at him. Grim, drawn expression, but resolute and focused. But it wasn't just the way Joshua looked. Ford *knew* it was his brother. As much as he knew himself. Time, distance, nothing changed the unbreakable bond of brotherhood.

"What's in the bay?" Ford asked. He shook his head to clear the rain from his eyes.

Joshua slowed and looked out over the choppy waters. "That." He pointed just offshore.

Ford scanned the waves. Something poked out of the sea. Rigging. Maybe an upper deck. A ship. But the hull was missing. It disappeared beneath the surface of the water.

"A sunken boat?" Ford asked. "What happened to the sub? Is it still damaged?"

"No, it works just fine. It's half boat. Sails, deck, hull. But it seals up and dives like a sub. C'mon." Joshua waded in a few steps into the waters of the calmer bay. Using only his left arm, he swam out to the exposed rigging.

After the sea monster attack, how could he swim out into open water without a glance back? Ford kept his eyes on his brother, looking for any sign of distress. The man had nearly passed out just minutes ago. Once Joshua was at the rigging, he stood and waved Ford over.

Ford waded into the water and swam to his brother. Just laid out on the surface like bait. Easy pickin's. Joshua had better have taken care of the creature. Ford, arm over arm, powered through the waves. The special boots gave him an extra boost until finally he reached the deep waters. Gasping for breath, he got to the boat without encountering sharp teeth or spiked tail.

He climbed over a wooden railing and sloshed across the deck. Joshua held onto the mainmast as the boat rocked in the swells. From the sails, it looked to be a sort of clipper, at least the biggest clipper Ford had ever seen. At Joshua's feet, where the cargo access would have been, was a raised, circular access hatch.

Joshua leaned over, yanked on a handle with his uninjured arm, and lifted the door. "Follow me." He climbed into the opening and descended a wooden spiral staircase. "Close the door behind you," he called up.

Ford nodded, stepped onto a platform and pulled the door closed over him. He turned a lever to lock it, then circled down the staircase. At the bottom, Joshua tossed him a towel.

Ford caught it, letting it hang limp in his hand. "How did you . . . the sea monster . . ."

"Yeah, it's a great story. Suffice it to say, I would have drowned if they hadn't come along. You think your speargun is something." He nodded at the weapon attached to Ford's waist. "They have something bigger and more effective than cannons. Spears, attached to rope, that shoot out from the sides of the ship like cannons. Nahesekai didn't stand a chance."

They stood in the main hold of the ship, soldiers darting around them. Portholes, like the ones in the tunnel, showed blue sea beyond.

"You killed it?" Ford asked.

Joshua shook his head. "I don't think so. But it'll have second thoughts about attacking any boats in the near future." He grimaced and drew his right hand to his chest.

Lucas bounded up, with Anna right behind. "Glad to see you, Ford," he said.

Anna noticed Joshua's injury right away. "Lucas," she said, staring at Joshua's hand. "Bring the healer."

"Why?" Lucas followed Anna's gaze and his smile faded to a grim line. He nodded and dashed back the way they had come.

"What is it?" Ford asked, stepping around Anna to be closer to his brother. "It's not a burn?"

Anna shook her head, her brow creased with worry.

Within just a few minutes, Lucas returned with an elderly man with snow-white hair and a leathered face. "What do we have here?" he asked, his voice softer than his grizzled features. He lifted Joshua's arm and turned his hand over, then glanced at Lucas. "Bring me my bowl."

Lucas disappeared again.

The man continued to tug on Joshua's arm, looking at it from different angles. It had to be an optical illusion, but the mark seemed to cover more of Joshua's hand.

"I'm Father Braden," he said without stopping his inspection.

Joshua's face was gray and he swayed. Ford caught him again.

"The captain's cabin will be a quiet place for me to work," Father Braden said. "Anna, see that someone brings my bowl."

Anna ran off in the direction Lucas had gone.

"Let's get him somewhere comfortable, shall we?" Father Braden said.

Ford and the healer helped Joshua to the aft of the ship and through a doorway into a dark, quiet room.

"The captain won't mind?" Joshua croaked.

"You know? She never uses it."

Joshua groaned as they lay him on a bed against one side of the cabin. Ford kneeled at Joshua's feet while Father Braden crouched at Joshua's head. His brother writhed, his eyes squeezed shut, trying to pull his hand away from the healer.

"What's wrong with him?" Ford asked as he gripped Joshua's shoulders so Father Braden could look at his hand.

"Schade poison." Father Braden glanced up at Ford. "He threatened the Schade? Got near enough to be touched?"

Ford nodded. Joshua was near enough because he had to save his reckless brother.

Why didn't I stay in Silom?

Lucas burst into the room with Anna on his heels.

"Father Braden, I have it," he said breathlessly.

"Very good. Bring it here."

Lucas handed off a wooden bowl filled with a clear liquid.

"What is it?" Ford asked. Surely the medicine here was better than back home.

Father Braden took a small towel, dipped it in the bowl, squeezed off the excess and lay it over the wound. Then he pressed his hands over the towel and looked at Ford with a half smile.

"Water."

"What?" Ford stood up.

Joshua's eyes fluttered open. He finally lay still.

"Right." Ford wiped at his face without taking his eyes off his brother. Joshua was alive and safe. Ford was one for two so far. Now they just needed to get Lily.

"Have you seen any sign of the others?" Joshua asked, his voice raw. Father Braden still held his hand with the medicinal . . . water.

"Others? Here?" Ford blinked away the mental fog.

Joshua frowned. "Peter, Ava, Harel, Fitz. You know, our crew?"

"Right, sorry. It's just—"

Joshua shut his eyes and grimaced. "It's okay." He shifted and opened his eyes, gazing hard at Ford. "I understand, you know. Not wanting to wait I mean." His voice gained strength. "But you have to know that what's happening here is bigger than us. We can't just make choices based on what we think we know."

Lucas took the bowl from Father Braden. "We spotted boats on the river. They should be here by sundown."

"If I'd waited a day," Ford said, "maybe the Schade wouldn't have attacked. You wouldn't have had to . . ." He gestured at Joshua's hand.

"As it so happens," Anna said, "we did not know where you might be. When we saw you, we knew to anchor here and not continue to the deeper bay. It will be a shorter travel for Harel and the others."

"Glad I could help," Ford mumbled, glancing at Joshua's blackened hand. "Will he be okay?" he asked Father Braden.

Father Braden sighed. "If he rests." He began wrapping Joshua's hand. "If we can get him to a healing house, we should be able to keep it from spreading."

"You can't eliminate it entirely? He'll always have that?"

Joshua held up his hand and looked at it. "Not much of a tattoo."

Ford rolled his eyes. "No, it's like a solid bruise. And it's getting bigger."

"I'll be okay." Joshua grunted as he sat up. "But I can't lay still. I will go after my daughter as soon as we reach the catacombs."

Father Braden nodded. "I will do all I can. If I can contain the infection, even without curing it, you should have use of your hand." He looked up at Lucas. "More tonic."

Lucas nodded and left.

"I'll help the captain prepare to dive," Anna said and followed Lucas out.

Father Braden looked after her. "Those two are the reason we are here. They know the *Sealight* inside and out." He looked between Ford and Joshua. "They work together. Which is what you must do."

"We have to trust each other," Joshua said.

Ford narrowed his eyes. "Trust only each *other*? Doesn't it seem like there's something bigger at play here? A larger plan?" He waited to see if Joshua caught his meaning. All this talk of Arkonai, the confrontation at the beach, finding Joshua. He wasn't in control. But something was. Or someone."

Joshua gave him a half smile and lay back, closing his eyes again. "I think you know the answer to that."

Ford didn't entirely. But he was starting to.

"Ford!" Ava burst into the room and threw her arms around his neck. "Thank God you're okay." Then she pulled back and punched him in the chest hard enough for Ford to rock back. "That's for leaving."

She glanced down at Joshua as Peter brushed past her and kneeled at the bedside.

"Joshua! You're alive!" Peter gripped his shoulder.

Joshua gave him a faint smile. "Mostly."

Peter looked down at his wrapped hand. "What—"

"Long story. Where's Harel?"

Peter nodded and stood. "He's with Fitz and Sabel and the captain. We're supposed to meet with them to go over our plan."

"We have a plan?" Ford asked.

"If you'd stuck around—" Ava began.

Ford raised his hands in petition. "I know, I know. Won't happen again. How did you get here?"

"When we saw you were gone, Sabel rallied us and took out after you," Ava said. "The captain sent a boat to get us from the beach."

Ford started to mention his leaving was the catalyst to them all being here and on their way, but Ava's scowl held his tongue. Instead, he looked at Peter. "You were saying you had a plan?"

"We don't have all the details worked out," Peter said. "You okay to join us?" he asked Joshua.

"Yep." Joshua waved Ford over to help him up. He leaned heavily on Ford, but he got to his feet. He felt his waist and then glanced around the room.

"Missing this?" Father Braden stepped out of a corner and handed Joshua his sword.

"Thank you," Joshua said, then raised his bandaged hand. "For everything."

One by one, Peter, Ava, Joshua, then Ford left the captain's quarters and went straight to another stairwell. They rounded upwards and arrived in another chamber. No cot or wash table. Just tables, papers scattered across them, lined the perimeter of a long, narrow room. At a center table a slim woman with sharp features and dark brown hair pulled back in a tight ponytail watched them file in. She wore the same tunic and pants everyone else wore except for a short jacket with an ornamental belt. Fitz stood next to her with Harel and Sabel across the table.

"Ah, here we all are," she said with a glance at Harel. When her gaze fell on Sabel, it turned to ice. "And a few extra."

Harel marched straight to Joshua and grasped him in a tight hug. He looked down at Joshua's hand and his expression turned grim.

Fitz shouldered Harel out of the way. "Joshua," he said with a relieved smile. "Great to see you whole. You beat old Nahesekai for the second time!"

"No time for leisurely reunions," the woman in the snazzy jacket snapped. "I am Captain Jenat." She glanced between Joshua and Ford. "Ford and Joshua, I presume?"

"I'm Ford. This is Ava and Peter."

Captain Jenat nodded and then held out a rolled page to Joshua. "This will be for you."

"What—"

"It is a map," Sabel said. "I am Sabel of Silom."

"Good to meet ya," Joshua said.

"It is a map of the catacombs," Captain Jenat clarified. "We expect you to be our guide. Of the four temporals, only you have navigated the tunnels."

"Captain," Ford stepped further into the room. "I'm not sure you're aware of what happened on the beach. His hand." He gestured at the mark on Joshua's hand.

She flitted her eyes to it. "I am aware. If he wishes to stay aboard . . ." She raised her eyebrows at Joshua.

"No," Joshua said.

Ford touched his brother's shoulder. "Josh, maybe you should—"

"What? Trust my baby to be rescued by someone else? Anyone else? Ain't happenin'"

Captain Jenat nodded curtly. "Very well. Hold on to something." She crossed to the back of the room, where a chain dangled and gave it a sharp yank.

The *Sealight* shuddered. Ford grabbed hold of a table and reached out for Ava, pulling her to his side. She gripped his bicep. He tightened his hold.

The ship pitched downward at a forty-five degree angle. With a great groan, it lurched forward. The aqua light spilling in from the portholes turned navy blue, then midnight. Ford's ears popped. He held onto Ava after the ship leveled. She patted his arm and pulled away. He was reluctant to let her go.

Captain Jenat sighed deeply and looked at Harel. "It's a wonder we are still seaworthy after being so close to the reef."

Harel nodded and his jaw tensed. "We are on our way now. Thanks to Arkonai you knew where to find us."

"Agreed. Now, gather around." Captain Jenat glanced at each of them. "I will fill you in on our plan."

No one interrupted as Captain Jenat laid out their strategy. She detailed the moment they entered the bay outside the catacombs until they sailed back to Kulum. She didn't mention Lily's rescue or her being among them when they left. The captain either assumed their rescue would be successful or it didn't matter when it came time to exit the catacombs and flee the Schade.

"What caused the damage to the ship back at Endyle?" Ava finally asked after Captain Jenat discussed how they would get back to the boat from the catacombs. "Are we sure something won't happen again? We should have a back-up plan."

Captain Jenat gave her a shrewd look, then her expression cleared and she looked at Harel. "I like her."

"It would be prudent," Fitz said. "I think we should meet at the river. But that would mean crossing the Rift on foot."

"Indeed," Harel said.

Captain Jenat gave Ava another look. "If it comes to a battle on land, I hope you like Velare enough to call it home. It is where you will be buried."

Twenty-Five

"You need to concentrate," the elder mage, Faida, snapped at Lily.

Lily nodded and looked down at the scepter. They were so bossy. Especially Faida. But something was working. The harder they pushed her, the more she could do.

She and Faida faced each other in a low-ceilinged cavern beneath the cliffs. It was vastly different from the large one in which she had awoken so long ago. It contained small, dark pools throughout. The purple light radiated within some of the rock formations, but Faida lit a lantern, anyway.

Lily put all her focus on the pool of water at her feet. The scepter warmed her hand. Any minute. She'd see the—

Droplets rose out of the water. A few. Then a small spout of water twirled up and danced across the surface. She grinned and looked at Faida.

Faida clicked her tongue. "Discipline!" She pointed at the water.

Lily looked down. The spout was gone. Lily sighed and forced herself to make eye contact with the displeased mage. "Not exactly parting the red sea, but it's more than I've ever done before."

"If you would focus, you might drain the Kaidilas dry."

"Why?" Lily asked, heat rising in her cheeks. "Why is it so important I know how to do these things?"

Faida puckered her mouth and narrowed her eyes as she stared at Lily. She gave a slow nod. "I questioned if you would be the one to bring peace to Velare. Not only I. Many doubted. But your mother insisted."

"But why?" A headache flitted about her temples. "I haven't seen any conflict that I would need to bring peace to."

Faida cocked her head, but shooed her from the cavern. "Haven't you? Earth Apparent has seen its share of war."

A laugh burst from Lily as she walked toward the stairs back to the cliff. "You're saying that's what I'm meant to do? End conflict on Earth?"

"Our hope is for you to be capable of so much more."

Lily mounted the first step and turned to her teacher. "I'm just one girl. I'm nobody. Until a few weeks ago, I didn't even know this place existed. It's all happened so fast. I just don't think I'm who you want me to be."

"That could be. There are others. Those with as strong an ancestral line as yours. Perhaps stronger."

Lily fought a rise of jealousy. Weird. She didn't want to have so much expectation on her shoulders. But she didn't want anyone else to take her place. "I want to help. Really. I just wonder sometimes if I even belong here."

Faida's mouth quirked to one side. "So do I."

Lily used the bare tree to brace herself as she climbed down into the hole that led to the dragon eggs. Her favorite place in all of Velare. Since the ceremony, she and Jonah had traveled to the Rift and on to the dragon nursery almost every day. She had few duties to attend to. Her mom, even Dr. Charles, didn't seem to mind. As long as she worked with the high mages to learn the uses of her scepter, they left her to do pretty much anything she pleased.

After several hours spent with the elders, Lily was ready to be far away from the cliffs and the catacombs. In fact, she was living two lives. As she trained in the catacombs, she was both powerful and drained. She had learned to move small pebbles without touching them and parted water when she stood in the underground pools. But afterward, it was as though her spirit had run a marathon. She slept for hours, curled up on her bed, dreaming of a table full of food surrounded by a family she was sure she knew at one time. But each person became consumed by a dark smoke creeping in from the edges of the room. She awoke gasping for breath, looking for the shadow in her room.

Exploring the coves and the caves with Jonah had the opposite effect. Her muscles ached by the time she went to bed, but her heart was full. Images of a man with stern gray eyes rose as she drifted to sleep.

She and Jonah had explored near the opening of the cave where a few of the eggs incubated, but Jonah had come banging on her door this morning with the promise of finding the entire clutch. They'd rushed up shore, across the rift and straight to the den, bantering about what they would find. It was dark and cramped, but with the dusty clay crumbling beneath her fingers, Lily's heart pounded as she slid down a gravel slope and dropped into a shallow chamber.

She hadn't believed Jonah when he'd first mentioned dragons. *Come on, dragons?* Maybe a Komodo dragon. But that was just an oversized lizard. Not winged. Not fire-breathing. But Jonah had assured her the eggs contained monsters that did both. She'd read stories about dragons. The man with gray eyes held a book as she sat at his feet with another girl. That's how she knew of Smaug. This man told her dragons were responsible for the volcanoes in Earth Apparent. But she hadn't believed him. Hadn't believed a lot of his tales. She wasn't even sure *he* was real.

But the dimensional realms were real. And so were the dragons. At least the eggs were.

"Where's their mom?" Lily stepped over a jagged rock. Jonah held a lantern aloft, but Lily didn't need it. The dragon den was filled with purple light.

"The dragon dame?" Jonah ducked under a low spot in the tunnel. "I've never seen her. The elders tell stories of her return just before the eggs hatch."

"Do you think she's a good dragon?"

"I told you, dragons aren't good or bad. But they can be controlled and manipulated." He was quiet a moment. "I think she'll be good."

"I thought you said—"

"Here!" Jonah darted right through a narrow slot.

Lily squeezed through and gasped. Purple light illuminated dozens of eggs, green, yellow, orange, all the size of a car tire, spread out over a deep chamber.

"Jonah," Lily breathed. "There must be . . ."

"I know, maybe forty. Or more."

She bent down to an egg the color of new grass and ran her hand along—"Scales!"

"Yes, these are older than the ones at the den entrance."

"Would that mean the mother, the dragon dame, might be back soon?"

Jonah's eyes were wide as he nodded. "I think so."

Lily looked up at the chamber ceiling as though in a rush of great wings, the mother might descend on them.

"But . . ." Jonah bent down and touched the egg, his fingertips brushing hers. "Remember, if even one egg is missing, none can hatch."

Lily frowned. "Who would take an egg?"

Jonah shrugged.

"Jonah, my boy!" Dr. Charles called out as he squeezed through the fissure and both Lily and Jonah shot to their feet.

Dr. Charles made his way to them, holding out a lantern in front of his face. He picked his way over the boulders and stalagmites, out of place in his slacks and loafers.

Jonah gave Lily a side glance. How is it the good doctor always interrupted what promised to be some great insight?

Dr. Charles reached them, huffing and puffing. "Exciting times!" he said with a radiant smile. It faltered as he looked around the nest, but he recovered quickly. "But we have some unfortunate developments. I need for you to return to the upper cliffs right away."

"What developments?" Lily asked, following the doctor, but casting a glance over her shoulder at the nests. Jonah was right. The baby dragons would be good. They would both see to that.

She jogged to catch up with Dr. Charles. "What's the development?"

"It seems we might have visitors."

"Is that good?" She gave Jonah a quizzical look. He seemed just as confused.

"Are they Velarean?" he asked as they entered the tunnel.

"They have yet to announce their approach," Dr. Charles said. "But they are coming in from the sea."

"By boat?" Lily asked. Her stomach twittered. By boat, unannounced. An image of the man with gray eyes surfaced. He was sailing the *Black Pearl* into the Schade Harbor. She smiled. Just as suddenly, the image was gone. Fewer and fewer memories surfaced. But the warm feeling hung around this time.

"Yes," Dr. Charles said. "But they are still far offshore. We have time."

"Time for what?" Lily asked.

"To prepare for any hostilities."

They came to the end of the tunnel, filtered sunshine marking the opening. Dr. Charles scrambled out first, sliding on his slick soles. Jonah followed and finally Lily, blinking back the bright light.

They traveled due south toward the sea, a half-day's walk from the dragon nursery. A narrow forest obscured their view of the water. But the sparkling blue glimpses between the trees revealed no boat cutting through the waves.

"Come!" Dr. Charles was already rushing across the Rift. "We can make it back by evening if we hurry."

They traversed the shore and crossed the river, covered in a strange mist. Lily kept her eyes on the Kaidilas. She couldn't quite remember who she expected to see. Even as the sun sank behind the cliffs and they crunched the gravel shore in front of the opening to the catacombs, no ship arrived.

But Dr. Charles was frantic to get them inside.

"I don't see anything," Lily argued as they entered the catacombs. Jonah took her hand.

Dr. Charles scowled and gave her a firm push. "That does not bode well. Hurry."

Bode. Lily shivered.

"How do you know anyone is coming?" she asked as they came to the winding staircase.

"The Schade know," Dr. Charles murmured.

Goosebumps rose on Lily's arms. She hadn't encountered Bode, or any of the Schade since her first few days in Velare. In fact, she had barely given them any thought at all.

Dr. Charles rushed them up the steps. At the top, as twilight set in, he gripped Lily's shoulders. His blond hair was messy and his blue eyes wide with fear. "Go home to your mother. Stay there. Whatever happens, don't leave."

"But—"

"It'll be okay." He gave her shoulder an awkward pat and something like a smile lifted one side of his mouth. He licked his lips and turned to Jonah. "You too. We'll see the strangers off soon enough."

Jonah opened his mouth as though to argue, but glanced at Lily and nodded. "Be safe," he said and darted away.

Lily followed the path back to her home.

No, her mom's home. She might have gone through an induction ceremony and some weird lessons on magic tricks, but did that make this home? Of course it did. She was always confused after spending time away from the cliffs. She was meant to be here. They had important work to do.

She came to the door and hurried inside.

"Oh, thank God," Amy breathed and pulled Lily into a tight hug.

"Do you know who it is? Coming in from the sea?"

Amy shook her head. Though unsurprising, her mother's lack of knowledge sent a wave of irritation over Lily. How is it she knew so little of Velare, the Schade, of the cult with whom she had partnered?

"Didn't you ask?"

"We'll learn soon enough."

Her mother just trusted because she *didn't* understand. It was easier to have someone else call the shots. But the more Lily learned from the mages and felt the power from the scepter, the more she wanted to know.

"Let's have some dinner," Amy said.

"Yeah, sure mom." Lily trudged to the washroom. She'd have to rely on Jonah for answers. Everyone else wanted to speak in riddles.

All was calm through dinner. They sipped at the brew her mom made with the seripyn seed. It tasted better than the soup. Lily relaxed and cupped her hand around the mug.

"Do you think they were mistaken? About the boat?"

Amy squinted her eyes and looked into her drink as though thinking was a strenuous act. "Maybe. Everyone has been so on edge. You know, Dr. Charles actually yelled at one of the elders today?"

"Wow. I think of him as a big Labrador. Happy, but maybe not that bright."

Amy snorted. "That's not nice."

Lily shrugged. "I like labs well enough. What'd he yell about?"

Amy set her mug down and stood up, stretching her back. "Oh, I don't know." She began clearing their dishes. "I heard him say something about a silo. Mean anything to you?"

"Yeah," Lily said slowly. But like a spooked rabbit, the memory bolted as soon as she got near it. "Maybe. We can ask him tomorrow."

"Sure, honey."

The drain her lessons took seemed especially strong tonight. Lily tried to help clean up after dinner, but she couldn't stop yawning and her eyes drooped.

"Sweetie, get some sleep. They ask a lot of you."

Lily nodded and slumped to bed. But as soon as her head touched the pillow, the fatigue evaporated. She lay awake, listening for shouts, scuffles, anything. But all was quiet. Why was Dr. Charles so panicked?

She finally got up, dressed, and started for the door. She tiptoed back, grabbed her pack, and tucked her scepter into it. If something was about to go down, she might as well be equipped. After easing the door closed behind her, she made her way from one stone house corner to the next until she was crouching at the cliff edge. A full moon shone across the water. A wind howled across the bay. Waves slapped at the shore . . . where dark shadows gathered.

The Schade. As though consuming any moonlight, an ebony line of Schade stood between the waterline and the catacombs. Individual forms, yet interconnected. They were waiting for something.

Lily looked back out at the water. Choppy, black, but otherwise undisturbed.

"Lily?"

Lily gasped and turned, losing her balance and landing on her rear. "Jonah!" she hissed.

He put a finger to his lips, then pointed to the water.

Just offshore, something broke the surface of the water.

A ship.

The *Black Pearl*.

Twenty-Six

Ford gripped the railing as he followed Joshua down the stairs from the nav room. The air was heavy, like being down ten feet without clearing his ears. It was the same feeling as on the beach. His legs were weighted and his lungs refused to expand. The Schade. They were near. The effect wasn't as strong as when he fought the shadow-Josh, but definitely noticeable.

The *Sealight* was at full speed and angled slightly upward as they made their ascent. They had a plan. Or at least Sabel and Harel had a plan. It sounded like they were to just follow instructions.

Fine, what did he know about catacombs and fighting interdimensional shadow people?

"So we're just going to surface and say 'surprise!'" Ford asked, tightening his backpack. He checked his hip for his speargun. Ava and Peter followed closely behind, also with their weapons. They each carried a backpack with refreshed supplies: a flask of seripyn, water, blankets, some dried meat and fruit.

"We have to assume they already know we're coming," Joshua said. "It's less about surprise and more about resolve. We can't let up until we find Lily."

They circled down one more set of stairs until they were just outside the infirmary. Ford peered inside. All six cots were full and Father Braden bustled around the small room handing over mugs to patients. He glanced at Joshua, who was also looking into the room.

"The sea dragon did a number on the ship." Joshua looked down at his bandaged hand. The wound had spread and seeped out from the bandage onto his wrist.

The ship angled more. Joshua turned and strode toward the crew's sleeping quarters where he and Ford had first entered from the deck.

"But half the beds were already full when they rescued me," Joshua continued. "The damage . . . nobody thinks it was an accident."

They skirted around Kulumans and Silomites crowding in the space, waiting for the moment the *Sealight* rose from the sea.

Ford opened his mouth wide and popped his ears. Any minute, they would rise to the surface. The ship angled even more. Any minute . . .

Everyone looked up at the small hatch from which they would have to exit at full speed.

"Ford," Ava said, her voice tight as she slid close to him and held his arm leaning against him.

Ford touched a dark curl that hung in her face. "Just stay with Josh. You're safest with him and Harel."

A grin twisted her mouth. "You mean I'm best suited to protect them."

Ford pulled her into a side hug. "Absolutely what I meant. They wouldn't have come up with half the stuff you did for the rescue."

Ava shrugged. "I—"

Harel and Sabel rushed up. "We've entered the bay."

The boat surged forward. Harel bolted up the stairs, followed by Sabel. Ford leaned forward and gripped the handrail, pulling himself up to keep from tumbling back into Joshua, Ava and Peter.

Harel threw the hatch open as they broke the sea's surface. Ford leaped from the boat as the waters parted from the bow. Single file, the soldiers poured out onto the deck. Ford gripped Ava's hand and ran to the rail as the ship leveled. He looked forward, but any details of the cliff hid in the darkness. Ford looked up into a sea of stars. A full moon shone above the tall, frowning cliff. The moonlight spilled over the water, silvery and bright. Ford could hardly draw a breath. He struggled to keep his legs under him.

"Harel and the captain know how to make an entrance," Ford mumbled as Joshua stumbled up next to him. Harel, Sabel, and Peter joined them.

Joshua winced and shook his head. "I don't like being out in the open," he said to Harel, then drew his sword with his left hand.

"Stealth does not matter," Harel said, then looked at Ford, Peter, then Ava. "They know we are here."

Ava drew her dagger. "Then we should assume they know *why* we're here."

Peter nodded. "That's right." He looked at Joshua. "You have the cave map?"

Joshua nodded.

"You're the only one of us who's been through the catacombs," Peter said, as though Joshua needed reminding. "We'll be right behind you."

"Just stick to the plan," Sabel said. "I will handle the Schade. Harel and his soldiers will see to any Velareans."

The boat pulled to a stop as they weighed anchor.

Joshua gave a curt nod. "We all know our part. Find Lily and get out."

Maybe no one else saw it, but Joshua was struggling. He had firmly rejected all pleas to stay on board. No one had pressed too hard. This was his child.

"Right." Sabel smiled, walked to the port side of the ship. She glanced back. "For the valor of Arkonai," she said and leaped.

"What the—" Ford ran to where she disappeared. She was running full speed. On top of the water. The other Silomite soldiers joined her, jumping off the ship and landing on the water. Two dozen warriors raced to shore.

Ford stepped back and ran his hand through his hair. "Glad I'm taking a tender. I don't think I'm the walking on water type."

Harel put a hand on his shoulder. "You might surprise yourself. For now, the boats that will take you to shore are on both port and starboard sides. Give Sabel time to make the way safe."

Joshua nodded. "I hope Sabel's recon was accurate."

Panicked shouts from Sabel's soldiers carried across the water.

"They have made it to the shore," Harel said. "It is as I thought. The Schade protect the catacombs."

"So we continue with the plan," Joshua said. His face was slick with sweat.

Harel nodded. "Ford and Peter, follow Fitz." He pointed to starboard. "Ava, Joshua, and I will reach the catacombs from the south."

"Joshua," Ford said, blocking his way. "You don't have to go. We've got this."

Joshua leveled his gaze at Ford. Behind the steely stare was fevered pain. But Ford simply nodded and moved aside. Joshua and Harel ran across to the port side.

Ava gave Ford a quick hug. As she turned to follow Joshua, Ford caught her arm and pulled her back. He stared into her deep brown eyes, then pulled her into a fierce embrace before letting her go.

He ran for the narrow starboard boat hanging from the rail. It was made of the same smooth wood as the main vessel. He jumped in with Peter and Fitz. Two soldiers lowered the boat to the water, and they raced away, Fitz steering them due north to shallower waters. It was a simple propulsion system that forced the water through a narrow tube out the back. But Ford had a feeling they were lacking a motor. Fitz might not be walking on water, but his boat was.

Ford clutched the side of the boat as it hurtled across the waves, pounding down only to lift and gain air before hitting the water's surface again. They had to make it to shore without encountering Nahesekai. Joshua wouldn't survive another battle with the sea dragon. None of them would.

Ford's stomach soured. Joshua might not survive this rescue.

Fitz slowed down and guided them to a channel and up onto a gravel beach. He was out with his sword drawn before Ford could get his legs under him. Stumbling over the rocky shore, he drew his speargun and followed Fitz. Peter brought up the rear with his staff held ready. The shouts and clashes of battle echoed into the night ahead. They were still distant, but not for long.

The ruse had to work. Otherwise, three coming in from the south and three from the north, sneaking past the Schade and any Velareans would prove to be a foolish plan.

The Schade didn't matter. Neither did the Velareans. Just Lily. They had to find his niece and get back to the ship. Sabel had some idea where they might be holding her. Through the catacombs, up a set of stairs, down a path, into a stone house.

Ford blew out a breath. *Nice and vague.*

They ran in the blue moonlight across a sandy beach. The cliff grew before them. They didn't speak. Didn't stop. Just ran until they came up on the cliff and pressed against it, gasping for breath. Fitz got them to the cliff wall with no resistance. Hopefully, Joshua and Ava could say the same for Harel.

More shouts from the water's edge. It was a good sign. Sabel and the others had the Schade and Velareans engaged. But the six of them still had to get through the catacombs with Joshua guiding them.

They hurried along the cliff wall. A pungent, rotten odor rose the further they traveled. Then an ice cold breeze hit Ford in the face, blowing back his hair. He gagged and stumbled.

"I see movement ahead," Fitz whispered.

"Joshua?" Ford asked.

"I think so. I—" Fitz drew up and stopped short. A shadow darted out of a crevasse in the cliff wall and stood facing him.

"Well, hello there." A man in a button-down shirt and khakis grinned down at Fitz. Before anyone could react, the man thrust his arm toward Fitz's stomach. Fitz gasped and went stiff. He pulled at the man's arm and shoved him out of the way. The man fought, but Fitz, now holding his gut, rammed at him with his shoulder.

"Go," Fitz gasped. He yanked something from his stomach and approached the man standing between him and Ford and Peter.

Peter shoved Ford forward. Ford ran his hand along the cliff wall as they shuffled on in the sand. They couldn't be more than a hundred yards from the battle. Finally, Ford's hand slipped and he reached into empty space. He and Peter tumbled sideways into a massive, arched opening in the cliff. Ford gagged again and clambered to his feet.

"Fitz," he whispered, covering his nose and mouth with the crook of his arm.

Peter put a hand on Ford's shoulder. "He'll have to handle whoever that was."

Ford gritted his teeth. "I think I know who it was."

"We have to find Joshua. It's a labyrinth of tunnels in there. We'd never make it out."

A shout, closer than the Schade skirmish, came from ahead. Then another. Joshua.

Ford slipped on the slick cave floor as he scurried out of the cave, toward his brother's voice. Josh couldn't end up like Fitz. He was already so weak. They should have never split up.

Three shadowed forms ran straight at them from several yards away. A glint of metal. Then another.

"Josh?" Ford called as loud as he dared.

"It is us," Harel said. They came into the moonlight, Joshua leaning heavily on Harel.

"We were attacked by soldiers," Ava said, wiping her blade on her pants and then sheathing it. "Not Schade—" her voice caught. "I couldn't . . . I had to . . ."

Ford drew her in and hugged her tight. "You had to," he whispered.

Joshua tugged on Ford's arm. "This way. The center arch."

Ford nodded. He fought the impulse to hug his brother. He looked at Harel "Fitz, he . . . someone attacked him."

Harel nodded. "We'll go back for him. Lily first."

Ava ran past Joshua and took Ford's hand. The four of them followed a darkened tunnel, the moonlight quickly fading away. How Joshua knew where he was going, Ford could not fathom. Maybe a father's instinct. Maybe a temporal's intuition. Josh knew the map. Knew where to go. They reached a staircase, spiraling up into the moonlight.

Joshua charged up the steps, sword drawn, with no hesitation. Whatever might be waiting for them at the top, Joshua would run into, headlong.

"Hello?"

Lily's sweet voice echoed down the steps. When Ford reached the top, Lily had stepped back, watching Joshua, then Ford, Ava, and Peter warily.

"What's going on?" she asked.

She was dressed in the same kind of tunic and pants as every other Velarean. She held a gold rod with a gem adorning one end. A boy a little younger than she stood next to her, holding her hand.

"Lily, it's me. It's dad. I've come to take you home."

Lily frowned, obviously confused.

"Lilliput," Ford said, moving to stand next to Joshua.

Lily's gaze alternated between Ford and Joshua, then Peter and Ava.

The boy backed up a pace, pulling Lily with him.

"Hey, kiddo," Joshua said softly and took a step toward her as he sheathed his sword.

Lily blinked and she looked once more at Ford.

"Uncle Ford?" She cocked her head.

"That's me." Ford gave her his goofiest grin.

She smiled back.

"Dad!" She hesitated once more before running at Joshua, flinging her arms around him. Joshua stroked her hair.

He held her at arm's length with his left arm and stared at her. "How? Where—" He shook his head. "Doesn't matter. I've got you. We need to go."

Lily turned around and looked at the boy, then shook her head. "No. Dad, you've got it all wrong. Mom's here. The Velareans, they're helping. They're . . ." A frown creased her brow as she seemed to search for the right words. "They were looking for me."

"Of course they were," Joshua growled.

"Uncle Ford!" Lily's face lit up as it always did when she was about to appeal to him for some hairbrained idea. "You've got to understand. They want me here. They need me here."

Ford stepped up to her and touched her cool cheek. "It might seem like that's the gig. But we've got an injured Velarean who would say otherwise."

Joshua shot him a surprised look.

"Fitz. Some guy looking like a used car salesman attacked us." He glanced at Harel. The Velarean frowned but nodded and said nothing.

"Temporal?" Joshua asked.

"Had to be. Khakis, white shirt—"

"Dr. Charles?" Lily gasped.

"You know 'em?" Ford asked.

"Yeah, he . . . but there's no way he would hurt anyone."

"We'll let Fitz know on our way out." Ford grabbed her arm and pulled.

"Wait, Uncle Ford, my mom, she's here. I can't leave without her."

Joshua's eyes widened. "Your mom?" Then he glared past Lily, as though looking for his ex-wife. "She brought you here," he growled.

"No," Lily shook her head vehemently. "She was already here, working with Dr. Charles."

"The one who just attacked Fitz," Ford said.

Peter stepped forward. "Look, we're wasting time. Sabel can only hold off the Schade for so long."

Lily blinked. "The Schade," she said as though trying to remember something.

"You know," Ford said, still loosely holding her arm, "spooky shadow people? Not an entity we want to tangle with."

Lily nodded slowly, frowning in confusion. She glanced over her shoulder, then drew up, looking her dad straight in the eye. "I'm not going anywhere."

Twenty-Seven

Joshua rubbed the back of his neck. "You can't stay here." He tugged on Lily's arm.

"You don't understand." Lily's voice quivered. "Everyone here, Velareans, temporals, Cliffers, we take care of each other. We all have jobs to do."

"The jobs of which you speak only usher in destruction," Harel said.

Ford put a hand on Harel's arm, shook his head, then jut his chin to Joshua.

"Sweetheart," Joshua said. "You belong with us. In Earth Apparent. Home. I don't know what they told you, but it was all lies."

"Nooo!" Lily sobbed, pulling at her dad. "Please, this is my family."

"What's that make your dad?" Ford grumbled, unable to stay silent. "You can't really think we're going to leave you here." He stepped up next to his brother. "I made a mistake, okay? Letting you come with me on the dive. It's my fault you're here and I'll set this whole place of fire to get you back home safe."

"Dive . . ." Lily looked over Ford's face like she was seeing him for the first time. As though it took every ounce of concentration to understand what he was saying.

What did they do to her?

Then Lily looked at Ava and finally at Peter, her eyes growing wider. "Uncle Peter . . . Miss Ava."

"That's right," Ava said, taking a small step toward the girl as though trying not to spook a bird.

"Here," Peter said, digging into his backpack. He withdrew his flask of seripyn. "I don't know if they're giving this to you, but it might help. It always clears my head."

Lily took a step away from Peter. "I am taking the seripyn. I don't have the headaches anymore."

Peter held out the flask. "Just try. For ol' Pete." He gave her one of his disarming grins.

Ford looked from Peter to Lily. If he could convince her, that was points for him.

"Lily," the boy said and grabbed her hand.

"It's okay, Jonah." She looked down at him with a look of affection she sometimes offered Holly.

Lily finally nodded and took the flask. She took a small sip. "There, happy? I don't know why—" She blinked and looked at the flask, then at Peter, Ava, Ford, then her dad.

"How did you . . . what was that—" She looked down at the baton with renewed wonder.

"That stuff's the real deal," Ford said. "Now, you ready to go?"

"I can't." She shook her head, tears filling her eyes. "I can't leave . . . without mom."

Joshua heaved a sigh and wiped the sweat from his brow. "Okay, tell you what, go with Uncle Ford and Miss Ava. Uncle Peter and I will find your mom. But Lily"—he put a hand on her shoulder—"I can't make her come if she doesn't want to."

"Great plan, bro, but how do we get out of the catacombs?" Ford glanced down at Joshua's arm. He needed the healer. The longer he delayed, the more it spread.

"I know the way, Uncle Ford," Lily said, then turned to her dad. "Tell mom she has to come. Promise me."

Joshua flashed a dark look at Ford, both a plea and a warning. Protect Lily at all costs. "I'll do my very best," he said to Lily.

Lily nodded, tears streaming down her cheeks. She pointed east. "Fifth house on the right." She shook her head. "There are so many here. Jonah . . ." She looked at the boy and cried harder.

Renewed shouting came from the beach below. The Silomites were fierce fighters, but there was no telling how long they could hold off the Schade.

"We're out of time," Harel said.

Ford pulled firmly on Lily's arm.

Joshua looked at Ford. "I'll be right behind you."

"We won't leave without you."

"Hey!" an unfamiliar voice shouted from the direction Lily had pointed. "Who are you?"

"Cliffers," Lily murmured and moved as though to meet whoever shouted.

"It's Thomas," Jonah said to Lily. "Here!" he yelled, waving over the newcomer, only a silhouette in the moonlight. A rumble of voices followed. A crowd was gathering.

Joshua nudged Lily on and drew his sword. He looked at Peter. "Ready?"

Peter gripped his staff and nodded. He and Joshua took off at a jog, disappearing into the darkness, into the mass of people.

"Lily," Jonah pleaded as he took two steps in the same direction. "What are you doing?"

"I . . . I know it doesn't make sense. I mean, it does, but probably not to you. Hey, come with me!"

Jonah's face darkened, and he shook his head. He glanced at Ford, Ava, and Harel and then once more at Lily. He shook his head, turned, and dashed away.

"Jonah!"

Ford grabbed her before she could run after the boy.

Harel stepped in front of her. "He cannot understand. He is in the sway of the Schade."

"We can't force him to come with us, Lilliput," Ford said. "Harel's right. We're out of time."

He glanced at the sea. The moon had settled on the horizon, bloated and yellow. He turned to Lily.

"We'll get you to the boat and wait for your dad there."

"He won't hurt anyone, will he?" Lily asked.

"What? Your dad?" Ford asked.

"Of course he won't," Ava said and wrapped her arm over Lily's shoulder. She guided Lily to the top of the steps. "We'll let you lead the way."

Lily nodded. With one last glance toward the oncoming crowd, she scurried down the steps. Ford grabbed Ava's hand and hurried down a few steps. As soon as they entered the darkness, Ford's skin prickled. Something was here. It was just like what he felt when hunting for ghosts. Only worse.

"I'll seal the entrance to the cave," Harel said. "I'll meet you at the bottom."

"How will Joshua and Peter get back?"

Harel waved him away. "They have the tools to break the shield."

"Of course," Ford mumbled as he and Ava darted down the steps. "Lily," he reached out as he staggered on the last step.

"Over here," she said.

Ford tightened his grip on Ava's hand and followed Lily's voice. He listened for her footsteps on the hard cave floor. As they wound through the tunnels, her steps became fainter and fainter.

"It's okay, Uncle Ford," Lily said, her voice echoing in the blackness as she drew away.

Something slithered to their right.

"I'm not so sure about that," Ava whispered.

"Keep moving," Harel ordered in a low voice.

"Lil?" Ford whispered.

Nothing.

"Lily!" he hissed and stopped.

A sucking, slurping noise, like a gurgling pipe backed up with some nasty sludge, came from their left. A dry chuckle resounded through the cavern like the rustling of dead leaves still clinging to a dormant tree.

"Harel?" Ford called.

"Here," Harel said softly and a blue light flickered to life. Harel held a driftwood branch above his head, illuminating his haggard face. The pale flame sent dancing shadows across a high-ceilinged cavern.

A shadow shifted in the corner where a giant stalagmite rose out of the ground. Ford pulled his gun from its holster. Ava withdrew her dagger.

From behind the formation, Lily crept toward them, dragging her dive tank behind her.

Ford let out a breath and rushed over and lifted the tank onto his shoulder. Harel took Lily's vest from her and Ava held out her hand for Lily to take.

"I can't believe you still have this," Ford said. "Our gear will be the only way we make it back through the portal."

"I'd forgotten all about it," Lily said.

They exited the catacombs to the beach, cooled by a steady wind. The moon had finally given up the night. Though the darkness was nearly complete, Harel doused his light. Fighting on the shoreline had reached a fevered pitch. The Silomites had done exactly what they had planned. Kept the Schade occupied. But that didn't guarantee they would have a clear path to the boat.

Ford led them back along the cliff wall.

Please let us go by without being seen.

As they jogged, bent over and silent, Harel ran alongside them. "I will create a shield for as long as I can." Without breaking stride, he lifted his free arm.

Ford couldn't tell he'd done anything. Like a thousand slithering snakes made of smoke, the Schade fought to overtake Sabel and her soldiers. But in the darkness, the fighters seemed only to battle each other.

One fighter dropped back from the fray and nearly backed into Harel, but stopped just short. He glanced over his shoulder and his eyes widened in recognition. He touched his forehead and ran back into combat. There was no clashing of swords, only shouts and calls for aid.

Finally, Ford reached the spot where Fitz had gone down. Two dark shadows, bodies, lay sprawled out on the ground. Ford dropped the tank, went to one, and turned him over.

"Dr. Charles!" Lily gasped and kneeled next to him.

Ford felt for a pulse. Nothing. He moved to the second body and lifted his hand. Would a Velarean have a pulse?

Turns out, they did. Fitz's was weak and thready. He moaned. Ava knelt next to him and looked over his body.

"Here," she said grimly. She pulled her hand away from his stomach. Her fingers were covered in blood.

Ford nodded and gently lifted the warrior over his shoulder. Ava took Lily's vest. Harel hefted the tank onto his shoulder.

"I can no longer hold the barricade," he gasped.

"It's okay," Ford said. "We're almost there." Ford did his best to hurry without jostling Fitz. "Hang in there, buddy," Ford whispered. "We're going straight out to the water."

But after only a few steps, smoke wound its way around them. It pooled at their feet and drifted up their legs.

"Harel!" Ford shouted.

Harel dropped the tank and held out his hands. The smoke halted but didn't dissipate.

Ava dropped the vest and pulled out her dagger. She sliced at the darkened mist at her knees and, with a flash of light, it withdrew. She continued slashing, but the shadow smoke was thick. A form took shape between them and the sea.

Ford eased Fitz to the ground and drew his gun. He tried to clear his mind. Focus on the sound of the voice he heard at the pool. He took aim as wispy, black arms reached out for him.

Lily refusing to leave. Joshua taking off with Peter.

No, no focus!

Fitz on the ground dying. Lily standing vulnerable behind him.

Trust. Trust the voice.

Heat rose in his chest. His fingertips tingled.

"For the valor of Arkonai," he whispered.

He fired once. A bright light blazed for a moment and then it and the form were gone.

"Let's go," Ford said as he picked up Fitz and started forward, wading through the smoke.

But it was too much. It was like wading through knee-deep quicksand. Ford's legs burned. Ava gave Lily her vest and tried slashing at the Schade to make a path. She kept them moving with sparks of light. But they had a long way to go, and the mist was gathering.

"Harel!" Ford gasped and glanced at the Velarean.

Harel bent over with the weight of the tank, slogged his feet forward. He didn't even look up.

Ford looked around. The Silomites. They were at a distance, still fighting off the Schade further down.

The smoke billowed up again. It drifted up Ford's legs, squeezing, gripping as it went. Ford's feet went numb.

Spots winked in and out of his vision.

I'm gonna pass out.

"Sabel!" someone called out, but the voice was slipping away.

Ford went to his knees, with Fitz still on his back. He let his eyes slip closed.

Then the pressure was gone. He opened his eyes. Sabel stood over him, her spear piercing the Schade mist all around them. Three or four other soldiers joined in. Lights flashed like fireworks.

"Go!" Sabel cried. "Get to the boat!"

Ford forced one leg, then the other under him and stood with a grunt. He glanced around. Ava, gasping, stood with her dagger in one hand and Lily's hand in the other. The vest lay on the ground. Harel was pulling the tank onto his back.

"Everybody with me?" Ford asked.

Nods from Ava and Harel. Lily gazed at the Schade mist evaporating under the strikes of Sabel's small army.

"Lil?" Ford asked.

She looked at him and gave a small nod.

Ford shuffled forward and was heaving for air by the time they reached the boat. He waded out and, with Harel's help, eased Fitz into it. Ava climbed in and braced Fitz's head with her leg. With one last look back, Lily jumped in with Harel right behind her. Ford climbed into the back. Easing the lever down, as he had seen Fitz do, to start the flow of water to propel them to the ship. But nothing happened.

"Um, Harel, a little help?"

Harel nodded and leaned over, touching the lever. The boat sputtered forward.

Harel shook his head. "I have so little strength left." He smiled grimly. "We will get to the *Sealight*. But it will be slow."

Harel steered them into the deeper waters, coming within a few yards of the ship. A dark form broke the surface, blocking their way.

Harel jerked the steering handle, barely missing the shape even as it disappeared below, sending a rolling wave, forcing everyone to one side of the boat. Ford quickly recovered.

He balanced himself on his knees and drew his speargun, but the dark waters closed over whatever was there.

"Not far," Ford said, glancing up. "We'll make it—"

The boat slammed into something and lurched starboard. Ford grabbed Lily as she tumbled dangerously close to the edge. He scrambled to the bow, aimed,speargun, and fired. The spear rocketed into the waters, but the line hung loose. Ford drew it back. Harel guided the boat back toward shore, away from the ship.

Billowing from the catacombs was the Schade mist. It swirled up like a tornado and moved across the shore.

"The Schade!" Harel shouted. "We cannot go back!" He maneuvered the boat back out to sea.

"Come on, come on," Ford whispered. He tried to concentrate on the powerful feeling that had given him success with the Schade, but panic scattered his thoughts, leaving his mind empty except for the image of the dark, ridged hump receding beneath the waves.

Another bump tipped the boat. Lily gripped Fitz and pulled him with her as she and Ava attempted to counter the leaning craft. The ridges of a scaley back surfaced, then disappeared. The tip of a spiked tail. Then it was gone, leaving its wake trailing behind it, heading back to the ship.

Away from the Schade.

Ford fired again, and Joshua's determined, trustworthy face swam into his mind. He willed the spear to find the beast. The line went taut. He had it.

Now what?

He yanked, as though pulling in a largemouth bass. It yanked back. Ford let the line play out. At least until it ran out.

He pulled again, harder.

Trust the weapon.

Ford nodded, agreeing with the voice.

He flipped the lever so the line could wind back into the gun. Holding the grip with both hands, he glanced at Lily, then Ava. He had no way to protect them. But if his love for them could, then they would be safe anywhere, in any dimension. The line tugged. A rush of warmth traveled from his chest, down his arms and into his hands. The gun yanked hard, but Ford held tight. He braced his thighs against the bow of the boat and let Nahesekai pulled them toward the ship.

"The Schade are gaining!" Ava shouted.

A hissing whisper drew close.

As the boat slowed and drifted near the ship, the line whipped, pulled taut once more, then went slack. It wound into the reel. The spear hurtled out of the water and found its place in the holster.

"There!" someone shouted from the boat deck above them.

Ford helped haul Fitz up the ladder as the sailors grasped for him and pulled him from Ford's arms. The mist rolled over the waves, only fifty yards from the ship. Ford yanked Lily, then Ava, onto the ladder. Harel was right behind them as they scrambled up. They raced across the deck, leaped down into the hatch, and into the belly of the ship.

"Uncle Ford! We have to go back for dad! We have to get Uncle Peter and my mom! Dad promised he would get her!"

Ford held the sobbing girl as she gripped her scepter to her chest. They sat on the cot of Captain Jenat's quarters. Ava paced around the small space.

Tears of his own streaked down his face. He'd found his brother, only to lose him again. And he'd left Pete behind for good measure.

"We will get him. But right now we're trapped." Ford glanced at the porthole. It should have shimmered midnight blue from the water, or sparkled with the stars. But it was black. Swirling, menacing black.

Lily followed his gaze. "How come the Schade can't get in?"

"The openings are protected." Captain Jenat swept into the room. "But the *Sealight* will neither sail nor dive. Not with the Schade attached to the hull."

"How's Fitz?" Ava asked. "And Harel?"

Captain Jenat nodded. "Father Braden is attending to them both. Harel only needs rest."

"What about Sabel?" Ford asked. "Couldn't they fight the Schade off the ship?"

Captain Jenat was already shaking her head. "Much like Harel, they will be depleted from fighting the Schade on shore. More so, I would warrant. I don't know what such a small troop could do."

Lily wiggled her way out of Ford's arms and went to the window.

"Harel asked for you," Captain Jenat said to Ford. "All of you." She glanced at Ava and Lily.

"Are you sure they can't enter the ship?" Lily murmured without turning. She gently touched the window with her fingertips, the scepter at her side. The gem seemed to swirl in time with the mist at the window. Ford leaned in for a closer look, but it was only a large, polished smoky quartz.

"I am sure," the Captain said, but frowned at Lily.

"Come on, Lily," Ford said, standing. "Let's go see Harel. Maybe he has a plan for getting us out of here."

Lily continued to caress the window.

"Lily?"

She jerked like he'd poked her, then turned. "Right. Maybe he'll know how to get to my dad."

Ford exchanged a meaningful look with Ava. They'd get her another dose of seripyn.

They made their way down one level to the infirmary. Fitz lay on a low cot along one wall. Harel sat next to him, holding one of his hands.

"How ya doin'?" Ford asked as he squeezed in behind Harel. Ava and Lily waited in the doorway.

Fitz opened his eyes to slits and took a shallow breath. "I have had better days."

Harel looked over his shoulder but did not meet Ford's eyes.

"We completed our quest," Fitz whispered. His eyes shifted to Lily, and he smiled faintly.

"Yes, we did, my friend," Harel said.

"Harel!" Lucas burst into the room, shoving aside Lily and Ava. "It is Sabel. She and some of her troop have made it to the ship!"

Harel stood and followed Lucas out. Ford glanced once more at Fitz who gave him a weak wave to go.

Ford nodded and left the room to catch up to Harel who was already at the crew quarters with a disheveled Sabel and barely more than a dozen soldiers.

". . . there are so few," Harel finished saying.

"How?" Ford blurted. "How did you get through?"

Sabel's eyes filled with tears. "At the cost of many of my soldiers. My friends. Myrel fell overboard—" A sob caught in her throat.

Harel gripped both her shoulders and looked down into her eyes. "We will see them again, yes?"

Sabel nodded and wiped at her eyes. "Yes, of course."

"But if you got through," Ava said, "couldn't we escape?"

"We barely made it to the hatch," Sabel said. "I and those standing before you made it into the *Sealight* while the others combated the Schade. The door shut before they could make it inside. And you?" She finally looked at Ford, Ava, and Lily. "You rescued the girl." Her expression finally softened.

"Yes, but my dad and my Uncle Peter are still there," Lily said.

Sabel nodded. "Much has been sacrificed."

"We're going after him." Ford said firmly.

Sabel raised her eyebrows. "Not today. The Schade are gaining strength. It is only a matter of time before they gain access to the ship."

"The Schade have us captive," Captain Jenet said as she strode up. She looked at Harel.

Without a word Harel brushed past her, heading back toward the infirmary. The captain then looked at Ford and her darkened expression was all he needed to know what she'd communicated to Harel. He glanced at Ava and Lily, and the three followed Harel.

The infirmary was darkened. Only a lantern hung over Fitz. His eyes were closed. Ava slipped her hand into Ford's.

"Fitz?" Harel asked as he sat on the adjacent bed.

His eyes fluttered open. "Sabel?"

"Safe."

Fitz barely moved his head in a nod and he closed his eyes again. "We can go home."

"Not without my dad," Lily said.

"Not with the Schade holding the ship," Ford said.

Fitz took a deep breath as though it drained every ounce of energy and he opened his eyes again. "Your father is a great warrior," he whispered, then took another shallow breath. "Part of the Cord of Alnok"—another breath—"He and Peter will find a way to survive until you return for him."

Ford let go of Ava's hand. He sat down next to Fitz, across from Harel. Fitz's face was devoid of color, and blood tinged his lips. He gave Ford a weak smile and moved his hand over Ford's own.

"Do not despair," Fitz said. "Greater is he who is in you than all the Schade in Velare."

"He, you mean Arkonai?"

Fitz smiled and nodded. "I think I shall take a rest now." His hand fell away from Ford's as he closed his eyes. His chest continued to rise and fall in rattling breaths.

Harel kneeled on one knee next to Fitz's head and cradled it. "Farewell, brother. For now." He kissed his forehead, then stood and left.

Sabel entered, then the other soldiers. Even stoic Captain Jenat came around and gave a terse speech. Through it all, Fitz lay still. Ford didn't move from his station and watched Fitz's chest until it stopped moving.

Twenty Eight

arel joined Ford, Ava, and Lily in the captain's quarters. They had stayed in the crowded infirmary until Captain Jenat had Fitz's body covered with a sheet.

"The *Sealight* is being pulled under," Harel said. Some of the fire had dwindled in his hazel eyes.

"What do the Schade mean to do?" Ava asked.

Harel shook his head. "Eventually, they will find a way into the ship. Without a means of escape, we will drown."

Goosebumps spread over Ford's body. What a way to finally go.

"There has to be a way," he said.

Ava began pacing, but Lily drifted again to the window where the Schade clung to the outside of the gelatinous window. She held the strange baton at her side. Again, the quartz stone seemed to swirl with some internal mist.

"Lily," Ford said. "What is that?" He pointed to the baton.

Lily turned around, then looked at it. "My scepter? It's a gift from the Cliffers." She shrugged.

"Okay, but what is it?"

"Just a ceremonial thing."

"Can I see it?" Ford held out a hand.

Lily recoiled so suddenly, even Ava gasped.

Ford waited with his hand out.

Lily shook her head.

"Ford—" Ava began, but Ford shook his head. He was going to try something.

"You understand the Schade are not just keeping us from leaving. They're keeping us from getting to your dad."

Lily frowned and glanced over her shoulder, at the window, then back at Ford. "You think my scepter has something to do with the Schade? They weren't even a part of the ceremony. I haven't had anything to do with them."

"Haven't you?" Ford asked. He finally dropped his hand. "Seems like maybe they've been running the show all along."

"No . . . I haven't . . . they haven't—"

Ford gave her a hard stare. "We cannot get your dad until the Schade let us go."

"So what can I do?" Tears leaked out onto Lily's cheeks.

"I don't know, but they wanted you very badly."

"What are you saying?" Lily shouted. "That this is my fault?"

"No, but they're keeping you separated from your dad. From Uncle Peter. They're in danger as long as we're trapped on this boat."

Lily's face flushed. She spun around, the scepter gripped in her hand. "Let us go!" she sobbed.

Ford touched her shoulder. "Hey, sweetie—"

She swiped off his hand. "Let us go!"

"Lily, we'll find a way," Ava said.

Lily stepped closer to the window and held out her hand toward it. "Let us GO!"

The boat shuddered. The swirling mist stopped as though frozen. Lily held her position.

Then the mist dispersed and disappeared. Lily's knees buckled and Ford lurched forward to catch her. He looked up at Ava.

"Tell Captain Jenat we should get moving while we can."

Ava nodded, glanced at Lily, and then hurried off.

"Lily?" Ford said softly to the slack girl. "Lilliput?"

"Uncle Ford?" she murmured. "Are we going to get my dad now?"

Ford's throat nearly closed over his next word. "Soon."

"How did you know?" Ava asked as they stood at the aft porthole in the captain's quarters. They were traveling so fast the water was nothing more than a blue, foaming blur.

Lily was still sleeping.

"I thought she might have some insight into the Schade and how to get them to release the ship. I had no idea *that* would happen." He gestured toward the window.

Ava nodded.

"Joshua will hang in there until we come for him," Ava said.

Ford looked down at her. Her face was pale, a frown stitched between her brown eyes.

Ford slipped an arm over her shoulder, just as he would do when trying to convince her of a particular show idea. "My brother has probably already beat us to Endyle." He smiled but it took more strength than he had to hold it in place and he let it fade.

Ava sighed and laid her head against Ford's chest. "Wouldn't that be something?" She pulled away and looked up at him. "You hang in there, too."

"Of course. I always do."

But he wasn't hanging in there. He was dying inside. First, Ford was forced to tell Joshua he had lost his daughter. Now he had to tell Raelyn he'd lost her husband and her brother. He didn't deserve Ava's encouragement. He didn't deserve anything. Ford slid his arm from Ava's shoulder.

"I have to get Lily home."

"Of course we do. That's why we came here."

"I promised Josh."

"We will. One thing at a time."

Ford sighed. "That's why you're the boss. You see what I can't."

The *Sealight* rose once more, docking in a cove just off the shore of Endyle. As they disembarked, through the thin, silvery light of morning, Ford could see the tower of Kulum in the distance.

At once, new repairs began. They had no time to rest or recover. The Schade were coming.

"We will gather your gear from the tower," Harel said. "We can waste no time. Though we have seen no sign of the Schade for many miles, that does not mean they are not fast approaching."

"Or they are already here," Lucas added.

"The traitorous Velareans will have joined them," Sabel said with a scowl. Her right cheek was blackened and her right eye bloodshot. It was the same deep burn mark as Joshua. "I'll leave you to your preparations," she continued. "I must meet with Jonis. We will send a scouting party ahead to assure your safe travel to Kulum. And we must join our defenses. If this is farewell"—she bowed her head—"for the valor of Arkonai."

"Yeah," Ford said, "Uh, you, too."

They gathered Lily's gear but left their Velarean packs behind. All but Lily's, with, despite Ford's objections, her scepter tucked safely inside.

"Lily's out of air," Ava said quietly. "She'll have to use Joshua or Peter's."

Lily was already shaking her head. "Then how will they get back? How will mom come home? We can't take their only means of returning!"

"We'll plan for that when we get home." Ava turned to Ford. "We can bring extra gear back, right?" Her wide eyes begged Ford to agree.

"I don't know." Ford glanced at Harel.

"Perhaps," Harel said. "But I cannot make guarantees about how the portal might work each time. I am amazed the tanks made it through this time."

"Not helpful, Harel," Ford said under his breath.

"Then we have to go back for Dad and Peter now," Lily said, with that same determined, stubborn look Joshua always got, her gray eyes stormy and hard.

"No," Ford said, clenching his fists. "I promised to get you back home. I promised my brother I would see you to safety. I'm not breaking that promise." He didn't voice what surely they all knew. His brother might not have made it out at all.

"I'm not leaving here until I'm sure they have a way to come home." Lily looked from Ford to Ava to Harel.

Ford heaved a sigh. "I have another idea. But we need to get to Kulum." He glanced at Lily, Ava, then finally Harel. His chest tightened. Standing next to Harel should have been Fitz. "Let's get to shore. I'll tell you on the way."

He needed to get Lily moving. He had a plan, yes. But she wouldn't like it. None of them would.

They sat low in the boat as a lavender sunrise tinged the blue sky. They headed directly for Kulum. Ford could only hope whatever had happened with his gun had taken care of Nahesekai. At least for now.

The boat slid onto the beach and Harel was jumping onto the shore before it stopped, pulling it out of the water. They had to grab their tanks and fins from the tower, head down the steps and into the waters. Ford didn't voice his next concern: was the portal open?

It had to be.

Ford had just hauled Lily's tank and vest from the boat when a shadow rose up from the waters, moving like a tidal wave, blackening the twinkling sunlight.

"Move!" Harel bellowed.

Ford dropped the gear, grabbed Ava's and Lily's hands, and together they raced for Kulum tower. They passed the stone wall and dove through the doorway. Harel ran past them to the secret panel. He opened it and they all dashed in.

"I'll hold them off," he gasped.

Already, a stealthy slithering sound came from outside the room. Harel rushed to the hole at the center of the chamber. He grabbed the bucket of sand and sealed the door, the sand transforming into the gelatinous substance as it had before. Then he pressed his shoulder against the door for good measure.

"Can we be sure the portal's open?" Ava asked, standing helplessly beside their gear that had been stowed in the corner of the small room.

"Give Lily mine," Ford said.

"Uncle Ford, no," Lily said. "You're just going to have to leave me."

Ford shook his head. "You forget my lung capacity. I can hold my breath."

"Ford!" Ava said. Then she looked between Lily and Ford and pressed her lips together. What could she say? They weren't leaving Lily.

"No time to argue," Ford snapped, pointing at his tank. "Get geared up. Now," he added when Lily paused.

Ford turned to Harel. "Ava's right. What if the portal isn't open?"

"You'll have to open it."

"Me?" Ford choked.

Harel glanced at the speargun on Ford's hip. "You are well equipped."

Ford scoffed. "I don't know how you expect me to—"

"I don't expect you to. Remember the weapon's source of power." He stared hard at Ford. "Finish what you came here to do. Save Lily. Get her out of Velare. Fulfill your promise. I'll hold them here."

Ford nodded and turned. Ava and Lily, tanks on their backs, masks on their heads, and mouthpieces dangling on their shoulders, waited for him to take the lead. Ava scooped up their fins, handing Ford's to him.

"We have fins." He pointed at his boots.

Ava nodded and dropped them.

Harel, his feet planted, shoulders hunched, continued to hold the water in place, covering the door.

"Hurry!" he grunted.

They sat down around the hole, feet dangling in the water. They had one shot. But Ford not only didn't know how to open the portal. He didn't even know where to find it.

He looked at Ava. "I was unconscious by the time I came through the portal."

"I know," she said. "Remember what Harel said. Let your weapon guide you."

Ford took a few steady breaths. "Like dousing rods?"

Ava rolled her eyes. "There's a source of a lot more power than a couple of metal rods."

"Arkonai," Ford murmured.

Ava nodded. "Our Creator."

The time for any argument was long passed. He'd have to trust.

"Okay." He leaned forward and looked at each of them. "Keep a hand on me. Don't let go." He took a deep breath and blew it out, glancing at Harel. He took another breath, drawing in all the oxygen he could.

With one last breath, he plunged in. The Velarean suit held off any cold. He could see through the water enough with the rising sun above, even without a mask. Ava's hand rested on his back to his left and Lily's hand on his arm on his right. Ford looked for the blue light.

Nothing.

Not a glow, not a pinpoint. Just blue water, fading to black.

Then black surrounded him and cut off his sight completely.

The Schade.

Ava's hand slipped away. Something glinted in the shadows as she disappeared. He grabbed Lily with one hand and reached for his gun with his other.

With his chest expanded, he was in control of his sustained breath hold. But with every beat of his heart, he spent precious oxygen. At this rate, he'd have ten minutes at best.

I need an escape. I need the portal.

I need to find Ava.

He kicked his legs, going deeper, and raised the gun. Lily pulled, or was pulled, away from him. He gripped her hand harder and fired out at the mass of shadow.

The cord unraveled, but found nothing. He hit the switch and wound it back.

He could do this. He'd hit his mark on shore. With Joshua.

He fired again. Nothing. Not even the vibration.

Spots twinkled in the darkness as the tingling of lightheadedness started.

He kicked harder, searching below him for the blue light. Willing it to appear.

Lily was yanked from him.

No!

Ford fired again. The shadows parted, revealing long blonde hair as the spear barely missed her head. Ford swam to her and wrapped an arm around her waist. He turned and fired again. The shadows parted again. Ava was slashing at the inky substance around her. She looked up and slashed again and the shadow drew away from her.

Help me find the portal. Ford sent the prayer to Arkonai. The Author. The Creator. God.

He fired directly between his feet. A blue light pulsed, illuminating the sea floor. The Schade retreated, then surged again, blocking the light.

The air in Ford's lungs fought to be released. It pressed against his throat and nose, demanding to be let out.

He wound the cord and fired again. The light pulsed, but didn't fade completely. The Schade couldn't obscure it this time. Ford tried to shove Lily ahead of him as air leaked from his pressed lips, but she held on. He would have to take a breath. He tried to force Lily toward the light once more. But she yanked her mouthpiece out and shoved it into Ford's mouth just as he took a heaving breath in. He grabbed the mouthpiece and pushed it back into Lily's mouth.

Ford glanced around for Ava. He spied her, still fighting off the Schade, but she was too far away. Already the breath he took was fighting for escape. He swam toward the bottom of the sea. Toward the light.

He'd get Lily there. He would save her, just like he promised.

It seemed as though the shadows were descending again, crowding out his peripheral vision. Eating away at his sight. He kicked toward the light. He let Lily go and she swam ahead of him.

Ford kicked once more. The darkness closed into his vision as the light overtook him.

Twenty-Nine

"**F**ord..."

A name. His name. Someone calling from a great distance.

Ford tried to open his eyes, but they were sealed shut. He tried to take a breath. He needed to answer the person speaking to him, but his lungs wouldn't obey.

Then something pressed against his lips. Air was forced into his mouth, expanding his lungs. He needed to cough, but his bloated lungs held on. His chest would burst.

He parted his lips. The cough would not be denied. Warm liquid filled his mouth and bubbled over his cheeks.

"Ford!"

The voice, closer. Urgent.

He tried again to answer.

Another breath into his mouth. Another cough. This time rough, expelling the liquid in a spray. He coughed again. And again, taking in deep, gasping breaths.

"Wha..."

"Shh, don't try to talk," the voice told him.

A warbling howl pierced his ears. Rough hands pulled him away from the voice. He struggled to stay.

"I'm right here," the same voice said, so Ford settled down and let sleep take him . . .

"Ford?"

"I'm awake," he croaked, his throat burning. He forced his eyes open. A blurry, glaring light filled a white room. "Am I dead?" he whispered.

"Nearly. But no, you're in the hospital."

A hand, small and warm, took his. He blinked the room into focus.

"Ava," he croaked.

"Yes," she nodded, and tears filled her eyes.

Everything flooded back. The sea. The portal. The Schade. Ford struggled to sit up, fighting with a tube attached to the back of his hand. "Lily, Joshua . . ."

"Lily's fine. She's in the next room."

"Josh? Peter?"

Tears filled Ava's eyes as she shook her head.

Ford fell back against the pillows. He'd gain one and lost two.

The room, smelling of disinfectant and alcohol, was quiet and cramped. The walls, covered in a wallpaper with small flowers, meant to feel homey no doubt, did just the opposite. He had to get out of here. He had to get back to Velare.

He took a deep breath. "I have to talk to Raelyn."

"She's been here."

"What'd you tell her?"

"As much as I could. It's all still fuzzy. She didn't say much, but she seemed to understand."

Ford shook his head. She could understand only one thing. His failure. He'd saved Lily, but traded in Joshua and Peter.

"Really," Ava insisted. "She said one way or another, this was all bound to happen."

"The police. What did you tell them? They had to be confused as to how we found Lily."

"Yeah, about that"—Ava leaned in close—"turns out, time doesn't exactly track the same in Velare as it does here. As far as they knew, we were only gone about twelve hours. I just told them we found Lily on the other side of the lake. I think they were so relieved she was safe and relatively unharmed, they didn't press for details."

"Not even about Joshua?"

Ava shrugged. "As far as they know, he's a distraught father who'd gone home to grieve. Raelyn and I assured them we would get Lily home safe and there was no need for them to talk to him."

"Wow."

"The police were easy. The other guy that came around. He's a different story."

"Oh?"

A nurse hurried into the room. Ava slipped out of the way and stood near the window.

"How're we feeling?" the nurse asked.

"Much better."

"Hungry?"

Ford hadn't considered it. But his stomach grumbled. "Yeah."

"Lunch in about an hour." She busied herself taking his pulse, blood pressure, checking the monitors. "Doing good. The doctor will be around soon."

She left as quickly as she came.

Ava sat back on the bed. "Same guy who was there the night, well, last night, when Lily disappeared. The one from B&K. Dr. Kabal or something. He wanted to talk to you when you woke up."

"I bet he does. Ticked off about us being in his lake."

Ava chewed on her lower lip. "Maybe. He was acting weird. He actually seemed less worried about his lake and more about Joshua and Lily. Raelyn stopped him before he went into Lily's room to talk to her."

Ford nodded. "My brother knows someone who used to work for them. I met him once. Gabe something or other. It was their LHC that opened the portal to Alnok. Maybe Dr. Kabal was a part of it. As the top dog, he must have some idea about what went on."

"Yeah, we'll have to make up something. I don't want him nosing around. I didn't want them to find out about the ghost hunting. But now, that's probably the best story we have."

He gave Ava a hard stare. "I'm going back for Joshua."

"Of course we are."

"Wait, we?"

"Like it or not, I'm just as much a part of this as you are. You can't go alone. Who else would believe you?"

Ford smiled at her crossed arms and shrugged. "I wouldn't want anyone else. Really. But there are others. Gabe being one of them. Maybe you don't have to risk it again."

Ava cocked her head. "You know, I—"

Approaching footsteps clicked down the hall. Then the swishing of a long, purposeful stride. A man rounded the corner into the doorway. A tall, graying man with a stern frown. "Mr. Montgomery. I hope you remember me. Dr. Kanabel." The CEO of B&K Sciences strode into the room with his hand out, ready to shake Ford's.

Ava stood in front of Ford. "I really don't think this is appropriate—"

Ford grunted as he lifted himself up higher in the bed. He touched Ava's arm. "It's okay. He deserves an explanation." He looked around Ava at the scientist.

"What can I do for you?"

Dr. Kanabel gave him a thin smile. He cocked his head, and though he appeared aloof, his eyes were sunken and his skin pale. "Answers, Mr. Montgomery. You can provide answers."

"I'll give you all I can."

Dr. Kanabel narrowed his eyes. "Very well. Why did you ignore our requests to stay away from the lake?"

"We did trespass on your land to get to the lake. But you already knew that. I had one opportunity to research Iron Town. I hope you'll accept my apologies." Ford took Ava's approach. A good ghost story. "When we reached the bottom, we didn't see anything, but once we got to the house, well, let's just say I got more evidence than I ever needed.

"So," Ford continued. "If you would like to file a trespass charge, be my guest. Just remember"—he gave the doctor a pointed look—"we found more down there than the police would expect."

"Or the federal government," Ava added. She seemed to catch his angle. Accuse and threaten without really going that far.

Dr. Kanabel's face went red. "I won't have you trespassed. Yet. I hope you found what you were looking for. Now you can stay away."

Ford shrugged. "Iron Town doesn't really hold much of my interest anymore."

Dr. Kanabel glared at Ford. "You don't get off that easy." He lowered his voice. "I've lost someone I care about. And it seems you have too. Neither of them are coming back," he whispered.

"I'm sorry for your loss," Ford said. "But as for my missing person, she's in the room next door, safe and sound."

And I'll get Joshua back even if I have to hold my breath and swim through the portal alone.

Dr. Kanabel stared down his nose. "We'll see about that." Then he spun around and stalked out.

Ava turned, her eyes wide. "What does he mean?"

Ford pushed his hair out of his eyes, his hands trembling. "Not sure. But I think our next dive will be much more difficult."

"You think he caught your meaning? That we'd expose the LHC?"

"Oh yeah, I think he caught it. But we need to watch Lily even more closely. They may not want us near the lake, but they still want her."

Thirty

"Pass the rolls, please?" Raelyn asked Ford.

He considered throwing one at her, but changed his mind. No one felt like laughing. It was Thursday night. Family dinner. Raelyn, Holly, and Lily sat in their usual spots. Ava sat in Peter's. Joshua's chair was empty. They'd both been gone, left in Velare for three days.

This was the first time they had all been together since returning from Velare. They had told Raelyn what had happened over and over, making sure no detail was left out. Ford listened carefully to Lily's recount of the ceremony in which she was given the scepter. It seemed a basic initiation, but he hadn't seen the scepter since they'd returned.

Ford handed Raelyn the breadbasket. As she took it, something glinted at her throat. He held the basket as she tugged on it.

"What you got there?" He let go as she took a roll.

"What?" She touched the round charm hanging around her neck. "This?"

"Yeah, I've never seen you wear it." Something about it was familiar.

Raelyn glanced at her girls and then at Ava. "It's a gift from my time in Alnok."

"Oh?"

"It, um, helped me find my way. Sometimes Kade, our guide, couldn't be with us, so it was up to me to find the portals."

"And that helped?"

"Yeah, well, not this one. I wore Kade's. But it turns out, Moses and Nahor, the last remaining temporals in Alnok, returned to Earth Apparent with one. They melted it down and used it to create one for each of their children and it was passed down." She looked at Holly and then Lily. "Grandpa Fulton gave me this."

Ava had gone still and quiet, staring at the amulet.

"Why'd you start wearing it?" Lily asked.

"Actually"—Raelyn pressed her fingertips on it—"I heard it. It was vibrating from inside my jewelry box."

"When Joshua went to Velare." Ford didn't need her to answer. But she did.

"That's right. As one of the Cord, I knew, as long as it was humming, he was okay."

Ford's stomach turned. "And now? What's it doing?"

Raelyn's chin quivered. "It's quiet . . . but warm."

"That's good, right mom?" Lily asked as a tear trailed down her cheek.

Raelyn reached across the table and took her hand. "It's very, very good. Now, eat up. Uncle Ford, Ava, and I have some planning to do."

"Mom—" Lily began, but Raelyn flashed a warning look and she fell silent.

They finished the meal and Lily and Holly left to get ready for school the next morning. Raelyn heaved a sigh.

"Joshua's folks are coming over later. I think we should tell them."

Ford frowned. "Tell them what? Their son is trapped in another dimension?"

"My dad knows. My mom did too. I don't think they'll be all that surprised. They cared for Lily when Joshua was gone all that time destroying the portals in Alnok."

"I just think the less complication the better," Ford argued. "They can't help. And they just might hinder our rescue."

Raelyn nodded. "Okay. For now. But if I think they can offer us anything to help us get Joshua, I'm bringing them in."

"Fair enough."

"Also, I don't think you and Ava should go alone. I know I can't"—she rubbed her baby bump—"but the other three members of the Cord should know what's going on. I think you should at least talk to them."

"Gabe?"

"Yes, and Jinny and Avery."

Ford ran his fingers through his hair. "Talk, yes. Join, maybe. They may know more than me, but Velare is different. If they aren't experienced divers, they might just get themselves in trouble."

"Okay." Raelyn nodded. "Do you have a plan?"

"Go to Velare. Get Joshua and Peter. Come home."

Raelyn blew out a breath. "Oh, boy."

"Okay, okay," Ford sat back from the table. "We have to find a way into B&K. I don't know if we can get to the portal from the lake. They'll be watching it too closely. You said that's how you got to Alnok, right?"

Raelyn pushed her food around her plate with her fork. "It was. But after the Upheaval, the government dismantled their LHC."

"Does anyone here believe that?" Ford asked.

"What if they just moved it to beneath the lake?" Raelyn sat her fork down. "Either way, the warehouse or the lake, both will be impossible to get into."

"Don't worry, sis." Ford leaned near. "He's my brother. If anyone can get him and get out, I can." He took both her hands. "Trust me." He looked at Ava who hadn't said a word.

"You okay?" he asked gently.

Ava looked from Ford to Raelyn and back. She shook her head and opened her mouth, shut it, then opened it again.

"What is it, Ava?" Raelyn asked.

"That necklace. The amulet."

Raelyn touched it again. "The Durinial?"

Ava nodded. "I have one just like it."

Epilogue

Lily took her time getting to her room as she listened to the last of the adult's conversation. They were discussing the possibility of not taking her to Velare. They couldn't stop her. She was going.

But the draw to her room was stronger than her desire to eavesdrop. She closed her door and locked it. She went to her closet and pushed aside some shoe boxes. At the very back was the Velarean backpack.

She pulled it to her and peered inside. The scepter was crammed in sideways. She withdrew it. She traced the intricate pattern engraved into the cool metal and let out a contented sigh. A cold, but not unpleasant shiver coursed through her body.

It was silly to be so secretive. Uncle Ford hadn't even asked about it. The concealment was excessive, but somehow, completely necessary. A constant knot in her stomach kept her awake at night and preoccupied during the day. Unless she was touching the scepter.

Holding it, touching the mesmerizing rough-cut, clear stone capping off the rich gold baton, eased her fear for her dad. In fact, she hardly thought of him at all. What came into sharp focus was the elders and all they had taught her. The other Cliffers, her friends. The dragon eggs. Everything about Velare rushed back to a comforting and vivid memory. The salty, humid air. The dry desert of the Rift. Her home with her mom.

Lily sniffed. She wiped her cheeks and looked at her wet palm. Why was she crying?

She stood up and walked to the bed, holding the stone up to the light. It wasn't clear exactly. Floating inside was a dark, wispy formation. Once or twice, it had seemed to shift like smoke caught in glass, but of course she was seeing things. It was just a flaw in the stone.

She was supposed to be doing homework. The scepter needed to go back. She returned to the closet and kneeled down. Her hand was reluctant to let go, as though someone else controlled it, keeping her fingers curled around the metal, now growing warm.

Lily's face flushed. The pulse she felt when she was training with the elders prickled her fingertips and her palm. Shadows gathered in the corners of her closet, twisting and coiling like serpents ready to strike.

"Lily?" Holly called through the door and knocked.

"Just a minute!" Lily's voice quivered. "Let go, let go," she whispered, trying to peel her fingers off of it.

Loose hangers swayed wildly. Her stack of shoeboxes vibrated and fell to the ground as though caught in an earthquake.

"Lily, I need your pencil sharpener!" Holly insisted.

Lily's heart pounded. She pried harder at her hand. The shadows grew, sending dark vines of mist, like searching hands, toward her.

She thumped the scepter on the carpet and it fell free. The shadows withdrew and disappeared. The vibrations stopped. She kicked the scepter into the closet and slammed the door closed.

Still shaking, she scrambled away and leaned against her bed.

"Lily!" Holly banged on the door.

Lily got to her feet and unlocked her door, opening it to her frustrated sister.

Holly glanced past Lily. "What's going on?"

Lily frowned and moved to one side, letting Holly in. "Nothing. Why?"

"Sounded like you were playing the drums or something."

"Just cleaning up. You needed my sharpener?"

Holly produced a yellow pencil. "Yep."

"Got it." Lily went to her desk drawer. Her hands trembled as she shoved aside papers and paperclips.

"Hey, I'm really glad you're back," Holly said softly.

Lily found the sharpener and turned back to her sister. Holly stepped forward and wrapped her arms around Lily's waist, burying her head in her stomach.

Lily blinked and then relaxed and hugged Holly tight. "Me too. Now"—she pulled Holly from her"—you've got homework, too." She held up the sharpener.

Holly grabbed it and grinned. "I might need help with math." Then she skipped out of the room.

Lily gazed after her sister before her eyes were drawn to her closet. She shuddered. The shadows, the vibration, it was overwhelming. She looked at her hand that had held the scepter. A hint of the scroll was pressed into her skin. It was dangerous. She was just asking for trouble.

And she couldn't wait to hold it again.

Also by SL Dooley

Coming 2025
Haunted: Echoes from the Depths
Haunted: Shore of Shadows